A REVIVED

MODERN

CLASSIC

SHE WAS A QUEEN

MAURICE COLLIS

SHE WAS A QUEEN

WITH AN INTRODUCTION BY LOUISE COLLIS

A NEW DIRECTIONS BOOK

Manufactured in the United States of America.
New Directions Books are printed on acid-free paper.
First published in 1937 by Faber and Faber Limited. Reissued as
New Directions Paperbook 716 in 1991 as part of the Revived Modern
Classics Series.
Published simultaneously in Canada by Penguin Books Canada Limited.

Library of Congress Cataloging-in-Publication Data

Collis, Maurice, 1889-
    She was a queen / Maurice Collis.
        p.   cm. —(A Revived modern classic) (New Directions
    paperbook ; 716)
    "First published in 1937 by Faber and Faber Limited" —T.p. verso.
    ISBN 0-8112-1169-X
    1.   Saw, Queen of Burma, fl. 1287—Fiction.   2.   Burma—
History—To 1824—Fiction.   I.   Title.   II.   Series.
PR6005.O366S5   1991
823'.912—dc20   90-21153
                                                                       CIP

New Directions Books are published for James Laughlin
by New Directions Publishing Corporation,
80 Eighth Avenue, New York 10011

Though to the moonlight my sleeve but narrow lodging can afford, yet might it dwell there for ever and for ever, this radiance of which my eyes can never tire.

Tale of Genji. Waley.

To
GORDON LUCE
in memory of
old fellowship

A NEW INTRODUCTION

BY LOUISE COLLIS

My father Maurice Collis had an unusual apprentice-ship. Born and brought up in Ireland, he joined the Indian Civil Service in 1912, being posted to Burma. He had chosen this career in a youthful spirit of adventure and romance. Also, the pay was good. His literary inclinations at that date were vague and indecisive: he wrote a short book on the Napoleonic legend as developed by nineteenth century poets and could not find a publisher for it.

On closer acquaintance, the Orient turned out to be both more and less exciting than he had expected. He suffered much from the loneliness of country stations where he might be the only educated person for a hundred miles. He was a sociable man: congenial company and conversation after the day's work were essential for his happiness. Then again, his mind was always hungry and it was difficult to obtain sufficient books and magazines to occupy the long, dark evenings, to overcome a feeling of being cast away in jungles and mangrove swamps. He wrote melancholy poems, in Spencerian mode, full of Celtic Twilight and Druids. These did not express his real personality which was fundamentally optimistic, energetic and much given to laughter, though there were storms.

By 1922 he felt a great longing to leave the civil service and settle in London. His dream was to become a writer and to take part in the efflorescence of intellectual and artistic life which characterized the twenties and early thirties in Europe. He was on home leave at the time, spending part of it in Paris in a daze of excitement at the new ballet, the new theatre, the new exhibitions, buying the latest novelists and poets, the literary magazines, getting married. But he could not find any suitable job and although he managed to get his poems published, the lack of public interest and the cruel things the critics said were most debilitating.

In spite of his dissatisfactions, the Orient enchanted him and he returned to Burma. The stream of books ordered from London included many on the art, history, literature and philosophy of Asia. He devoured all these works with the greatest enthusiasm, becoming widely and variously learned. He observed Burmese village life, its customs and festivals, the elaborate traditional dramas played by travelling bands of actors. He had his horoscope drawn on a palm leaf by one of the last survivors of the royal astrologers of the court of Mandalay.

By the late twenties Maurice had risen to the position of magistrate in Rangoon and his feeling that he was in the wrong career was strongly reinforced by his superiors. He passed the same sentence, for instance, on a European who ran over some Burmese as would have been inflicted on a Burmese who damaged Europeans. He gave a nominal sentence to an Indian political agitator on the grounds of lack of proper evidence. These rulings could not be challenged in law, which made matters worse. He became far more friendly with prominent Burmese and Chinese residents of Rangoon than social custom allowed. He published humorous stories in local newspapers. Although these activities earned him a special place in popular opinion, they resulted in his next posting being to a country station, far to the south of the capital, on the borders of Siam, a considerable demotion.

Yet it was here, in the remote port of Mergui, that he finally was able to embark on his true vocation as a writer. The place had been a noted pirate stronghold in the seventeenth century, the chief figure being Samuel White, a renegade from the East India Company. Maurice discovered many relics of those times, such as cannons, wine bottles, candlesticks, kitchen utensils and Mrs White's grave, complete with inscription. He read all the contemporary accounts of White's adventures which had culminated in furious engagement with an East India Company flotilla and a simultaneous massacre of his followers by the Burmese. Maurice was tremendously excited by all this. Wherever he went, he was treading in the footsteps of Samuel White. His house was on the site of White's headquarters. Three of White's cannons were outside his door and ceremonially fired on the Burmese new year. He was told that the town was pestered with ghosts who could not be propitiated by any Buddhist prayer because they were aliens, the relic of some great battle in a fabulous past.

As he gathered more and more information, it dawned on Maurice that this official banishment was to be his salvation. He had spenty twenty years turning himself into an orientalist and, at last, he had found the subject of his first book. He resolved to write it during his next long leave and, if he could get it published, to leave the civil service and begin the literary career he had so long desired. He saw that Spencerian poems and amusing short stories were a mistake; that the history of Asia provided an infinity of possible subjects, untouched by other modern authors. As he stood on the wharf receiving a farewell address from the local people, he knew that the long time of uncertainty was over; that at the age of forty-five he was going to begin an entirely new life in which the haunting presence of the East would become a memory and a powerful inspiration.

Once arrived in London, he set to work with characteristic energy and singlemindedness to turn the dream into reality. At times, he was troubled by difficult questions such as, what if it doesn't work out? Will it bring in enough to keep the family going? Suppose it's another false start? He banished such thoughts. And he was right. *Siamese White* was published in 1936 to a chorus of praise from the right critics. The publishers begged him to hurry up with his next book. He could hardly believe it as he began the first chapter of *She Was A Queen* without a moment's delay. He chose the subject simply for its appeal to his romantic temperament and wrote with enthusiasm. This book is among his best: full of curious adventures, curious learning, beautiful prose and a fast narrative pace. Now read on.

Preface

The narrative which follows is founded upon certain episodes related in a Burmese history called the Hmannan Yazawin or Glass Palace Chronicle. That chronicle dates from the year 1829, when King Bagyidaw of Burma appointed a committee of scholars to draw up a definitive history of what had happened in Burma from the earliest times to the date of writing. The committee met in a sacred chamber in front of the royal Palace of Glass, as the palace at the then capital, Ava, was called, and after sifting the existing records and consulting learned monks, the college of astrologers and antiquarians of note, produced a book in several volumes which was submitted to Bagyidaw, 'Sovereign of Umbrella-holding Kings, Master of the White Elephant and Captain of the Law.' The book became the official history of Burma, and there is no question that it recorded as closely as possible what was believed to be the historical truth.

The fifth volume contains an account of the fall of the Pagān dynasty, an event which took place in and about the year 1287. It is with that event that the present book is concerned. Working on the translation of the Glass Palace Chronicle made in 1923 by Professors Pe Maung Tin and G. H. Luce of Rangoon University, I have attempted to recreate a drama which has been considered the strangest and most memorable in Burmese history. With a few minor exceptions, the characters, the structure and story generally come straight from the chronicle, while twenty years' experience of Burma has given me the blood and spirit with which to animate them.

No modern history of the Pagān dynasty has been published and doubtless when, after an up-to-date collation of sources, one is published, its contents will differ materially from those of the 1829 chronicle. But if the reader of the following pages is given for truth what may eventually in part be called legend, he can console himself with the reflection that generations of Oriental readers have been content to probe no deeper and to take the chronicle as a veritable account of what happened when the great Kublai Khan turned his attention for a moment to Burma.

MAURICE COLLIS

Maidenhead
    September 1936

Contents

★ *Contents* ★

Illustrations

★ *Illustrations* ★

i
The Hamadryad

In the village of Kanbyu, on the lower slopes of Mount Pōpa, a farmer had his house. As he sat of an evening in the garden with its bushes of jasmin and hibiscus, smoking his cigar or playing his flute, his eyes would seek the mountain that towered above him or wander across the plain to the city in the distance.

The mountain was a solitary peak in the centre of Burma and seemed immensely high. Sometimes he saw it trailing a cloud, as once it had a cloud of fire, for it was an extinct volcano; sometimes it appeared to twist up into the pale blue like a horn, its spirals making for him a sound of music, which lifted him until he felt that he viewed the whole land.

The city, which he could see as he looked westwards, was the capital, Pagān, with the great river Irrawaddy flowing past it. When the light was good, he would distinguish spires tapering up, roofs of pagoda and ordination hall, roofs of monastery and elephant stable. When these glittered in their gold leaf behind the red walls, when he could catch the flash of the white bridges on the lotus-moat and of the finial of the palace where the King lived magnificently, his mind used to leave his mountain village and saunter on those streets and by those shining porticos.

But it also made him happy to watch his little daughter learning to walk, 'teaching the soles of her feet to walk', in the phrase of the poem he had composed on that subject. She came tottering to him one dusk as he sat by the jasmin, a naked child beautiful as a cherub. He lifted her onto his knee and, kissing her, said: 'I am ploughing to-morrow and will take you with me.'

Next day very early he caught his bulls and pressed their necks between the yoke-pins, mounting with his daughter into the cart. Together they drove to the clearing in which lay his rice-land. There he left the child on a mat under a tamarind-tree and, changing the bulls to the plough-yoke, descended to the field.

To him ploughing was more than churning the earth, for when he had the mud-puddle under his bare feet and as he pressed his toes into it he felt a seething there, a pulsing that would become his food and his blood. His practice, therefore, on first ploughing was to kneel a moment on the embankment, kneading the clay in his hand and identifying himself with it. This rite he performed that day, while the bulls stood with drooping heads, sunk in their being, as if they too were touched by a waft from the earth. When he was satisfied that between him and the clay there was interchange and passage, he rose from his knees, shook the reins and the three started to churn the rice-bed.

As he went backwards and forwards, calling on the bulls monotonously, his daughter fell asleep under the tree. He forgot her, his thin face intent on the ploughing; he walked almost in a trance, so intense was his concentration; and did not see that a hamadryad, the grandest of all venomous snakes, had issued from the wood and was approaching her. The snake slid on by stages, watchful and stately, and when it reached the child, made a circle round her with its tail and reared above her head its oval hood. There it remained, rising and stooping, waving over her face, but not touching her.

At a turn of the plough the farmer looked across the field and saw the hamadryad. Its pose was hieratic; it did not seem about to strike; it had a curious air. But it frightened him, for if his daughter should awake it might kill her, and he rushed from the field to drive it off. When it heard him coming, like the swish of a whip it disappeared into the bushes.

He took up his daughter and examined her; she was quite unhurt. She smiled into his face; she looked very happy. As he thought of what had occurred, it seemed strange. He had never seen a snake in that pose before. Unable to concentrate any longer on his work, doubtful whether it was safe to leave his daughter again under the tree, he gave up for the day and returned to the village.

On arrival at his house he recounted in detail to his wife what had happened. 'I think we should go and see the Abbot,' she said. Accordingly, that evening they set out for the monastery with a present of fruit and buds on a stick. Passing out of the village by the gate in the stockade, they came to a pond covered with lotus, clustered so thickly that the water was hidden. By the side of the pond stood the monastery, a rustic building of wood and thatch. They climbed the steps and entered a room, where an old man in a yellow robe was sitting alone. After offering the present, the farmer told his story. The Abbot listened with great attention. 'What you tell me', he said, 'is very surprising. I never expected anything of the kind in a little village. You are quite sure you have given me the details correctly? It was a hamadryad and not some other snake that you saw?'

The farmer assured him his account was exact; he would not dare to tell his Reverence a lie.

'If that is so,' said the Abbot, 'your daughter is marked out for a great career. The phenomenon you mention is given explicitly in the books. Though rarely seen, the sign is a major sign and has been commented on from remotest antiquity. The hamadryad as king-cobra is the symbol of a king. When it advances in unusual fashion to meet a person, it stands for the coming of a king. When, as in this case, it encircles a girl, seeming to protect her by its attitude, only one interpretation is given—the girl is destined to be a queen. No exceptions to this rule have ever been recorded.'

The farmer was not so surprised as his wife. During those hours in the garden, he had sometimes imagined his daughter in the capital. Its red walls had worked on him for that very reason. What the Abbot said seemed to confirm an inner certainty. But his wife was astonished—'A queen!' she exclaimed.

Old Burmese Lady on the way to a Shrine
with a Present of Flowers
From a contemporary fresco at Pagān
By courtesy of the Royal Asiatic Society

★ *The Hamadryad* ★

On the way home they decided to say nothing about the matter to their neighbours, but quietly to fit the child in some measure for what was to come. The farmer was the richest man in the village and he was able to afford to bring her up like a lady. He called her Ma Saw and kept a nurse to look after her. Later he employed a governess and two maids. As she grew up he gave her the best education available. At festivals she was better dressed than anyone else. And he told her that some extraordinary future awaited her. In spite of this unsettling attention, she remained unspoilt. She was noted for three qualities—beauty, calmness and good heart.

These events occurred when Kyazwa, the philosopher king, was on the throne, the king who wrote a handbook on metaphysics for the use of his concubines. When Ma Saw was about twelve, he was succeeded by his son Usana, a buoyant prince, the reverse of his father.

ii

The Dirty Pup

This Usana was a lively fellow. As heir-apparent he found the atmosphere of the court so stuffy that he made frequent tours all over the country. His father was a pedant. The book on metaphysics was a standing joke, not for its matter, which was scholarly and profound and included sections on psychology and physics, but because the concubinate was obliged to read it. In normal times a girl might hope to rise through the various grades of that body on the strength of her good looks or her wit, her manner of making love or some pretty way. But under King Kyazwa there was only one ladder up, a fluent tongue for learned patter. The book was called, alarmingly, the *Paramatthabindu*, and for years it was on the table of every one of the court ladies. Those who could not understand it learnt short passages by heart, which they would bring out even in the privacy of the bedchamber. An apt quotation went further than a pointed breast. But women are marvellously adaptive to circumstances. The ladies laughed among themselves, but acquired the technique of talking like pundits. After a time they began to think they were really learned and to look down on other girls who expressed themselves normally. A court jargon grew up which was quite unintelligible outside the inner circle which surrounded the King. The evening parties in his rooms were stifling entertainments. He would have spent the day in successive conferences with doctors of letters and would arrive with fresh interpretations of the classics and their commentaries. These he would ask the concubines and ladies to discuss. The brightest girl was the one he chose to go to bed with, but even in bed he continued his quotations.

This air was too overcharged for Usana and he was always travelling. He liked hunting and visiting local governors. Indeed, his father encouraged him in this, making him his deputy when local enquiries were necessary or where a point of law had to be elucidated by an examination *in situ*. Kyazwa loathed talking to country people. On one of these trips Usana found himself at dusk approaching Myit-tha, a village of rice-fields and betel gardens on a pleasant stream. The hot weather was at its height with the month of April, and, as to the year, Ma Saw was not yet born.

When he reached the cultivated land near the village, the sun's disk rolled under the plain. It was the hour of the evening bell, when dust billows into the sunset as the cattle are driven home across the stubble fields. In that twilight the lanes were full of their lowing. There was peace, the voices of people rising up, a pulse of gongs from the monastery hill. Scent of flowers was dropping; the warmth was steeped with it.

When Usana was near the village well, he halted his elephant and ordered a footman to bring him a cup of water. Considering his rank, he did not use much state. In fact, he had not more than a dozen men with him. As he liked the ways of rustic folk, he found a small escort conducive to easy exchange.

At the well was the usual crowd of villagers, mostly girls having a bath. They had old skirts tucked round their waists and were pouring pots of water over their heads. Among them was a girl who had finished her bath; she wore a red skirt and a red flower in her hair. She had just drawn a last potful to wash the skirt she had bathed in, when the footman asked her to fill the prince's cup. They had all seen His Highness arrive and were making broad jokes about it. He was known by sight up and down the country and was extremely popular, particularly with the girls. So when the footman held out the cup to be filled, she poured gaily, saying to her companions: 'I came out to bathe, but have become the maid of the White Umbrella.' With that, she smiled across to the road where the prince was waiting, and then turning her back, began to wash the skirt. Usana saw her hair knotted on the nape of her neck and the red flower of hibiscus over her ear. He said nothing at the time, and after drinking the water went on to the monastery, where he was staying the night. But after his dinner he decided to make her closer acquaintance, and sent a message to her father, whom he learnt was a turner, a petty craftsman of the village, a man with no land, without the status of a landowner. The turner was naturally much flattered. He borrowed some silk clothes for his girl and got her to powder and scent herself carefully. They set out together through the heavy night. 'Do all you can', said he, as they went along, 'to persuade the prince to keep you for a bit. Think of the other children; we're very poor. Even if he only kept you a month, it would make all the difference.' 'You're talking nonsense,' said she, as she hurried behind him. 'I shall be back for sure in the morning. The most we can expect is the price of ten baskets of rice.' 'Well, get that anyhow,' said he. 'There's not half a basket left in the house.'

They found the prince in the guest-chamber of the monastery. He was very affable to the father. The poor man was quite dazzled. 'What a lovely gentleman he is!' he said afterwards. The girl herself had a success. She had never read anything in her life, but she could talk. She told Usana what the other girls at the well had said when they saw him or rather what she thought he would like to think they had said. Her words, fresh from the earth and her own mind, seemed almost like wisdom after the court chatter. She was so bright and easy, attentive and light, that he did not part with her in the morning. When he had finished his business at Myit-tha, he took her back with him to Pagān.

There she was given a small appointment in his household; as under-maid she used to fan him at meals or in the evening when he was not attending court. As the words had come out at the well, jokingly spoken, so she was, the maid of the White Umbrella, or, at least, of the heir-apparent, who in due course would succeed to that style. She was a good girl, humble and affectionate, and though the prince paid her quite a lot of attention, her attitude to the other girls and to his wife was irreproachable. She also sent her father presents of food and she did not forget her brother, who was a monk in Myit-tha monastery. A vacancy was made for him in one of the grand brick monasteries at the capital, actually the foundation over which the Royal Chaplain presided. She was able to effect this act of patronage owing to an increase in her own importance, which came about in the following manner. One day when she was on duty with the prince, the even beat of her lacquer fan began to falter. She felt suddenly dizzy and sank down on the floor. As the prince had a mild fondness for her, he gave her a thought and it occurred to him what must be the matter. Accordingly he directed that she was to be relieved of her duties and looked after carefully by the head matron. One day when he had almost forgotten about her, they mentioned that a son had been born to him. Now he had had only one son, the Prince Thihathu, a son whom his wife had presented to him some years back. None of his concubines had borne him boys. The new arrival had therefore some importance, for he could be recognised as heir if the elder son died. It was regrettable, however, that the mother was of such a low class. A boy by some mandarin's daughter would have been more acceptable. Perhaps this slight disappointment caused him to choose the name he did, for he called the infant the Dirty Pup.

When King Kyazwa died and Usana succeeded, this boy had been at school for some years. The monastery where his uncle lived had been chosen; he had the advantage there of lectures by the Royal Chaplain, the most distinguished scholar and ecclesiastic of the age. As for his mother, she was not so fortunate. When Usana moved into the royal apartments, he took over the court with all the women. The turner's daughter now expected official recognition. After all, she was the mother of the King's second son. But the court was too snobbish to swallow her origin, for though good-natured and affectionate, she was as common as dirt. So they said, the grand ladies who had become so learned. In a weak moment Usana consented to retire her. She was given a small estate and sent back to Myit-tha.

iii

The Sleeve

When the court was settling down to the new regime and trying to understand what was expected of it, place-seekers began to draw certain conclusions and to adapt themselves accordingly. Usana was going to be an easy king; hunting was likely to take the place of philosophy; girls would be judged on their looks and wit. Drink, too, was coming in again; Kyazwa's court had been dry in every sense. It was further noticed that Thihathu, the heir-apparent, who was just of age, had turned out earnest like his grandfather, but far less good-natured. He considered himself a gifted administrator, a delusion his ancestor had never entertained. Though of some capacity, he had no presence, and his manners were awkward and sometimes rude.

The big person was Yazathingyan, the Chief Minister. Lightly built, with a strain of Indian blood which gave him a high nose and a dark skin, he was a man of great ability and ambition. He had been minister under Kyazwa, but Usana had appointed him President of the Council. Aged fifty, he had had wide experience. His private fortune was immense. His residence, situated within the inner or palace city, was extensive and well appointed. His household and servants numbered two hundred; he had numerous slaves, elephants, horses and palanquins. Not a great intellectual, his insight was deep into men and affairs, and like many of his type he was fond of dabbling on the fringe of literature. For instance, he had always been interested in symbolism, and though extremely practical in his outlook was known to contemplate a treatise on signs.

So imposing a Chief Minister was not to Prince Thihathu's taste. It meant that his influence in the administration was of the smallest. He used to see Yazathingyan frequently closeted with the King; he did not know what projects they were concocting; and when he made proposals himself the King invariably withheld sanction until he had discussed them with the Chief Minister. The prince even found it difficult to get appointments for his people. All this irritated him to a degree. Not that he had just cause for irritation; it was not customary for the heir-apparent to stand between the King and his advisers; but he was a wrong-headed young man and did not understand his position. There was small excuse for his self-assertion. As the only legitimate son he had no reason to apprehend rivalry or intrigue. His half-brother by the turner's daughter did not count. All he had to do was to enjoy himself at court, a court which was likely to become most entertaining. But instead of taking things easily, he thrust himself forward and invited the slights which he invariably received. There were many little unpleasant-nesses between him and Yazathingyan, but it was not until the fourth year of the reign that a serious passage occurred.

Early in December of that year, Usana, who had fixed the following week for the annual ascent of Mount Pōpa to consult a state oracle which was situated on its shoulder, received in public audience the many notabilities who had come into the capital to join in the expedition. Public audience in Pagán was attended with a great deal of ceremony. It took place at dawn in the outer hall of the palace, a large, pillared apartment open on three sides and with a back wall, through a window of which the King showed himself. No ladies were ever present, but the Council, the courtiers and the whole of the mandarinate assembled in the hall, and, when the King became visible by the drawing up of the curtain over his window, prostrated themselves on the floor. As a rule the King then addressed certain formal questions to the ministers and, after noticing shortly the visiting officials, disappeared behind his curtain. The ceremony was calculated to impress persons who did not see him frequently.

On this occasion the audience proceeded in the usual way. The occupants of the hall lay face downwards before the curtained window; music sounded; the curtain was drawn; Usana was seen above them seated in his window like a statue of the Buddha looking from its niche. He had grown plumper, but he was clearly a man who enjoyed great vigour. His face had the glow

of perfect health, though he found the gold crown and
heavy robes tiring, more tiring than a march on the
back of an elephant.

Yazathingyan was below him on knees and elbows,
his hands joined in front of his bowed face. Dressed in
a silk robe with wide sleeves and a pointed hat, he had
touched the floor three times with his forehead when
the King was revealed. Close to him was Thihathu in a
similar posture and, behind, the mandarinate, lying as
thick as strewn flowers, the floor strewn with the colour
of their robes and sleeves. Above them rose the red
lacquered or gilded pillars into the roof. It was a calculated scene and suggested, as it was meant to suggest,
supplication to deity. Yazathingyan himself had stif-
fened the ceremonial where this allowed, as the more
elevated above mortality the King could be made to
appear, the more actual power there remained for his
agent, the Chief Minister, to wield.

When the usual questions and answers were over
and the King had addressed formal welcome to the
governors of outlying provinces, he began to speak of
the expedition to Pōpa.

'It is our intention,' he intoned, 'in accordance with
our practice and that of our ancestors, to make the
ascent of the sacred mountain, when the moon is full.
The oracle there may have something weighty to impart to us as heavenly regent. No one can tell what it
will impart, but as the realm is calm and prosperous we
have no reason to apprehend that its words will be disturbing. Had our ministers less application, our Chief
Minister less acumen, we might feel more uncertain,
but in the circumstances of a loyal Council and an able

President, we regard the present expedition in the light of routine.'

At the conclusion of these highly flattering remarks, which were as grateful to Yazathingyan's recumbent back as the sun's rays on a winter morning, conchs were blown, the curtain descended and the King disappeared. The audience at an end, those attending it were free to disperse. But the Chief Minister remained where he was, stretched on knee and elbow, his wide sleeves carpeting the floor about him, for he desired by prolonging his obeisance to emphasise the compliments of which he had been the recipient. Thihathu, rising to depart, was irritated to observe that he blocked his path. He waited an instant to give him time to get up, but Yazathingyan did not stir. The prince, already put out by the praise of the minister, concluded that his immobility was a calculated slight. When this mistaken notion entered his head, his irritation passed beyond control. He felt a tearing at the roots of his mind. Reckless wild thoughts rushed through it. So it had come to this, he was no more important than one of the carved figures on the walls. He might not exist for all the minister cared. Sunk in exaggerated obeisance to the father, he refused the common courtesy of passage to the son, spreading his sleeves to trip or force aside the heir-apparent. It was past bearing, beyond all insolence. Grimacing in the suddenness of his rage, he spat on the sleeve in the sight of the whole mandarinate. There was red juice of betel in his mouth and the silk brocade was stained suddenly as by a splash of blood.

At this atrocious insult there was a hush. The mandarins were frightened, but they were also interested.

Yazathingyan felt their prying eyes, their mocking
spirit. Instinctively hiding his rage and mortification,
he said mildly to Thihathu: 'The prince must forgive
me if I failed to see that he desired to pass.'

Thihathu had been sobered by his very act. When he
saw the red stain he knew that he had committed an
unpardonable indiscretion. At the tone of the minister's
voice he shuddered; the restraint of it was dreadful.
But as what he had done could not be undone, he
sought to revive the indignation which had given him
his courage, and pushed roughly out of the hall. The
mandarins shrank from him, knowing it was dangerous
to have seen the Chief Minister's humiliation, and slunk
away and dispersed into the town. Yazathingyan was
left in the empty room with his minions.

When he was alone, an inward paroxysm seized him.
He seemed to see the lacquered pillars on all sides
twisting, to see them writhing in motion like the trunks
of elephants. But this pressure became eased and he
said harshly to his servants:

'Bring me a chest!'

When one was brought, he took off his court dress
and placed it in the chest, looking the while intently at
the sleeve, where the splash of betel redly showed. Then
he straightened himself and faced his men. They did
not know his object in placing the robe in the chest,
but he had an air of menace as he did so. Putting on a
fresh robe, he signed to them to shoulder the box and
follow him to his residence.

That the heir-apparent had spat on the Chief Minister
was rumoured at once through the whole palace-city.
There was laughter in the bazaar. Old women, shout-

ing hoarsely, told stories of great ribaldry to account for the assault. A couple of girls began acting the parts of prince and minister. One spat at the other; indecent words were exchanged in jest; until one of them, angered by a thrust she thought was personal, dragged down the other's skirt and they came to blows, fell into an open drain and there fought on naked.

This licence spread through the streets, leading to further breaches of the peace and much hilarity. In due course the news reached the monastery, situated at some distance outside the walls, where the King's younger son was boarded. The prince, still known by the nickname his father had given him—Kwéchi Min or Prince Dirty Dog—was leaning over the wall which surrounded the garden. Girls were passing along the road. It was something to do, watching them go by. He was seventeen years old and bored with his books, bored with the monastery, longing to get out. Besides, he knew several of the girls. One of his sweethearts he now saw approaching from the direction of the city. She sold pineapples in the bazaar, a sprightly little thing. When she was level with him, she called from the road: 'Have you heard the news? It's most amusing.' She came up to the wall and told him what had happened. 'Yazathingyan is said to be half mad.' And added: 'Why don't you go and do something instead of sticking in that monastery?'

'What do you mean?' he asked, for he was not very bright, but the girl slipped away and was off up the road.

The prince, his ugly little face puckered with excitement, hurried into the monastery and told his uncle.

The monk was by no means intelligent, but when he heard the news, he had an intuition.

'I think we should go at once and condole with the Chief Minister,' he said. 'You see, it's like this. He'll be looking out for a way of paying back Thihathu. What better way than taking you up?'

The youth was much impressed by this suggestion.

'Do you think we ought to consult the Royal Chaplain first?' he enquired. 'He's reading in his room at the back of the circumambulatory.'

'I don't think we need. It's too lay a matter. He'd never give us his attention.'

They were talking in one of the cells off the main hall. Not wishing to be seen leaving by the front entrance, they turned into the corridor which surrounded the statue of the Blessed One, intending to go out by the side door near the Chaplain's room. But if they thought that he was immersed in his books they were mistaken, for as they reached the side door and glanced back to make sure that they were not observed, they saw him standing near the entrance to his chamber. He did not speak, but his right hand was raised in the gesture that betokens the taking away of fear. They prostrated themselves at once, but when they looked up again, he had disappeared. Hastily going out, they made a circuit through the grounds and struck the road to the city lower down. The sun set as they hurried on their way.

It was only a mile or so, and they reached Pagān before the gates were shut. Passing through the outer to the inner city, they approached by devious ways Yazathingyan's stockade. It was now dark, but when they explained their identity the watchman admitted them into a garden of shrubs and pots of flowers, deep in which loomed the house, wooden and high roofed. They halted at the porch.

In an upper room Yazathingyan was seated with members of his household. The chest was in the corner, spread with a scarlet canopy. Women came and went silently or in shadowy background lazed with cigars. The minister himself was brooding on the morning's insult. Shielded from the pert eye of public curiosity, he had lowered his guard. That he deeply felt the humiliation was written in his pose. News of merriment in the bazaar, of chatter on pagoda steps, had been carried to him by his familiars and thinking of the necessity of appearing as usual next day, he wondered if his nerve was strong enough to armour him against such derision. Some one whispered to him then that the Kwéchi Min was downstairs. An illumination spread over his face; he rose to his feet and descended to welcome him.

'My uncle and I have called to condole with your Excellency,' began the young prince, speaking with deference. 'We were shocked to hear of Thihathu's behaviour this morning. That such a lout should be heir to the throne!'

He was able to put such a note of respectful sympathy into his voice that Yazathingyan, tired and upset, was moved. It was like a hand-touch to one about to weep.

To expose the details of the interview which followed is hardly necessary. Suffice it to say that they came to a close understanding. The King was only thirty-six years of age, so that the question of the succession did not enter either of their heads. But the Kwéchi Min wanted to leave the monastery and be set up like a real prince with a household and estates. This exactly suited Yazathingyan, who sought a counterpoise to Thihathu, a method by which he could gradually undermine him. Who could tell—the cards well played —the heir-apparent might be tempted into some abortive rebellion? Then perhaps the Kwéchi Min might supplant him as heir. That would be a pretty revenge. But one must not look too far ahead. The first move was to get the younger prince an establishment.

'Leave it to me,' said Yazathingyan in conclusion.

'If your Excellency can effect this, please always count on my devoted service,' replied the other.

With these assurances they parted, the prince and his uncle to sleep the night at a monastery within the walls.

iv
The Mountain Oracle

During the ensuing week Yazathingyan did not find the atmosphere of the court as disagreeable as he had expected, because attention was concentrated on the expedition to Pōpa. Of the spirits inhabiting the mountain the view generally accepted was that they were the ghosts of two persons, a brother and sister, who had been burnt long ago in the far north of the kingdom, when their souls, instead of passing into the normal cycle of rebirth in this or some other world, had become earth-bound on the site of their death, where they haunted a tree. They were then malevolent ghosts, for any man or beast who entered so much as the shadow of the tree was blasted. But later, professionals who knew how to protect themselves against the evil of the occult dug up the tree and threw it into the river Irrawaddy, on the tide of which it floated to Pagān. There the authorities conceived the idea of carving from its wood statues of the brother and sister, in the hope that, if respect was shown, the ghosts would lose their evil character. That they were potent ghosts was indubitable, and if their potency could be enlisted in the public interest they would become a valuable national asset. This calculation proved to be correct, for the spirits, after their statues had been set up on the shoulder of Pōpa and provided with a shrine, where offerings of fruit and flowers were laid, consented annually to possess mediums, through the mouths of whom they gave intelligence often of much value, for it was prophetic in character. As time passed they came to be regarded as an oracle, which informed the monarchy and through it the people of what was likely to occur during the current year. They were named the Mahagiri.

In justice to the established Church it should be insisted that members of its holy order extended no official recognition to such rites. Its doctrine taught an escape from the world's illusion to absolute truth by meditation and good works. The Mahagiri could have no significance. The expedition to Pōpa, therefore, was no festival of the order, the members of which did not attend it. In short, it had no religious character, but, for the court, was a social excursion of an arresting kind and, for the people, an occasion when their rustic predilection for the occult and the pagan could be indulged.

Yazathingyan was hurrying on the preparations. The headmen of the mountain region were ordered to build the usual two camps, one at the foot of Pōpa, where the King would spend the night before the ascent, and the second on the shoulder adjacent to the shrine. The mediums were selected, and these, with musicians trained in the old music of the earth-rites, were sent forward to await the King's arrival. Dancers and drummers left daily in carts, with loads of hangings, lamps, cushions and wine.

At first light on the morning of the full moon day of December Usana mounted his elephant at the door of the private apartments, and took his seat on the roofed saddle, beside which was spread the White Umbrella. In front of him, on the elephant's head, was a driver, his legs under the ears. A large procession formed about him. There was Yazathingyan on his elephant, a regiment of the elephant-guards, a regiment of the horse-guards, with mandarins and musicians, ladies in palanquins and umbrella-holders walking. Everybody of importance at court was present, from Thihathu, the heir-apparent, to the Mayor of the Palace and the Captain of the Boats.

A start was made, and they passed through the town, music playing. Usana, on his tall elephant with its gilded tusks, was level with the roofs, which seemed to flutter as their winged eaves lifted them up. So they paraded till they reached the Tharaba gate in the outer wall. It was remarked by some as they went under it that bees were building a hive on the lintel. But they said nothing, for it was a bad sign and had the King seen it he might have turned back.

Crossing the lotus-moat, they entered the plain and made east towards the rising sun. The bulk of Pōpa straddled before, its western flanks dark in shadow, the cone rising tremendously overhead. But though its pressure seemed upon them, not until evening did they reach the village at its foot, where the first camp had been pitched.

The headmen of circles and villages were in attendance. Though Usana was obliged to use state on a country tour of this significance, his manner to the people was easy and pleasant.

'What news', he asked, 'for the climb to-morrow?'

'There is no news in particular, Lord of Life,' intoned the elders. 'All is ready, the Mahagiri wait.'

'On an occasion of this kind,' he smiled, 'I should have been glad to hear of some propitious sign.'

He knew how to talk to rustics, thaw their nervousness, draw them out.

'Your Majesty permitting,' murmured the oldest man, very prostrate, 'we have heard it said that in Kanbyu, a village of this mountain, there is a jasmin bush which has flowered in three colours.'

'Indeed,' said Usana pleased, for he liked country marvels. 'To whom does the bush belong?'

'It was planted by a landowner's daughter called Ma Saw and stands in her father's garden.'

'What do you think of that?' the King asked Yazathingyan. It was the minister's special subject and he replied:

'As Your Majesty is aware, the interpretation of signs is not concerned with cause and effect, but with juxtaposition in time and place. The present phenomenon of the three-coloured jasmin primarily concerns the owner, not us. She is evidently about to come by some extraordinary good fortune.'

'It will be interesting to follow this up,' observed the

King. 'On the descent from the mountain, we might visit Kanbyu.' No more was said and they entered the camp, where in bamboo and on a miniature scale a model of the palace at the capital had been constructed.

At sunset, when he had finished supper, Usana came out upon a dais to witness the ritual dances, which always took place on the full moon night before the ascent to the oracle. The dais, an arbour of flowers, of which trunks of plantain were the pillars, their leaves a canopy of waving spires, stood in a courtyard before a stage on which the dancers would appear. Along the sides of the courtyard the officials and the ladies were accommodated, while seated on the ground were hundreds of villagers.

After the King was well set, he said to Yazathing-yan, who was close below him:

'My offering to the Mahagiri is five hundred lamps. Light up now, touch the drums and let the dancers come out.'

The lamps were lit and night fell apace, for the shoulder of Pōpa stood against the rising moon. Then was heard a burst of that old music which had been in the kingdom before the pure knowledge of the Blessed One was brought from the south. Wild it was, and as if blowing from far places; those who heard it awoke to the world of spirits. Their eyes opened on a great distance; they were aware of calling and laughter. It was as if their souls came flooding up, as if they drowned in some nethermost tide. Yet as the King listened, there seemed to him some dissonance in those notes, voices that did not chime, colours of clanging shade; and he saw animal forms and heard patter of feet.

The dancers were now moving through a measure, which, square at first, became a fretted circle as the full moon lifted from Pōpa, a moon of power which quenched all lamps but those in the palm-shadows. There was a low cry from the people, as if they had been sucked into the two circles, and with the moon and the dance were floating in a plenitude. With a coiling movement the dancers changed the meander. A sigh went up. So from pattern to pattern the dances continued till the invocation was complete.

The King retired for some rest after midnight and before the first glimmer of day was on his elephant, for it was customary to reach the second camp on the shoulder soon after dawn. As they brushed through the forest the dew lay wringing wet on the fronds. It was a rugged narrow path and the procession was strung out to an immense length, men, horses, palanquins, elephants, winding through the trees. Though the moon still held, her light was changing, hardening, her silver turning grey. Suddenly the earth gave up her odour more strongly and as men looked they saw that what had been blurred was distinct, for the dawn had come.

When the sun was clearing the tree-tops they reached an open space high on Pōpa's shoulder, in the centre of which was the shrine which housed the wooden shapes of the Mahagiri. The procession was brought to a halt. A great crowd of people had already arrived and an undercurrent of drums spoke of rising excitement.

The King entered his camp, which was a replica of that at the bottom of the hill, and, dismounting, enquired whether the mediums were present and when the ceremony would begin. He was informed that

43

everything was in readiness and that as soon as he was seated on the dais, which faced the shrine, the mediums would come out. There was a short delay and he took his place.

The mediums now advanced to pay their respects to him before they began their dance. They were stoutly built women of the lowest class and about fifty years of age. Dressed in finery after the style of court ladies, but with bony jaws, low foreheads and creased faces, they had an air of effrontery which contrasted with their elegant clothes and tall head-dresses. As they approached, their lips smacked out rollicking phrases, for both of them had taken drink.

When below the King's dais, they went down on hands and elbows, touching the ground many times with their foreheads. Then rising, they postured before him, saying heartily, with all the licence of the occasion:

'The King of the World has come up to Pōpa with his queens and maids, concubines and ladies. But they cannot help him to-day. He must have us,' and they capered and grimaced, 'nobody else can amuse him here. We are his maids, will he take us now?'

It was etiquette to laugh at this boisterous address and for the King to answer:

'Can I steal from the sky? The esteemed ladies are promised to the Mahagiri.'

'The King is master of men and spirits,' they shouted back, making obscene gestures. More drink was brought to them by a boy of ten.

But a maddening burst of the drums announced that the dance before the shrine was about to commence.

The sun poured down a dazzling light on the open space in front of it. The images were in shadow within, but their forms could dimly be perceived. Surrounding the space were the local villagers in hundreds. The slope of green behind was chequered with them, all ages from dim old men to children at the breast. Looking over their heads were the royal elephants. The woods, stretching away endlessly over the mountain landscape, enclosed them all as in a magic circle.

In the centre of that circle the mediums began to dance. At first their steps were slow; their arms, twisting and sinuous in spite of age, marked the poses; it was a measured rite they were accomplishing. Slowly expression left their faces; cheerful insolence was gone, the music had welled over them. Now the tempo increased; their movements were of delving inwards; their eyes had become glazed. At any moment the Mahagiri might possess them, so it seemed. The crowd on the periphery, straining to hear the imminent cry and the strange voice, as the spirits entered and addressed the King, felt themselves swinging round the centre as if the circle had become a revolving wheel. But the dance continued; still no voice was heard. A movement of alarm passed like a little wind. Was something wrong? Was the incantation miscarrying? The court was looking fixedly at the mediums, who seemed abnormally distressed. No one noticed that some of the village people near the forest margin had fled, nor that the elephants had coiled up their trunks. Then through a gap in the spectators were seen approaching two tigers. At leisure they sauntered to the mediums and, suddenly fatal, struck them down.

There was a vast shout of horror: 'The Mahagiri have entered the tigers.'

Panic followed, for it was not forgotten that in old days the Mahagiri had been evil spirits. The crowd of villagers plunged into the jungle, dragging their children after them, blind with fright. The court was thrown into confusion by a stampede of the elephants, which, squealing, had rushed down the slope, scraping off their howdahs as they crashed under the branches. Horses fought with grooms and broke for home. Men ran to yoke bulls and drove away furiously, standing in the carts the better to urge the animals. A mat caught fire by the kitchens and immediately the whole camp went up in flames. There was every reason for a speedy evacuation. Yazathingyan managed to rally part of the bodyguard and ordered them to carry the King away in a palanquin. He himself followed on a horse which had remained eating grass throughout the turmoil. Meanwhile the tigers tore the mediums to pieces.

V

The Jasmin Bush

When they reached the camp at the foot and Yazathingyan had time to think, he saw at once that the irruption of the tigers could have only one meaning. He had not the smallest doubt that Usana's days were numbered. True, he had not seen his master's horoscope. The contents of that document were kept a close secret by the Royal Chaplain. But the strange episode on the mountain was ample evidence that an event of mortal significance to the King was just under time's horizon. In the whole course of his experience he had never observed a more startling piece of symbolism. As a rule signs were less obvious, beehives in the ceiling or apparitions in the throne room, though there had been, of course, some very striking examples in history. He recalled to mind, for instance, how it was recorded in the annals that before King 'Kanlat's death an ogrish fiend had wandered laughing over the whole realm for seven days, those who heard the laugh not daring to sleep; and announcing King 'Kanlaung's passing, waves had boiled up furiously in the river on a calm day; and there was the well-known case of the so-called Golden Coconut king, when a tiger had entered the palace itself, thereby symbolising the very arrival of death. But that morning's work was the clearest sign of all. For tigers to break into a crowd was unheard of in the normal practice of those animals. There was only one reasonable explanation. The Mahagiri, to demonstrate what they had to impart, had enacted the King's death by analogy.

But putting aside the occult interpretation, the phenomenon as such remained. The science of signs was a science of sequences following upon observed phenomena, sequences tabulated over centuries. It was not necessary to look beyond the fact of the sign. Founding himself on the empiric, Yazathingyan was forced to the same conclusion as he had drawn from the supernatural. All the old treatises, all his experience, all analogies told him that what he had seen was a mortal symptom; the King was doomed.

That being the case, where did he himself stand? In a slippery place, he felt, for Thihathu was the heir-apparent. If the prince came to the throne, his first act would be to dispense with the services of the Chief Minister. His succession was ruin. But could he be displaced in time by the other son? It might be very difficult. If the King was to die shortly, it would be impossible. The moment they got back to Pagān he must get in touch with the Kwéchi Min. How fortunate it was that they had already had that interview.

He was unable to continue his train of thought because at that moment he received a message from the King that his attendance was desired. On his way to the royal quarters he decided to make light of the day's happenings and if feasible to distract his master's attention to something else. In that manner he would have a freer hand in the eventualities.

Usana's disposition was naturally sanguine, but he had received a shock. 'A disastrous consultation!' he exclaimed without ceremony to Yazathingyan, as he came in. 'You know that I am not easily upset, but the turn taken by the séance this morning was hardly reassuring. Do you think we are in for a bad time?'

'Not necessarily at all,' replied his minister. 'There may be some natural explanation of what happened. Perhaps the music was incorrectly played, or the mediums by means of arts unknown to us tampered with the rite.'

'That seems unlikely,' replied the King. 'I followed the music carefully; there was no mistake. As for the mediums, they were tried women.'

'Once you begin dabbling with the occult, you are on doubtful ground. I think the Church is very wise to avoid such practices. After all, we know nothing of the Mahagiri nor do we know what passes in their abode. It may be the tigers were possessed by other spirits.'

'No other spirits have ever been reported on the mountain. But the appearance itself, what does it symbolise, for we must assume that so strange an event is a symbol of something?' Usana had always accepted Yazathingyan as an expert in that branch of empiric science.

49

The latter now assumed a sophisticated air:

'I doubt very much, you know, whether we should take a serious view,' he said. 'Admittedly the phenomenon belonged to the category of unpropitious manifestations, but my experience is that an evil sign of the first magnitude is generally insidious. It does not blazon itself on the attention in quite the manner of the tigers. Speaking as a person with a tolerably long experience in these matters, I should advise calm.'

'It is rather a coincidence', observed the King thoughtfully, 'that while I was listening to the earth-music last night I had a curious premonition of animal forms and the patter of feet. I now wonder whether this had to do with what we have just seen or refers beyond to what is symbolised. It almost suggests that I am in danger from an animal.'

'With great respect I submit that Your Majesty should not give way to such fancies. They become a a habit, they poison existence. With signs one at least has the considered data of the past, but premonitions are not amenable to any check.'

Yazathingyan paused here, and then, in a tone graded to be mildly provocative, he added: 'We have had such a morning with unpropitious signs that it might be of interest to explore what appears to be propitious. The old headman yesterday mentioned a jasmin bush the flowers of which were in three colours. When Your Majesty expressed a wish to visit Kanbyu village where the bush is situated, I caused enquiries to be made. My informants assure me that the story is true and add that the farmer's daughter is exceptionally good-looking. Accordingly, I made bold to arrange an excursion there for to-morrow morning. If the girl is very attractive and is going to be very lucky, it might be worth Your Majesty's while to consider taking her into the palace. There are cases where association with a lucky person brings luck.'

This suggestion appealed to the King. A strange bush, a pretty girl—it would be better than returning dashed to Pagān. Usana was never depressed for long. He readily agreed and the minister departed to make the arrangements.

Kanbyu village lay on high ground not far from the royal camp. The inhabitants were well aware of the King's arrival in their vicinity, and news of the catastrophe on the mountain had reached them, carried by persons who had fled from the tigers. Everyone had enough knowledge of signs to know that what had happened was highly ominous. It was whispered that the King's life was in danger. In anticipation that his demise would be followed by disorder, certain men of disrepute were already in consultation, and the headman was considering whether the stockade required strengthening. The matter of the triple flowers, which had been exciting them all for days, passed out of mind, and they were surprised to receive Yazathingyan's message that the King might be expected the following morning. In fact, it seemed so unlikely that he would come after what had happened on Pōpa, that they made no preparations and did not inform Ma Saw and her father. When, therefore, a man posted on the lookout ran in to say that he had seen the King's elephant in the distance mounting towards them, there was some confusion. The farmer was hurriedly sent for and the headman with his council, after slipping on their silk clothes, made for the gateway at their best pace.

They were hardly in position when the royal procession rounded a corner of the road. The King had chosen to dispense with state; only Yazathingyan was with him and a small body of armed men. There cannot have been more than twenty-five in the party.

When they reached the gate, the Chief Minister, sitting his elephant, addressed the prostrate elders, using one of the King's titles which consorted well with the simplicity of the occasion.

'The Future Buddha', he said, 'has had the complacence to interest himself in your bush. He understands that it has blossomed in three colours of flowers.'

'That is true, your Excellency,' enunciated the elders as well as they could from their position on the ground.

'Show the way, then. The Lord of Paradise is in a hurry.'

As they entered the village, Yazathingyan beckoned to the headman. The man climbed onto his elephant and knelt on the haunches.

'The Ma Saw who planted the bush, who is she?' the minister asked confidentially.

'She is only a young girl, hardly grown up, but there is something vivid about her. She is like the daughter of a happy spirit. That man walking there is her father, the man with the soft face of a flautist.'

'Let me talk to him,' ordered Yazathingyan. The farmer was told to approach and walk close to the elephant.

The minister, bending slightly so that he could speak

in low tones, asked: 'What do they say here is the meaning of the bush?'

'The Abbot said that my daughter's fortunate time had arrived.'

'Arrived? Then you had earlier reason to think she would be lucky?'

In reply the farmer told him briefly the story of the hamadryad. Yazathingyan was deeply interested. He asked a number of questions with animation. The whole affair was going to make a first-rate chapter in the book on signs which, as had been correctly rumoured, he was compiling.

'It may well turn out', said he, 'that you are quite right, for possibly His Majesty may summon your daughter to the palace,' and broke off the conversation, for they were close to the house.

Ma Saw was still in ignorance of the King's arrival. Her father had been too absent-minded to send her a message. In the fresh morning air she was gardening in front of the house, quite unconscious of what was happening at the village gate. In her hand was one of those sticks on which buds are strung when an offering of flowers is made to pagodas, and with this she was making holes in the earth of pots and boxes. A maid was standing by with various kinds of flower seeds. Ma Saw had a busy and jovial air. She pursed her lips as she popped in the seeds. A puppy gambolled near her feet. She had had her bath and coiled up her hair, but was wearing the simplest costume possible, a hand-printed cotton skirt falling from her waist. Palms waved above her, and as she bent over the pots the golden skin of her back was mottled in light and shadow.

In this way she continued artlessly to garden as the royal procession moved through the village, but at the unaccustomed tramp of feet, she looked up from her work and saw the heads of the elephants over the hedge. In a flash she was aware of the White Umbrella.

Now she had been brought up to believe that an extraordinary future awaited her. During the last week the interpretation put upon the freakish flowering of her bush had excited her a good deal. In fact, as she gardened, she had been wondering when this long-foretold fortune would arrive. At the sight of the King she knew it must be close, but felt she was hardly dressed to meet it. Her first impulse was to run into the house. Then she thought, 'No, one should not be eager, nor should one meddle with the tide of events.' With her back to the King, who had now entered the garden, she continued for the moment to plant her seeds in the pots.

Usana remained seated on his elephant. He was aware of her presence, but he did not stare at her. Instead, glancing round, he observed gently: 'The high view from this house is very pleasant. What peace there is and freshness too. Some day', he continued, 'I must build hereabouts a pavilion and a little shrine. In the evening to sit and watch the sun fall into Irrawaddy as the smoke of cooking fires went straight up, how that would wrap one away from the travail of the world.' He spoke almost sadly; the shock of the previous day had left him less buoyant.

'And now', he added, 'show me this bush.'

The headman and elders made polite signs; it was a few steps down the garden; would the Future Buddha deign to look?

Usana dismounted and, with the White Umbrella held over him, stood for a moment surveying the house, a commodious wooden building raised on posts six feet high, the roof thatched, airy and clean. Ma Saw was now underneath it, kneeling on a mat, her hands joined in an attitude of respect. Usana let his eyes rest on her face an instant, that lovely face which was destined to be so famous. 'The daughter,' said Yazathingyan in a low whisper. The King said nothing, but walked towards the bush.

True enough, when he examined it, the flowers were of different colours, even their forms were not altogether the same. 'How very curious,' he said. 'This is really marvellous. Your daughter', he went on, turning to the farmer, who was standing near by with a detached air, 'must be allied to the influence which has transformed this common bush. These things are mysterious, but I cannot think that if some one else had planted it, there would have been such flowers. She must possess a hidden rarity which in this way is made known, as where a spirit passes the air is scented.'

These words, spoken in the melancholy tone the King had used since his arrival, sounded to the villagers inexpressibly gracious. To Yazathingyan it seemed that his master was becoming subject to an influence of another sort. At a convenient moment he whispered: 'Shall I make the necessary arrangements?' At the King's nod he withdrew a few paces and beckoned the headman.

'I am instructed to tell you', he said, 'that His Majesty is pleased with the way you have received him. You may present yourself to-night at the royal camp, when he will know how to reward you. The farmer should accompany you with those members of his family, including his daughter, whom he may wish to bring.'

The headman understood his orders perfectly. Shortly afterwards the King departed.

vi
Ma Saw's Elevation

When all was quiet again, Ma Saw climbed the stairs onto the house and seated herself in the centre of the large front room. She had gathered the purport of what Yazathingyan had said and knew that she was to go at least to the camp palace. Her father and the headman followed her upstairs; her mother, aunts and sisters crowded round her. Friends came in, looking at her with a new respect. It was her first court.

'Lady,' said the headman with a formality he had never used before, 'when you are at the King's side do not forget me. You heard how he spoke of a shrine and a rest-house. A word from you and I might get the contract.'

'I am not yet in the palace; I must first please the King,' she replied smiling.

'His Majesty seemed to me pleased already. He seemed very taken at the first glance.'

'Impossible,' laughed Ma Saw, 'with all his women.' But she felt the rush of overflowing spirits.

'I wonder what present the King will give to-night,' her mother was asking. For answer her father took up his flute and played an air from one of the operas. Under cover of the music some of the others tried to get Ma Saw's ear. For each of them she had a lively reply, as: 'Ask again when they have built a pagoda in the shape of one of my breasts.' Her manner was rich and broad. They retreated well satisfied. The stream of callers increased as the day wore on. The garden was full of people watching the house with fascination. They sat and smoked, saying little but missing nothing. One man attempted to pluck a flower from the bush, but that was prevented.

Later in the day the Abbot of Kanbyu was announced. He came in attended by an urchin carrying a great fan. Way was made and when he was seated apart on the best mat, he said: 'From Ma Saw's infancy there were hints of this, glints of light that were thrown forward in time.'

Then some one asked: 'But what about the Mahagiri? Can the King last, and if he falls what will become of our little lady?'

'Whatever happens, she must benefit,' said the Abbot. 'It is not my business to declare on the King's chances. But you must remember there are three kinds of flowers on the bush. That may very well refer to three periods, each highly fortunate, in Ma Saw's life.'

When the sun began to decline, a covered cart was got ready. Two fine bulls were yoked. Their humps were fat and stiff, their dewlaps loose and glossy. The cart, too, was gay, carved in flying lines, a carpet within under the thatched roof. Ma Saw, who had made an elaborate toilette, climbed in with her father and mother; her favourite aunt also accompanied them. The driver called to the bulls and made play to poke them with his stick. They left in a jingle of bells, trotting down the rough and dusty road.

As they approached the royal camp, the sun set over the plain. It was that enchanting moment of the day when, as at dawn, the scents of the earth are released. The stubble fields yielded their particular odour, as did the ponds and rushy places, and these seemed to mingle with the colours, making them richer and almost palpable. Through this countryside they drove on, exchanging remarks with those standing by the roadside, as, from them, 'How much did you pay for your cigars?' or, from the loiterers, 'Where are you taking that pretty girl?'

On arrival at the camp they were told to wait. It was now almost cold, and as they sat beside the cart, they wrapped shawls round their shoulders. After a time Yazathingyan sent for them. Darkness had fallen as they approached to kneel on the verandah of his mat house. He called them into a room and there in a tired voice said to the headman: 'The King has directed me to tell you that you should attend at the palace on a day to be fixed, when he will present you in audience with a silver-mounted sword. He has also desired me', he continued, turning to the farmer, 'to give you this in earnest of future favours,' and he handed him a small bag of gold. Dismissing the men, he then addressed himself to the women.

'The King is asleep. Recent events have tired him. You may go now to a room which has been prepared for you. In the morning there will be a conveyance to take you to Pagān.'

They withdrew after making a very low obeisance. The intelligence was highly satisfactory, for it meant that Ma Saw was to go to the palace. There was no question of her being only a night's amusement. In the room allotted to them, the three women were soon fast asleep on mats, wrapped in blankets they had brought with them.

An hour before dawn the bustle of departure began. By sunrise Ma Saw had completed her toilette and with her aunt and mother sat waiting orders. They were again summoned to Yazathingyan's presence. This time they did not actually see him, for he was engaged behind a screen, but he sent out word that a palanquin had been reserved for Ma Saw, and that she now should take her place in it. Her mother and aunt were to follow in a cart. The palanquin shortly afterwards came into view, borne by four men. It had open sides and a tiered roof. She took her seat joyously on its carpeted floor and when all was ready the bearers carried her away.

A long procession began to move out of the camp. For Ma Saw, who had never been beyond Kanbyu village, it was all new. She saw the King's elephant, surrounded by a troop of cavalry, in front. Yazathingyan was behind him. She tried to distinguish the palanquins of the queens, but the procession was so long, there were so many elephants, horses, attendants and carriages, that it was impossible to make out who was who. As the sun mounted higher and dried the dew, it became pleasantly warm. A strong wind began blowing from the north-east, carrying the dust in clouds over the bare fields on their left hand. The harvest was in; an air of plenty and delight lay over the land. Ma Saw sang as she was carried through scene after lovely scene.

Towards midday a halt was made for refreshment at a small temple recently built by the King. It was one of the hundreds for which the neighbourhood of Pagān was noted, and Ma Saw, accustomed only to the rustic shrines of Kanbyu, found it rich and strange. From her palanquin, now resting on the ground, she looked at the cement reliefs on the exterior. Over the doorway facing her was a long monster, its back hunched, its eye more roguish than wild. In its gaping jaws lions stood rampant, reaching at manikins dancing on its head. All up its back flames were curling. In the topmost of these was a dwarf on whose bulging cheek was genially seated a little demon looped in fat. Looking further at the pediments and friezes, she saw unicorns and flying elephants; spirits who were snorted from the jaws of dragons; deer or peacocks which jostled saints. At this cheerful medley her spirits bubbled over and she laughed outright. The most dreadful creatures, lions, dragons, harpies, were frisky and full of tricks in the presence of the gentle Buddhas housed within the temple.

Usana had dismounted and was now entering the doorway. Ma Saw, mingling with his train, peeped in to watch. The interior was like a cave. Beyond a small vestibule was a square central pillar surrounded by a corridor. She took courage and went in. Against the pillar were four statues, the four Buddhas who had been on earth, Kakusandha, Konagamana, Kassapa and Gotama. They sat there, back to back, facing the four quarters of the world, smiling a hidden smile, sheathed in the tranquillity of their *samādhi* trance. She observed the King on his knees, repeating the Three Gems and other versicles. Far removed was this from the previous day's attempted commune with mountain spirits, when for tipsy mediums the tempo of the music was wrought up to madness. Here was the peace of the Eightfold Path, of the Lords who possessed the Ninefold Glory.

But lest such abstractions should prove too cold she saw that on the walls in fresco were provided scenes which repeated the happy abandon of the reliefs without. To her left was a spirit flying downwards with tossing hands and feet flung up, graceful and young. It came from clouds, but clouds which, as you looked, took life. For she saw eyes staring from them, or were they the nipples of breasts? As she asked the question, she saw the clouds wreathe up more exuberantly into curling shells, which imperceptibly became owls and bulldogs and then bears and ducks. Letting her glance sweep with the line's rhythm, she found that these animals were now sprouting creepers from mouth or tail; that every being passed in and out of the vegetable world, trunks of elephants turning into palm-trees and human hair or finger-nails growing leaves. Yet it was no menacing jungle of the underworld, but a buzz of happy creatures rejoicing in the bliss of community with all things. And heartily Ma Saw thanked the dear Buddhas, who spread about them such concord.

The King had finished his devotions and moved further in to admire a fresco which one of his artists had recently finished. Beautifully coloured, the line abounding with life, the painting symbolised the defeat of illusion by the truth. Ma Saw followed in the crowd and heard the King say to Yazathingyan:

'Have you rewarded the man yet?'

'He was paid the usual fee.'

'Well, pay him again. This is a masterpiece.'

The picture was certainly remarkable. In the centre sat the last Buddha, Gotama, calm and smiling, the fingers of his right hand touching the earth. Towards him on the left were seen approaching the hosts of Mara, Lord of Illusion, riding on every animal they could press into service, camels and asses, even fowls and cobras. They had a cheerful look of effrontery on their faces, the men girt up to attack, shaking their spears or winding horns, the women in tight jackets, ogling as they advanced. Their rout then followed and they passed away to the right, more like a carnival troop than a broken army, for the women, as they fled, made play with their hips and bosoms, while the men, now disarmed, danced lightly or laughed farewell. If there was defeat, there was no malice; Mara had to be put down, but the Enlightened did not bully him; his presumption was judged no worse than an irreverent jest.

Ma Saw from her position behind the King was able to hear him say: 'It is in that spirit that I have tried to rule the kingdom.' Yazathingyan allowed an expression almost of warmth to suffuse his hard features. For a moment he was as fond of Usana as a minister can be of his King.

A move was now made towards the door. Merged in the crowd, Ma Saw left the building and returned to her palanquin. The long march was resumed, temples large and small becoming more numerous as the city grew closer. At sunset they crossed the outer moat and reached the Tharaba gate.

Now this gate had a well-known guardian. When it was built four hundred years earlier, a human soul had been bound to it. The art of binding a soul to a strong place, with the object of protecting that place, had been exercised from great antiquity. The pure religion regarded the practice as illusory and evil, but if it was in abeyance during Usana's reign its usefulness was not denied. The enslavement of a soul was carried out as follows. When the trench for the foundation of a treasure vault or gate had been dug, a man was taken (sometimes a criminal or sometimes a casual passer-by who was seized at a moment when by astronomical calculation it was clear that the rite would be efficacious) and was placed living in the trench, when the foundations were built on top of him. It was found by experience that the ghosts of persons so immolated did not wander away. They remained on the site; from time to time they were seen there and in moments of danger they gave warning. Such a soul had been bound to Tharaba. It's name was Tepathin.

As the King, seated high on his elephant, passed under the gate, he did not see Tepathin, but he heard a buzzing sound and ordered his driver to stop. Looking up, he noticed bees flying backwards and forwards to a hive, which they had built against the lintel.

'Did you see that hive on the way out to Pōpa?' he asked the driver.

The man trembled too much to reply, for he had seen it. Impatiently Usana beckoned to Yazathingyan to come up, and pointing to the hive said in a low voice:

'That hive must have been building when we passed outwards four days ago.'

Yazathingyan said nothing. He studied the hive. A tremor shook him. It was another warning, an urgent warning. A hive above the head was one of the most established of evil signs. That it was on Tharaba suggested that Tepathin had chosen to warn in that manner. Did it mean, on top of what had happened, that the King had left but a very short time? It was agitating, so much had to be done. He looked at his master, who seemed suddenly tired. There was nothing to be said. One could not belittle such a sign. Usana observed his reticence and exclaimed:

'Had I seen the bees on the way out I should have known what to expect on the mountain.'

Much depressed, he harshly directed his driver to proceed.

Ma Saw was too far back in the procession to see this episode. Her attention, indeed, was wholly occupied with the magnificence of the spectacle before her eyes, the great moat with its lotus flowers, the red brick walls stretching away on each side, crowned at intervals with towers. After passing through the Tharaba gate she saw the outer city, rectangular streets, broad and flanked with shade-trees, the wooden houses standing in their own gardens. They came then to the wall of the inner city and entering there she beheld the houses of the ministers and at last the royal residence itself, not far from the bank of Irrawaddy, a lovely work of art in wood, its central spire tapering up into the sunset sky, the roofs carved all over, in the manner of the temple mouldings, with every variety of scene from life and legend, depicted with the same laughing temper, but, perhaps, with more vibrant effect. It was of one storey, and the various buildings of which it was composed centred upon the two halls of audience, the outer with its pillars of red and gold lacquer now coming into view. The procession wound in. Usana, dismounting, disappeared through a doorway. The bearers of Ma Saw's palanquin carried her to a group of buildings further round, where in their separate apartments lived the queens, the concubines and their ladies-in-waiting.

Word had evidently been sent forward by Yazathingyan, for when Ma Saw was put down at a side door, she was received with broad kindness by an old woman, who led her into a private room. Two maids came forward and were soon busy with water for a bath, laying out in readiness for her afterwards a change of clothes. Carpets, screens, scent, powders were in profusion. Cigars and betel-nut lay on silver trays, flowers were arranged in silver vases. Two lamps before a little shrine provided enough light. The maids waited on her with pleasant flatteries. Supper, when it came, was excellent. She had finished and was smoking a cigar when they told her that her mother and aunt were accommodated in one of the Chief Minister's guest-houses.

Pagán City

A reconstruction by Thomas Yule, early in the nineteenth century
By courtesy of the Royal Asiatic Society

Half an hour later the old woman approached and said:

'A message has come that His Majesty will see you this evening.'

Now Ma Saw was only an adolescent of sixteen. She had had no experience of life outside a country village, but she possessed the secret of an intense femininity. Very close to the earth, she had something of its power. At this intelligence that she was to go shortly into the presence, she was not as abashed as she might have been. She had seen the King in public and had some clue of how to conduct herself with him in private. Moreover, she was very intelligent and had plenty of aplomb. Accordingly she replied to the old woman with a little pout: 'When the King calls, I am ready.'

It was not very much after this that the call came. The old woman bustled onto her feet. Ma Saw rose gracefully and followed her. They passed down corridors open on one side to the night and were admitted into the King's chamber by a side door.

Usana half reclined on a low couch. He was dressed negligently in loose silk and though fatigued and anxious wore his habitual expression of good nature. To one side knelt a couple of ladies-in-waiting. Otherwise the lofty room, carved and lacquered in low relief, was empty. The old woman retired, leaving Ma Saw just inside the door.

'Come and sit here,' said Usana, pointing to a rug beside him.

With a fluttering movement, bent double, her palms together, she approached and like a little bird lit on the mat. She smiled.

The King was pleased. He did not care for shy women, more particularly that night, when he was upset.
And she was very graceful, almost like that flying spirit
on the temple wall. He had sent for her because he
wished to distract himself from gloomy thoughts. Yet
he could not help speaking of what troubled him.

'You saw the bees this evening on the lintel of
Tharaba, I suppose?' he asked.

'No, Lord,' she replied. 'I was behind in my palanquin, singing. To one who had never beheld the Golden City, bees offered no distraction.'

'There was a hive. What would they say in your village to such a sign?'

'In my village we are poor trembling rustics. A leaf
cannot fall crosswise but we ask the reason, for a small
calamity is enough to ruin us. But the King of Burma
can laugh at bees.'

'Yazathingyan does not think so.'

'I have heard that the Chief Minister's amusement is
collecting signs. The gloomier they are, the more dra-
matic for his album. His interpretations therefore are
seldom cheerful.'

Usana began to brighten with the robust tonic of her
wit. It was surprising at her age. There were some
clever and amusing women in the palace, but she promised to excel them. Replying to her sally he said lightly:

'You think Yazathingyan likes to conjure up ghosts.
But what would happen to him if I went off?'

Ma Saw, however, was not to be drawn into so dangerous a topic. She said nothing and the King went
on:

'If he likes gloomy signs, he has had plenty of them

68

recently. You heard about the tigers? It was a shocking sight. They marched on like an hallucination.'

But she, in a half serious rich manner, replied:

'The woods of Pōpa are full of tigers. I have seen them in my village on a variety of occasions, at midday take the headman's pony, at midnight eat the clerk's baby. For us they are just hungry beasts.'

Usana found a comforting broadness in her unconventional manner. He dropped the subject of his fears and took her hand.

'Has she not a lively hand?' he said, turning to the two ladies-in-waiting, who knelt a few paces distant, an expression of indulgence on their charming faces.

'A lively hand to amuse a good-humoured King.' They quoted an old song. 'The King is so genial that the hands of those on whom he looks are lively as kittens.' And they struck an attitude as they knelt, heads on one side, wrist and knuckle joints turned back with extraordinary suppleness, the fingers in an arc, with tips approaching the back of their hands.

'Play something on the strings,' Usana told them. They reached for little harps like boats and plucked an air, which they knew he liked.

Ma Saw had now joined the King on the couch. She knelt beside him and had taken up a yak-tail whisk. There were a few mosquitoes about and these she dusted away, swinging the whisk in time with the music. Then dropping it, she pretended that one of the insects had bitten him on the arm. With playful concern she leant forward and rubbed the place with her tiny palm. As she did so, he breathed in her ear, 'Those hands, I knew they were lively,' in a tone which showed that the in-

fluence which Yazathingyan had seen approaching at
Kanbyu was clasping him now.

The ladies-in-waiting, happy that the master was
more himself again, began singing a popular song of
the day:

> *Our Father rowed to the Island,*
> *Where grows the rose-apple tree:*
> *The roses and apples were mingled,*
> *A marvel to see.*
>
> *O roses and apples, he chanted,*
> *For ever that cluster and swing,*
> *How is it I think of a finger*
> *That enters a ring?*

They sang this humorously, with its variations,
sometimes pressing the innuendo, sometimes pretending to disguise it, as if startled.

Usana complained at this stage of irritation on his
back. With quite an anxious look Ma Saw slipped off
her jacket, to have her arms free, we must suppose, and
leant over him. Putting her hand under the loose neck
of his shirt, she peeped in.

'I have the place,' she exclaimed.

'How did you know without my telling you?' He
laughed.

'The King has the softest skin,' she replied luxuri-
ously. 'I saw a red streak and knew the irritation must
be there. Let me massage it.' And taking a little oint-
ment from a gold box by the bed, she began rubbing
gently, letting her hand wander by degrees over his
whole body.

The ladies-in-waiting, who for all the licence of their
song had been watching the course of events with care,

now decided that they had done their part. They could withdraw without risk of disturbing the close understanding clearly established between their master and the new lady. Indeed, looking again they saw that it was imperative for them to withdraw at once. So harping a vigorous finale they danced into the shadows.

vii
The Royal Chaplain

Ma Saw's romantic discovery and sudden success provided the court with unlimited subjects for conversation. The flutter was increased a few days later by the King's announcement that he proposed to go south on a hunting expedition with her. As he said to Yazathingyan—'I can't sit here expecting something to happen. I hear the elephants are numerous this year at Dalla. Tell them to get the camp palace there ready. I leave in a week.' And he added: 'I am taking the lady of the bush with me. I find her a great distraction. She prevents me brooding over things.'

'Your Majesty will take the queens as well?'

'No, I won't. I want a holiday and no bickering; just fun with Ma Saw, fun and hunting. A couple of months of that and I shall be able for anything.'

So it was arranged. Yazathingyan was to stay behind with authority to carry on the government under the royal seal. To prevent the queens from feeling left out, the Mayor of the Palace had orders to arrange a series of entertainments. The King would have with him a contingent of the ladies-in-waiting, his servants, clerks, pages, chamberlains, he would have the guard, his favourite elephant, his trappers and his musicians, enough to maintain his state among the country people, but not so many as to turn into a royal progress what he wanted to be a hunting excursion with a favourite.

This announcement was followed four days later by the news that Ma Saw had been made deputy queen. Usana could not make her queen, as the number of queens was fixed at five and there was no vacancy. So he created the appointment of deputy and took her out of the concubinate. It was an astonishing elevation for a girl of her origin and standing in the palace. The assumption was that he was infatuated. Ma Saw, or Queen Saw as she was now to be called, took all this calmly enough, but the regular queens became uneasy and the concubines very jealous. Yazathingyan, however, was pleased, for it fitted nicely into the plan he had been evolving. In fact, one morning he waited on Queen Saw with a ring set with a great ruby, the colour of pigeon's blood.

'The stone', he explained, 'was recently bought for me by my agents. It has been admired by experts. I have been looking for an occasion to offer it to His Majesty, but if the Queen will accept it I shall be vastly flattered.' This little speech was repeated round the court. The impression gained ground that something was going on behind the scenes.

It is worthy of note that Queen Saw, in spite of the excitements of her new life, did not forget to send her mother and aunt back to Kanbyu with rich presents, nor to see that the headman got his sword. Thereafter she embarked joyously with the King on his state barge, Thonlupazaw, which, surrounded by the boats containing the guard and staff, left one morning for Dalla, 350 miles down stream.

Yazathingyan, who was on the wharf, watched the flotilla round Lokananda point, when he entered a palanquin and returned to his residence. There he summoned two of his aids, creatures whom he employed on confidential missions, called Tit and 'Nit, One and Two. They came in bowing and smiling and lay on a mat supported by their elbows, upon which, had their sleeves been rolled back, would have been found callosities, a skin almost as hard as the soles of their feet. Forty years of grovelling had done that for them.

'Go to the Royal Chaplain's monastery,' said their master, 'and tell him I desire to call and pay my respects to him to-night. I should also be glad to see his pupil, the Kwéchi Min. The side door may be left open. Use an absolute discretion.' The agents chanted compliance and slithered out of the room.

Later in the day they returned to report that the Royal Chaplain was at his disposal. Accordingly, after dark he called for his closed palanquin, a vehicle without distinguishing marks, and set out. Tit and 'Nit walked beside the bearers; otherwise he was unaccompanied. As he did not wish it to be known that he was getting into touch with the Kwéchi Min, he took a circuitous route through the inner city and passed

A Burmese Royal Barge
By courtesy of the Royal Asiatic Society

under the south-west gate, after Tit and 'Nit had shown
the council seal to the guard and hinted that the palanquin was going to fetch a lady in whom the third
minister was interested.

In the same manner the outer gate was opened and
they began to cross the plain. The moon was in its
fourth waxing and threw a feeble light from the
western heavens. As the bearers hurried on, temples
and monasteries, standing within walled grounds, appeared mistily on each side of the dusty track. From
some of them rose the chant of voices repeating the
scriptures. An occasional pedestrian was encountered,
singing to keep up his spirits in the dark, but who,
when he saw the palanquin of an official, slunk into the
hedge and held his peace.

After a mile or so the bearers turned into the garden
of the monastery they sought and, following the right
wall of the building, a massive brick structure, laid the
palanquin down at the side door. This was immediately
opened from inside and Yazathingyan stepped through
into the vaulted circumambulatory. To his right was
the entrance to the Chaplain's room. He entered at once
and prostrated himself before the figure seated on a
mat at the far end of the apartment.

The Royal Chaplain was a man of about fifty years
of age. In accordance with the rule of his Order, his
head was shaved and he was clothed in a robe of
yellow cotton. Though his expression was benignant,
there was a strange depth in his eyes and on his lips
something of disillusion.

'Rise, my disciple,' he said to his visitor, 'and seat
yourself near me.'

The minister complied and, after dismissing the attendants, the two began to talk.

'How is your Reverence's charge, the King's younger son?' began Yazathingyan.

'He is not as forward for eighteen as I could have wished,' replied the prelate.

'Is it inattention or backwardness?'

'I find it hard to say. He is certainly inattentive; backward he may also be, for he seems to have little real comprehension.'

'Is he not just a normal youth, rather stupid and fond of girls?' suggested the minister.

'He is fond of girls, and of food and drink, but he is not quite normal. He has done some queer things.'

This news was not exactly what Yazathingyan wanted to hear. An ordinary stupid youth would have suited him better, for his idea was not only to displace Prince Thihathu but to put in as king somebody who would leave everything in his hands. However, he had no alternative, and continued:

'About a month ago your pupil called on me.'

The Chaplain moved his head in assent.

'I gave him certain assurances on that occasion, promised to use my influence to get him estates. But matters have moved more rapidly than I expected. There is now an early prospect of the succession falling vacant. That, at least, is my reading of the recent happening on Pōpa. As keeper of the royal horoscope, it is in your Reverence's power to confirm me.'

'I cannot disclose to you the terms of the King's horoscope,' replied the Chaplain firmly, 'but it may interest you to know that I have carefully projected my pupil's.'

'Perhaps the Master would condescend in that case to give me a hint,' insinuated the Chief Minister.

'The calculations show that his hour of greatness has arrived,' answered the old prelate solemnly.

Coming on top of the rest, this appeared conclusive to Yazathingyan. His heart bounded, he had an instantaneous vision of the future, a grand future with himself as autocrat. He smiled as he thought of Thihathu.

'But', continued the Chaplain, 'I also made certain further investigations—into the Kwéchi Min's identity.'

'His identity?'

'Yes, who he was before he was born into this state of life. These investigations yielded curious results, and I think you should know their purport. Do you remember the prophecy which Our Lord uttered long ago on the top of Mount Tangyi? Perhaps not: well, let me recall to you the circumstances. The Blessed One came over to this country during his lifetime and in the course of his wanderings ascended to the top of Tangyi near this city. Like many others, that mountain had a spirit guardian, who in this case was not the spirit of a deceased, but a malevolent elemental. He was known among the rustics as "the ogre" and, indeed, his appearance—for he was frequently seen by those ascending the mountain—suggested a name of the kind. When the Blessed One, heated by the steep climb in the sun, reached the summit, the uncouth spirit appeared and held over him an umbrella made of leaves. This act of piety showed the Lord that though a lower being he had aspirations towards the higher truths, and to reward and encourage him he foretold his elevation thrice to the throne of Pagān. Students declare that the being has already twice been king.'

'What were the names of those two kings?' asked Yazathingyan, rather apprehensive of what was coming.

'One of them was Salé Nga Kwé, who reigned at the beginning of the dynasty. The other was Narathu, who died eighty-four years ago.'

'My recollection is that both of them left a bad reputation,' said Yazathingyan, still more perturbed.

'That is the case,' answered the Chaplain. 'Nga Kwé is chiefly remembered for the following anecdote. It appears that before he became king he was the slave of a hard master, a rich man of Salé. Later, during his reign, whenever he laid hands on men who resembled his late master, he had them thrown into a pond and there pierced them with his lance from the back of an elephant, calling them pigs. This sport was considered so disgraceful by his ministers that one day they induced his groom to cut the howdah girths when he was in the pond. The howdah slipped and the King fell with it. While he was struggling in the mud, they despatched him.'

'And Narathu?' enquired Yazathingyan. 'I seem to remember that he murdered his chief queen.'

'Yes, he stabbed his wife in the fourth year of his reign because she found fault with him for not washing; he poisoned his brother though he had sworn to stand by him; he was hated by the people and eventually was assassinated.'

'The story comes back to me,' said Yazathingyan. 'Both Nga Kwé and Narathu are generally held to have been half mad. But you are leading up to something, the third incarnation of the guardian spirit of Tangyi. Who is it? Don't tell me it is your pupil!'

The Royal Chaplain did not reply at once. Then he said:

'I should like to caution you. The science of identifying souls is very abstruse, the conclusions drawn are not always reliable. Moreover, the study of it is not reconcilable with the higher truth. I have been weak in wasting my time in its pursuit. But since I have begun to tell you the result of my researches, I may as well finish. There can be little doubt that my pupil is the third incarnation.'

'You are sure of this. The prince looks so mild and plain, a little rustic like his mother.'

The Royal Chaplain again paused before he answered:

'I think I am right. You may ask me how I know. But if you have never studied higher astrology, how am I to explain to you? I can only say that, when I came to examine all the aspects of his nativity and compared them with those of the two former kings, I found correspondences which can have but one explanation.'

Silence fell between the two men. Yazathingyan began to think that his plan for the succession was less brilliant than he had supposed. But unfortunately there was no other. To let Thihathu succeed was certain ruin. He must continue as he had begun. It remained to be seen how far he would be able to cope with the peculiar entity the Kwéchi Min was alleged to be. But the prince was very young and there was this point—Kings Nga Kwé and Narathu had both been assassinated. All

79

the same it was disappointing. With a sigh he raised his eyes to the Chaplain's and said:

'Is your pupil in the building? I should like to see him. He ought, I think, to proceed during the next few days to Dalla and join the King there. Should anything happen, he will then be on the spot.'

'I told him you would be here this evening and might want to see him,' replied the Chaplain, clapping his hands. A young novice entered and was directed to call the prince. He returned shortly and reported that he had gone out.

'Gone out, at this hour! What for?' asked the Chaplain.

'Sir,' replied the novice with unction, 'the others say that at dusk he saw two girls passing along the road and joined them. He has not yet come back.' He was glad to tell on the prince, who was a bully.

Yazathingyan rose. 'It is of no consequence. Your Reverence will be kind enough to give him my message. He had better go with his uncle, the monk, and secretly in a small boat.' He then took leave. Tit and 'Nit appeared at the door. They had heard the novice asking for the prince and now whispered, as they assisted their master into his palanquin, that he was in a pavilion at the other end of the garden.

'Is he alone?' asked the minister.

'No, your Honour,' they replied, 'he has two friends with him. We peeped through the curtain a moment. The prince was enjoying himself. Would your Honour like to peep?'

'Tell the bearers to hurry,' he ordered with dignity. 'I am already late.'

King Usana and his court had a lazy, pleasant voyage down stream. The Irrawaddy is rapid for such a great river and, rowing with it, fifty miles a day is not too long a stretch. But they did not travel at that pace, for halt was made at all the principal riverine villages. Usana enjoyed rural receptions. The mat houses under their palms on the high bank, the plain behind; on the wharf the bands and dancing girls and the orderly crowd, brightly clothed, cheerful but respectful—he loved those things and would land, converse with the headmen and elders, bestow rewards, ask if his officials were oppressive and admire the girls. A beauty generally had a chance of at least temporary employment in his train. And he made frequent benefactions to pagodas.

He soon got rid of the fears which had been worrying him. The charms of the countryside, but especially Queen Saw's good spirits, restored him to his usual buoyancy. He did not like her to leave his sight. For a man of his experience he was ridiculously fond of her. Though he collected from force of habit a number of women as he went down river, he felt no inclination to make their closer acquaintance. Not that Queen Saw was jealous. Landing with him at Prome she selected two charming girls and when he hardly noticed them, rallied him on his indifference. She already guessed that she was beyond rivals. Though very young, she was fully matured. She had great eyes, brown and laughing, a tiny mouth, and her wheaten complexion had a downy surface. In all her movements was an indescribable animation. Her hands have been mentioned, but not her budlike feet, the round of her arms or the weight of her hips. If other girls approached her in the form of these, none of them had her vivacity, her amusing tricks. So intense was her happiness that it increased tenfold the effect of her beauty.

On the twelfth day of the journey they reached Dalla. Near the river bank stood the hunting palace behind a high stockade of sharpened bamboo, resembling the camp on Pōpa, but larger and better appointed. The town itself lay around it on the land side. Everyone disembarked with pleasure. Accommodation on the boats had been restricted.

Next morning Usana sent for his trappers. They had arrived four days ahead of him and had been making enquiries. At no great distance from Dalla was forest land on which wild elephants were generally found. To catch these alive had from early times been a royal sport. The captives were tamed and used on state occasions or for war. A further interest attached to the pastime, for there was always the chance that a white elephant might be taken. It was accepted as established that a white elephant was one of the incarnations assumed by future Buddhas. To own a white elephant meant that living with you was the very entity (in a state of early development perhaps, but the very entity) which at last after many lives among men would attain to the complete enlightenment, the comprehension of all things. You could not tell which Buddha he was to be, whether the next or one of the many to come, but ultimately in endless time he would reach that delectable state. So to feel that eating his hay in your stable was a great spirit, which one day would save the world, was deeply comforting, for if you were good to him, treated him well, he might bless you then or later and at long last carry you with him to the incomparable bliss of Nirvana.

Usana's head trapper was an old man called U Nagā or, as we might say, Uncle Dragon. He was small and dried up; his skin was like tight parchment; a white moustache and a few white whiskers strayed on his face. Though fifty years of age, he could walk twenty miles a day. In the respectful but independent manner of his kind he replied to the King's questions.

'The news is good, Lord,' he said. 'In the jungle called Natsein a large herd is eating. Yesterday I myself peeped at them through the leaves of a banyan tree. I counted two hundred.'

'Were there any beasts of unusual quality?' asked the King.

'There were some great beasts,' replied U Nagā with caution, fingering his whiskers.

'Great beasts, yes, but can you be more precise?'

'There were tuskers,' admitted the trapper, 'and they spoke of a special creature, though I did not altogether see him.' That was enough for Usana and he gave his orders.

There were two ways of catching elephants. The most ordinary was to surround the herd with a ring of beaters and drive it into the mouth of a wide V, through the base of which a narrow passage led into a palisaded enclosure. There the animals were gradually tied up, starved at first and then fed and handled until they became docile. This method was the safest, as it was the most profitable, for by it fifty elephants might be taken at once, but it lacked the excitement of the other way, which was to penetrate the herd perched on the neck of a tame female elephant and cautiously creeping in choose the best animals and lasso them round the legs. Courage and skill were essential for this; it was far from safe, but it was splendid sport.

The existence of an elephant of exceptional proportions decided Usana to adopt the second method. Such an animal was worth lassoing. To drive him with others into a keddah was to throw away the chance of a sporting triumph. It may seem strange that the King at this time should have exposed himself to risks. If ever a man had been warned to be careful, it was he. We can only suppose that he found that form of hunting irresistibly exciting.

Next day he rose at dawn and, after being dressed by his maids in the simplest clothes, descended to the courtyard where a female elephant was waiting. Out hunting he dispensed entirely with ceremony, riding

Lassoing Elephants in Burma
By courtesy of the Royal Asiatic Society

alone on the neck of his mount. As a young man he had acquired great skill in directing these lofty brutes, and it was a pleasure to him now to tuck his feet under the ears and feel the heavy bulk below advance or halt, turn right or left, as he spoke or kicked with his bare heels.

The party consisted of U Nagā and four other trappers, each mounted on a female elephant. It was a tall jungle which they soon entered. Giant trees started up from the damp and gloomy undergrowth. One could not see far ahead. But U Nagā had made his arrangements. Men had been posted to give him news as the herd moved in its feeding. If to town-dwellers the forest seemed a maze, impenetrable and baffling, to him it was as familiar as his kitchen-garden. Signs invisible to the inexpert gave him all the information he required. He led the King on without pausing an instant.

After a two hours' march he announced in an undertone that the herd was not far off. The light breeze was against them and they made a detour to approach down wind. When they reached the bearing which U Nagā held to be the most favourable, a halt was made.

'Lord,' said the old man, pointing, 'the animals are feeding on bamboos about a mile from here. The forest will be too thick still for us to view the whole herd. We will have to mingle with it and search for the animal we want. The six of us should keep close together and allow our beasts to feed as we slowly creep in.'

They now lay down flat on the necks of their elephants. Each of them carried a spear in case of attack, but their weapon of offence was a coil of strong rope, one end of which was fixed to a girth, the other being a noose. As they approached the herd, which now could be heard cracking the bamboos, U Nagā adopted the formation he had always found the most satisfactory, putting the King half a length in front and supporting him closely on the flanks and rear. In this way they reached a point where the breathing and tearing of the hungry brutes seemed so close that they expected to see them at any moment. In fact, they were already within the orbit of the herd, for a female with her calf passed behind them. Their own elephants were now plucking the bamboos and lolled along with shoots streaming from their mouths, so like wild animals at ease as to be very deceiving. The matter of scent recurred, as they were encircled by the herd. But the hunters were favoured by the circumstance that the breeze had now fallen; moreover prone as they were on their elephants' hides, their particular smell was largely quenched in that of their mounts.

Proceeding slowly in this way, they came to an alley among the bamboos and there perceived a few yards from them a quantity of females and young males. But there was no sign of any tusker, such as might be supposed to preside over a herd, and they skirted the females in a leisurely manner, continuing their search methodically and without haste.

At the end of the alley was a small clearing. Once it had been cultivated for rice, but was now covered with grass. As they debouched into it from the leaves, they saw standing in the middle the animal they were after, a towering elephant with massive ivory. Trained, he would be a war-elephant fit to lead the guard.

★ *The Fatal Hunting* ★

With apparent aimlessness the six hunters strayed closer. The tusker inspected them casually and began to move off towards some bamboos on the far side of the open ground. They followed and came up with him on the fringe of the trees. The male now began to be attracted by the scent of the females, which for him predominated over that of their riders. Like all elephants, his sight was poor. It gave him no warning that men were upon him.

Usana held the noose ready in his hand and, as he came abreast of his quarry, let it trail on the ground. The tusker took a step towards U Nagā's mount and placed his hind foot right in the middle of the circle of rope. Usana pulled it taut and, paying out rapidly, retreated some yards, winding his end round an iron peg fixed in the girth. The moment the tusker felt the pressure on his leg, he became alarmed and tried to plunge into the forest. But the rope suddenly bringing him up, he was thrown on his knees. Scrambling to his feet and turning in anger, he raised his trunk high in the air and was horrified to detect the taint of humanity. On receiving this intelligence, he immediately decided to charge, but U Nagā with his five companions closed on him with precision. While two of the females jostled him, the riders of the rest had no difficulty in slipping nooses round his other legs. Then they all drew back a space, so that the captive was held from the four quarters and could neither move forwards nor backwards. Trumpeting, screaming with rage, he struggled, bending his shoulders in an effort to drag those who pulled him from behind or rising on his hind legs and striving to tear off with his trunk the ropes which gripped him in front. U Nagā held one of the front ropes and, calling to his companion who held the other to follow his lead, let out a few yards. The tusker, turning to flee sideways, was brought up with a jolt and flung on his shoulder. This was repeated several times till the animal was half stunned and stood there trembling, foam dripping from his pointed lip. He had been played like a fish.

U Nagā now ordered the riders of the two elephants which had jostled the tusker to approach him again. The men closed in, perched on the stern of their mounts to avoid his trunk. When these were in position on each side of him and leaning against him, the four who held the ropes eased them sufficiently to allow him to walk. A procession started. In the centre was the tusker, worried and shaken, while, squeezing him between them, the two females bustled him on. Ten yards ahead was U Nagā with one trapper, holding the two ropes which secured his front legs, while behind was Usana and the other trapper, handling the rear ropes. They had not gone very far when trackers whom U Nagā had posted came up. The captive was handed over to them to bring in, while the King returned to Dalla by a short cut, arriving in time for a late breakfast. It had been a great day's hunting.

That night after dinner he was sitting by a window looking over the river. The ebb had set in; an immense volume of water rolled to the sea. A very fine moon lit up the landing stage. Presently a small boat came alongside, from which stepped a youth and a monk of the Order. For some reason it gave the King a tremor to watch them. They entered his vision like actors in a play, when the story is about to take an unexpected direction. He was so much affected that he sent down to enquire their identity. The man did not return, but in a short time there was a movement at the far end of the shadowy room. Two persons came in and sat down. They were bowing towards him.

'Who is there?' he asked

'The Kwéchi Min and his uncle, the monk,' a voice murmured deprecatingly.

'The Dirty Pup,' exclaimed Usana heartily. 'Come up closer. How did you get here?'

The youth so named approached bent double and knelt below his father. The monk followed, but according to custom, made no obeisance. He had a bag in his hand from which he took out two bottles and laid them on the floor. The King glanced at him. Of course, he remembered now, it was the brother of the girl he had met long ago at Myit-tha well. What was it that had happened to her? For the moment he could not remember. He turned to his son.

'I thought you were at school, little bastard,' he said familiarly.

The prince did not very much like the expression. He seemed to wince under it. His eyes flickered. But he answered tolerably enough:

'The Royal Chaplain desired me to report myself to Your Majesty. My studies are finished.'

'So they must be, I suppose,' replied his father. 'Well, we are hunting now. You can join the expeditions, if you like. I shall consider later what provision to make for you.'

His son thanked him and added: 'My uncle and I

hope that Your Majesty will accept the present of these bottles. They contain a tonic wine of some reputation. My uncle has made a study of such wines. He can tell you the ingredients. I know they include rhinoceros horn. It is very stimulating.'

The monk looked somewhat sheepish at this testimony to his skill in compounding aphrodisiacs.

'The prince flatters me,' he said.

He was a small thickset man with a good-natured face.

Usana laughed and called for a wine-cup. There was a certain piquancy in taking such a wine from a monk. After a draught or two he felt the fatigues of the day slipping from him.

'You must stay on at court and keep me supplied with this,' he said.

Another cup seemed to make him preoccupied. Dismissing the two, he left the room in the direction of Queen Saw's apartments. A girl, smiling back at the company, carried the two bottles after him on a tray.

It was later than usual next morning when Usana appeared. He had a languid air, but he announced his intention of inspecting his captive of the day before. Where was U Nagā? The old retainer hurried to make known his presence. How was the tusker? He had given no trouble during the night, and was now in a large enclosure outside the town.

Presently, seated in the howdah of his favourite elephant, the King was driven out. On arrival at the enclosure, he could see over the palisade the tusker inside, his hind feet tethered to posts. He seemed very quiet.

'Open the gate, will you,' directed the King. 'I want to ride in and have a close look at him.'

'It is not altogether safe to enter,' protested U Nagā.

'What nonsense!' said the King. 'If it was safe for me to lasso him yesterday in the wild, what risk do I run now when he is secured by two legs?'

As U Nagā still delayed to open the gate, Usana with a movement of irritation told his driver to do so. He was the very man who had seen the hive on the Tharaba lintel.

Death is certain, but the moment of its coming is rarely anticipated. Unknown to U Nagā, the tusker was *must*. The peculiar frenzy of that state had seized him but a short time before, and as yet he had shown no outward sign of what possessed him. The moment, however, that Usana rode into the enclosure, he wheeled, snapped the tether, with a furious sweep of his head dashed away a tame elephant standing by and charged. The driver of the King's elephant had hardly a second in which to act. He managed to swerve slightly to the right, but as the *must* elephant passed on the left he slipped a tusk under the royal girth. The howdah fell and the King with it. From first to last it was a matter of seconds. U Nagā and his assistants flung themselves into the enclosure. But all was over; the King was dead; the elephant had touched him.

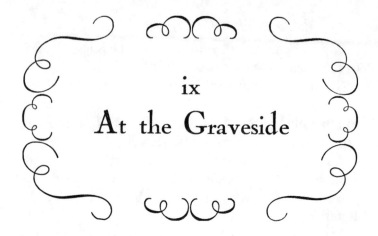

ix
At the Graveside

The news of the King's death was known in Dalla within the hour. Yazathingyan's agent heard it first, because he made it his business to keep his ear to the ground. His instructions were to come upstream to Pagān at once should anything of the kind supervene. Accordingly, after verifying the facts, he boarded a fast boat, which he had kept ready, and with oar and pole hurried north.

When Yazathingyan received the news he was not surprised. The critical moment for which he had been preparing had now arrived. His plans were mature, he knew what to do; but there is danger in any action, for human nature is incalculable. There was, moreover, the possibility that he might immediately be seized. On reflection he decided that this contingency was remote. Thihathu, though he hated him and intended to get rid of him, would do nothing before he was firmly established on the throne. Besides the prince suspected nothing. Yazathingyan had been very careful outwardly to heal the breach between them. After Usana's departure for Dalla he had made a great show of consulting the prince on matters of state. The Kwéchi Min's journey south had passed unnoticed, perhaps because a youth resembling him in appearance had been placed in the monastery.

As soon as Usana's death was made public, Thihathu, as heir-apparent, entered the royal apartments of the palace and took formal possession of the queens and the concubinate. The bulk of the court had remained in residence, though the late King had taken with him the best half of the guard. At an early date Yazathingyan asked to be received in private audience. Thihathu, who had no desire to drive the Chief Minister into opposition at this stage, consented to see him. He fancied that he could first make use of him to arrange the coronation.

Yazathingyan entered his presence with a wonderfully calculated air of pleasure and respect. After a slightly exaggerated protestation, more suited to public audience in the main hall, he condoled with him over his father's death and congratulated him on his accession. To this Thihathu made a gracious reply, pluming himself not a little on the impenetrability of his manner. He was a handsome man, only twenty-one. That Yazathingyan had resolved his death never entered his head.

The Chief Minister then disclosed the object of his visit.

'Your late father of happy memory', he said, 'has

died at a distant frontier town. The mandarins who were with him have attended his funeral, but those of us who remained at headquarters have not been able to pay our respects at his grave. I am giving utterance to the earnest desire of many of his late Majesty's officers when I say that we seek permission to go to Dalla and there before his mausoleum conform to the rites made obligatory by custom.'

Thihathu had not been expecting a request of this nature. He looked round at his household for advice, but there was no one present of much experience. Had there been, they might have told him that to let Yaza-thingyan join the bodyguard at Dalla, accompanied by the leading men of the realm, was clearly unwise. But his staff did not point this out and, seeing small reason to refuse, he sanctioned the proposal.

So authorised, Yazathingyan made rapid prepara-tions for his journey south. Messengers were sent out to summon the official governors and the headmen of important village tracts. During the ensuing week these notables rode into the capital. To all the same instructions were given—they were to accompany the Chief Minister on pilgrimage to the late King's grave. Within ten days they embarked on a flotilla of boats and, the north-east wind blowing, made rapid sail down stream. Yazathingyan travelled on his own barge. In the cabin was a chest covered with a scarlet canopy.

On the way halt was made at all the chief towns and villages, where the headmen were asked to join the pilgrimage. By the time they reached Dalla few men of note from the middle and south regions were not in the party.

Yazathingyan's first act was to wait on Queen Saw. The death of Usana had upset that young person. She had grown to like him, and though she was well aware that he was not in what was likely to be a lucky period, the arrival of death was just as shocking as it always is. It also left her position quite undefined. She had no one to turn to and awaited Yazathingyan's arrival with impatience.

When he was shown in, she said in her broad way:

'You are welcome to Dalla. Since the King's death I have heard more nonsense talked than during the whole course of my life. You have no idea of the confusion when the news came in. None of the mandarins had sufficient authority to cope with the situation. I was pestered with every sort of suggestion, but resolved to do nothing until you arrived. When I received your express that you were on the way, I shut myself in my rooms, where my women have brought me a stream of gossip. The Kwéchi Min has been drinking day and night with the dancing girls; his uncle has thrown off the yellow robe and joined in the fun; U Nagā hanged himself and the *must* elephant broke out and is now roaming the woods.'

Yazathingyan let her run on and then asked:

'What do you think of the Kwéchi Min?'

'He is an oafish person,' she replied promptly.

'It is about him that I have come to speak to you,' he said. 'If it should happen that the mandarinate and the headmen acclaimed him as king, what would you say?'

'It is no affair of mine. My intention is to return to my village.'

'Listen. His late Majesty's death has left us both in a precarious position. As for me, you may or may not know how I stand with the prince Thihathu. Suffice it to say that ruin and perhaps death await me if he is crowned. Your position is no less dangerous, for your sudden rise to favour has mortally offended the queens and leading concubines. If you return to Pagān, you will be ignominiously treated. You would be lucky to get back to your village unmolested.'

Queen Saw had already given her prospects some thought, and she did not now deny the truth of Yaza-thingyan's words.

He went on: 'I have reason to believe that the Kwéchi Min will be acclaimed. If so our prospects will be much improved.'

'How so?' said she.

'I shall not take up your time', he replied, 'with a disquisition about myself, but if you were prepared to accept the position of his Chief Queen, it seems to me that all your difficulties would be overcome.'

Queen Saw's first inclination was to ask a number of questions, among others how he proposed to get rid of Thihathu. But she forbore to ask them. All she said was:

'Then this is a rebellion.'

'It is a mistake', said he, 'to use terms of that kind. Let me put it like this. I want your co-operation in a little adjustment I am arranging. You may ask me why I set a value on your help. It is because I have formed a high opinion of your capacity and sense. The Kwéchi Min may lack both those qualities. If I could depend upon you to guide that "oafish person", as with so

96

much penetration you have described him, I should feel my position very much strengthened.'

Queen Saw could not help admiring the masterly way in which he presented his case. The fact was that he had flattered her with the greatest cleverness. She was not an intriguing woman, a pushing woman, but she knew her value. Indeed, having seen the court at close quarters and noticed the paucity of able men, she had become quietly aware of her own superior abilities. His proposal that she should become Chief Queen had not startled her for that reason. The only question was whether she should involve herself in an adventure of the kind he proposed. On the other hand, if Thihathu succeeded, she was exposed to terrible risks. So, after a little pause, she turned on him a humorous look and said:

'Very well, make your "adjustments" so that I can step in after an accomplished fact.'

He looked at her with great satisfaction. Her progress had been amazing. It was hardly three months since he had collected her from a mountain village. But there was a type of first-class mind, he reflected, which seemed to leap into understanding. Hers was perhaps of that class. He was profoundly glad.

'I can count then on your support,' he concluded. 'To-night I shall speak with the Kwéchi Min and in a day or so, when all the mandarins and country lords are met at the grave, I shall disclose my plans.'

With that he took leave to depart.

At dawn three days later an immense concourse assembled in the courtyard of the hunting palace. A procession was formed, which, besides the principals, included all the officials and landed gentry whom Yazathingyan had called in. A strong force of soldiers paraded with them. Queen Saw and her ladies followed in palanquins. They all passed through the town at a rapid pace in the direction of the late King's mausoleum.

When they reached the grave a square was formed. On one side of it was a pavilion and in this sat Yazathingyan, Queen Saw and the Kwéchi Min on a dais, while below them lay the mandarins and the rest of the notabilities. The ceremony of paying respect to the dead King was neither long nor impressive. Yazathingyan and those who accompanied him made a prostration, but as the band played the whole time in a loud declamatory manner, there was a certain informality and lightness in the proceedings. It seemed as if the company expected something further. When the Chief Minister, having stopped the band, opened his mouth to address them, nobody was surprised. They remarked that he leant his elbow upon a box.

He spoke for some time, but it will be sufficient to quote a few of his more telling periods. At an early stage he said:

'No one of you was as privileged as was I to enjoy our late master's confidence. Daily in contact with him, I could observe his easy justice, his regard for the country people. And if I was able from my close position before the throne to remark in him those qualities, the same proximity allowed me to perceive the lack of them in his son, Thihathu.'

A little further on, after painting a truly dreadful picture of the depravity of that prince, he asked:

'Do you know what will happen to you if Thihathu is crowned? Let me remind you of an episode which occurred a few months ago in the hall of audience.' He then related the affair of the sleeve, ending with the words—'the prince rose and, unable to contain his venom, pretending that I was in his way, that I blocked his way, spat betel-blood upon my lappet. Even when I took on myself the blame, he was not appeased, but with an insulting sneer swaggered away.'

At this point he moved his elbow from the box and threw up the lid. Every eye followed him as he took out an embroidered robe, as he held up the sleeve and pointed to the blood-red stain, which still clearly showed.

'If when he was only heir-apparent he spat thus upon the Chief Minister, what will he do to you, Ministers, to you, Mandarins, to you, Headmen, when he is crowned?'

Uttering these words, he looked round. It was clear that he had made some impression. He followed it up with a portrait of the Kwéchi Min, concluding as follows:

'Speaking with an old man's regard for virtue, you will believe me when I assure you that I have found in him those traits which the Religion admonishes us to admire—kindness, generosity, reverence to elders, pity for the unfortunate.'

Here he stopped. The drift of his address was patent to all. He had taken the precaution to salt the assembly with persons on whom he could entirely rely, men who had received advancement from him and looked to him for more, as well as minions directly in his pay.

★ *At the Graveside* ★

One of the former class now began to speak. Circuitously, at great length, in elaborate phrases he justified the minister's proposal, quoting endlessly from the sacred texts and from proverbs, relating interminable stories from the state histories. During this discourse, Yazathingyan's secretary, a man called Mahabo, slid from group to group making suggestions. With a suavity which was hypnotic he resolved doubts, flattered by an assent which at the same time twisted objections till they looked like concurrence, and marked down for future action the case of those persons who appeared likely to give trouble. Meanwhile the voice of the speaker droned on. When it ceased at last, a proper atmosphere had been created. Moreover, the household troops had moved up and surrounded the pavilion. Though on their faces there was nothing but a desire to hear better, it was evident that they were far from being in opposition to Yazathingyan. The more independent of the notabilities, particularly some of the headmen who exercised hereditary jurisdiction at a distance from the capital, had been inclined to whisper of illegitimacy and to respond grudgingly to Mahabo's blandishments. But when they saw the proximity of the guard, they waived their objections and tried to cover their first scepticism by a hurried compliance.

It was clear that the assembly was about to record a unanimous finding. Already some of the mandarins had flung themselves on the ground below the Kwéchi Min. Anticipating the issue, they wished to be the first to range themselves on his side, for so they could claim precedence when the new appointments were made.

100

Their example was rapidly followed; indeed, when those less nimble perceived the lead which had been gained on them, there was somewhat of a scramble. If any held back, they were in such a minority that nobody (except Mahabo) noted their names. The guard by now had broken ranks; some of the soldiers were striking attitudes or dancing; the band began to play again, and elephants, filling their trunks from an adjacent pond, squirted the crowd. The greatest hilarity prevailed everywhere.

In the midst of this enthusiasm, to seal with a symbol what was already an accomplished fact, Yazathingyan crawled over the dais towards the prince and touched the floor three times with his forehead. Throughout the proceedings Queen Saw had sat impassive and at ease, though she relished well enough Yazathingyan's comedy. When she perceived him grovelling before the oafish youth, without prompting she saw her cue and, infinitely graceful, went forward herself on knee and elbow. At the edge of his carpet she touched the boards with her pearl-strung head, and tuning her voice to a note held by the flute-players, who divined her intention, rolled out a great Pāli valediction. Yazathingyan lying there marvelled at her precocity. How had she learnt even a tag from the classic language?

But now an elephant with gilded tusks and scarlet caparison was led up to the pavilion. They intimated to the Kwéchi Min that he should mount it. As he rose to his feet he was closely observed. What would be the first act of his reign, what would be his first unconscious movement? From such a hint the course of events might be estimated. Observers were not to be altogether disappointed, for, as he walked mincingly towards the doorway through the excited crowd, a Tartar from beyond the frontier—what he was doing in Dalla no one knew—came in his way. The Kwéchi Min halted, looked down at the man, who was on his knees, and then stepped back, as it were to avoid him. The fellow, who was drunk, went after him and he tripped. This incident was not witnessed by many on account of the press, but Yazathingyan saw it and memorised the details. It was impossible to say at once what might be the interpretation, but it was suggestive enough to go into his notes.

At the doorway the Kwéchi Min mounted the elephant, sitting iconographically under a white umbrella held over his head by a man kneeling on the haunches. A troupe of Cambodian dancers recently arrived from Angkor assembled in front. These were agile girls, lithe but well formed. They wore high crowns of gold leaf, pointed at the top. The rest of their costume was beads, of which they wore three chains round the neck with a pectoral falling below the breasts, while across their hips again were rows of beads, a broad pendant dangling between their legs. Their faces were expressionless except for their eyes, which were nonchalant with their upward slant. Over their brown skins was dusted a powder. When the royal elephant began to move, they slid into their dance, darting, posing and pirouetting under its front feet. Like tree-fairies they darted in and out, the great beast minding its step so as not to hurt them.

After a time, when the band played with greater

An Indo-Chinese Dancer of the Period

liveliness, one of them seized the elephant's trunk and began to swarm up. As she did so, it hoisted her into the air and she, twisting round, sat the trunk like a celestial riding a snake. The elephant, with that roguish look which elephants sometimes wear, turned back its long nostril and touched her breast. So she balanced there singing, her arms in undulation, while the elephant dandled her as gently as might have a lover. The King-elect, so lately escaped from school, found this a joyous spectacle, but he had sense enough of etiquette to pretend at first to take no notice.

As they approached Dalla the enthusiasm increased, for a large concourse of people had surged out of the town. With these were more dancers, musicians and some acrobats. Many Hindus were in the crowd, for it was a place of trade with India. Their nautch girls were writhing and twisting, heavier beauties and more intensely physical, for the laughter of the Burmese and the Cambodians was irrelevant to their animality. Yet they were softer and sweeter, and, as they danced there naked by the roadside to welcome the new King, something of the all-embracing love of India, the Great Mother, animated their dark faces and their rolling hips. On a knoll behind them under a peepul-tree was an ash-grey ascetic. His arm was raised, but it had withered away, for he had held it in that position night and day for ten years.

The procession now entered the streets of Dalla. Here the excitement touched an even higher pitch. The elephants towered in the narrow thoroughfares, their riders sitting level with the balconies, which were crowded with women throwing flowers. The Cambodian girl still rode the trunk of the royal elephant and was singing in her foreign accent a Burmese song so coarse that, contrary to usage, it had not a double but a single meaning. In the course of it she turned and sprawled upon the elephant's forehead, looking into the face of the driver above her. The Kwéchi Min took, as he was meant to take, the song as a strong hint and made a note to have her registered on the permanent staff.

In this mood of hilarity they entered the palace. A great dinner had been arranged. Hundreds of dishes were served, the cuisine of India, Burma and Cambodia was ransacked, as was their repertory of entertainment. The Kwéchi Min ate and drank tremendously; he was like a youth giving his first party. As for Queen Saw, she knew what was expected of her. It was she who thought of new songs, new dances; and her repartee was the quickest, her invention the most inexhaustible. When at a very late hour the Kwéchi Min intimated that he wished to retire, she accompanied him into the private apartments.

By this time he was fairly drunk. Lying on a couch with two of the maids deftly massaging him, he began a long monologue. Queen Saw sat leaning against the couch; she directed the maids.

'My reign has begun well,' he announced to her rather indistinctly. 'Was there ever such eating and drinking! To think that I wasted all those years in the monastery, when my father might have had me at court. You have no idea what the Royal Chaplain was like. Not that I have anything against him, but he was always talking philosophy. Do you know, he expected

An Indian Beauty from the Ajanta Frescoes

me to read the *Abhidhama*! In fact, he had a fancy I
should master the whole *Tripitika*. And that reminds
me. Did you see the Cambodian girl on my elephant's
trunk? Did you ever see such a beauty? And did you
hear what she sang as she climbed up the elephant's
face? No, you couldn't have, of course, you were away
behind. Well, I'll tell you—what were the words now?
—I can't remember, but it was the dirtiest song I've
ever heard, a filthy song, a lovely song. I wish I could
remember the words. I wonder where the girl is now;
we could get her in. But I wish I could remember the
last line, anyway. How did it go?'

There was a pause; Queen Saw looked up; his eyes
were shut; he had suddenly fallen asleep.

x

The Rope Trick

So far, so good, thought Yazathingyan, and now for Thihathu. He had already issued orders that no one was to leave Dalla for the north on any pretext. The river was closed, guards lay across the various roads, for he was determined that no news of the usurpation should reach Pagān.

His next step was an ingenious stratagem. Desiring to avoid an open resort to arms, an advance on the capital with all its attendant risks, he planned to entice Thihathu to descend peacefully to Dalla. To him therefore he addressed a letter. Opening with a recital of his journey south, he recorded briefly the ceremonies of respect carried out over the late King's grave and then continued in these terms:

'Hardly had the last mandarin bowed his head before the royal mausoleum, when news was brought that a white elephant of great size with all the marks of authenticity upon it had been caught in the woods. This capture, coming at the moment of Your Majesty's accession, amounted to an augury of exceptional brilliance. We beseech Your Majesty to descend to Dalla and view the beast at once, so that with it in triumph you may return to the capital.'

Mahabo, the secretary, was sent with this letter. He was directed not to divide night from day and to reach Pagān with the utmost despatch. When he presented it he was to exercise to the full his gift of pleasing, to give a detailed and exact description of the capture of the alleged animal, a description exciting and full of coloured incident; to follow it by a learned catalogue of the elephant's points, that is to say of its esoteric points, the whorls in its hair, the sit of its ears, and the colour of its eyes; in his peroration to exhibit the extraordinary felicity of the occasion, astrologically and otherwise, using technical terms from the classical authors; and finally to point out that His Majesty had not a moment to lose, but should embark at once for Dalla, there to take possession of his astounding good fortune. A staff was to support Mahabo, persons with solemn, learned faces, and of an exaggerated respectability of demeanour, who, as he harangued the King, should interject remarks showing how heartily they rejoiced in the occurence. They were to add, if the occasion required, that Yazathingyan himself would have brought the glad news, had he not thought it necessary to watch day and night over the sacred beast, until such time as he could hand it over personally to his dear lord.

With the despatch of Mahabo there was nothing to be done for the moment but to continue the utmost vigilance on the river and on the roads. The guards were trebled and frequently inspected, but to distract attention from so unusual a measure a series of elaborate public entertainments was organised, nominally in celebration of the Kwéchi Min's accession. It had become obvious that he could no longer be called by that name, and Yazathingyan, after a confabulation with certain delegates from the Brahmanic College of Astrologers, decided that he should henceforth be known by the honorific title of Narathihāpaté. Every day fresh amusements were devised. The populace never seemed to go to bed. The prohibition against leaving the city passed unnoticed when it was everyone's desire to enter or remain there.

Yazathingyan was helped at this time by a fortunate chance. A travelling company of illusionists had arrived a few days previously from Bengal. These people were reputed to be adepts in the rope trick, a rare feat of which everyone had heard, but which no one had seen. The Chief Minister first satisfied himself through his agents that the Indians belonged to the esoteric circle of prestidigitators, and then arranged for them to give a demonstration in the open space before the palace.

At the time appointed a crowd collected, forming a semicircle from the covered platform on which Narathihāpaté, Queen Saw and the court were accommodated. The performers were two men only; their properties a rope and a vehicle like a cabin on wheels. This had a door, but no windows. The performance began by the men seating themselves on the ground within the semi-circle, where they remained quite motionless for a time, the rope coiled beside them. But some sort of a force appeared to vibrate in them, for they had not the appearance of persons seated firmly down.

After an intimidating pause one of them took up a flute and began playing an air. This had the effect upon the spectators that they did not seem to notice the passage of time, for perhaps half an hour passed in this way, everyone remaining very quiet. Suddenly the other man rose to his feet and took the rope into his hand. He stood there poised for a moment, his glance, as it were, inward, for he seemed very unconscious of the crowd, even of the court. Then swinging the coil with an easy motion, he appeared to let it go and it began to travel vertically into the air, not precisely as if he had thrown it, but rather as smoke rises or a fire balloon goes up. People said afterwards that at this time he uttered unintelligible words. The rope continued to unwind into heaven as if lighter than air, to a length which it seemed impossible could have been included within its original bulk. So it rose on, until the spectators grew doubtful whether they could see the end of it or not. A peculiar sensation came over them as they looked—a slight nausea.

The first Indian now put down his flute and went to the cabin. He opened the door and two tigers emerged. Yazathingyan, who was seated below the royal party, started somewhat when he perceived the creatures. The last tigers he had seen were the two on Pōpa. The present animals in their gait and expression reminded him of those beasts. They did not look normal. It was hard to say why, just as it is hard to say in what a madman who passes quietly by differs from a sane man. But certainly they were more horrible than common tigers.

They strode from the cabin towards the Indian who held the rope, placing one foot after the other in a hieratic manner. The flute was again sounding.

When they reached the base of the rope, which coiled on the ground, they sat on their haunches and looked up. A truly frightful expression came into their eyes. Those who saw it strove afterwards to describe it, but found no words nor any concept. All they could do was to declare their own reactions, some of them speaking of the increased nausea which crept over them, others of a diabolical excitement, of the sex and for destruction, by which they were possessed. There was utter silence, save for the note of the flute. In that pause, four of the King's elephants, which had been looking over the crowd, stampeded in horror.

The man holding the rope now bent his head and fixed his eyes upon the tigers. The creatures seemed to quail from him; they could not bear his glance. One of them, turning its head sideways and contracting its spine, gave a cry as it were a monster crying. Then unexpectedly both the animals were on the rope; they crawled up the rope like lizards climb a wall; fast, with a wriggling movement, they climbed on till they became indistinct, until they were like a faint blotch in the blue sky, and so evaporated away.

When they were gone out of sight, the man who held the rope let it go and seated himself upon the ground in the attitude of *samādhi*. The other took his flute again and played an air which no one had heard before and of which afterwards none of them could remember a phrase. Some felt that the music was the rope, and they found it impossible to say whether they were hearing or seeing the event; others thought that they had become the figure seated in *samādhi* and that they were equally the rope, the tigers and the flute. Yazathingyan was among the few who retained some control of his normal faculties. He had the sensation very strongly that they were dissolving, but before he plunged into an oblivion, he congratulated himself upon his showmanship—this unique entertainment would wholly cover his plot. He looked at Queen Saw and at Narathihāpaté. The Queen had let herself go into the enchantment; the latter was pale and sweating profusely.

In this tension the first Indian got to his feet and was seen climbing the rope. He did not clamber with hands and feet, but seemed more to slide up, or swoop up like a serpent, but it was impossible accurately to determine what means he used, for he went so fast. Like the tigers, he was lost to view in a few instants. A long pause followed, or what was apparently a pause, and then in the air was heard the sound of tearing flesh and cracking of bones. The rope turned red, it was running with blood; a pool of blood formed at its base and spread outwards. Into this began to drop fragments, fragments of flesh, bones that fell and splashed, lumps of intestine, and at last a human head, the Indian's head, horribly scarred as with claws, the hair clotted, the eyes licked out. During this rain of pieces, the tearing and growling continued, as if at the summit of the rope the two tigers were fighting over a kill. The flute music had stopped, for the phenomenon was established.

This ghastly scene had caused a number of people to faint. Yazathingyan, struggling for a lucid view, heartily wished that the Royal Chaplain was present. It was said of that prelate that, besides a knowledge of astrology, he possessed certain powers, but these he had never exhibited in public. His detachment would have been a solace now with a rope reaching into the sky and a rain of blood. The Religion taught that life was an illusion. What then was this enchantment that had the force of life?

But he was withdrawn from these speculations, for the tigers were descending, descending head first, haunches down, tail up, as if skidding on a steep slope. On reaching the ground they licked their lips, but appeared too sated to touch the blood or bones that lay scattered. They stalked heavily towards the cabin, which they entered. The surviving Indian shut them in.

When this man returned to the shambles, the rope sagged and fell down. Taking a roll of cotton cloth from his waist, he spread it over the remains of his comrade and, blowing his flute gently, sat down near by. When the air was played through, an air astringent in effect, he pulled aside the cloth. His comrade was disclosed unhurt, alive and whole. Together they hurried from the scene, drawing the cabin after them.

A sigh passed from lip to lip of the crowd. The royal party withdrew at once into the palace. Narathihāpaté was haggard; he had been sick. It was not the blood which had turned his stomach, but the psychic shock. But Queen Saw had not lost her aplomb. She went off the scene at a steady pace.

As Yazathingyan had calculated, this strange exhibition was the only subject of conversation for days. The closure of the roads, the usurpation, what Thihathu might do, were no longer debated. All that was said or sung turned upon the jugglers. In a week even the most impressionable had sufficiently recovered from the shock to enjoy themselves when the wags got to work on the episode. No popular entertainment was complete unless the clown brought a rope and threw it into the air. When it fell back on his head, entangling him in its folds, the crowd would laugh immoderately and the dancing girl observe that Burmans were no good, her next lover would be an Indian. In most houses children had string with cardboard tigers running up and down it.

xi
The Execution

While these relaxations were in progress a messenger from Pagán arrived. He reported that Mahabo's mission had met with instant success. When Thihathu was informed that the capture of a white elephant synchronised with his assumption of the White Umbrella, he exhibited the utmost satisfaction and in an uncritical moment filled Mahabo's mouth with gold, as a way of showing the value he put upon his words. He had scarcely patience to hear the whole, before he began giving orders for the preparation of his barge. The messenger added that he might be expected during the week.

It was, in fact, on the fifth day after the reception of this report that the royal barge was sighted far up the reach. Yazathingyan's arrangements were complete; the moment for which he had waited so long was at hand. His scouts reported that Thihathu, though ac-

companied by his father's five queens and a section of
the concubinate, had brought no soldiers with him except the usual guards. His army was composed of dancers, musicians and priests in anticipation of a festive
return to his capital with the white elephant.

When the royal barge came alongside the wharf,
there were drawn up on the bank those guardsmen
whom Usana had brought down, together with con-
tingents of elephantry, cavalry and foot. Yazathingyan
and the mandarins were waiting on their knees. Narathihāpaté, of course, was not present. A palanquin with
a seven-tiered gilded roof, the bearers kneeling, was in
a prominent position. As Thihathu landed, he was invited by Yazathingyan to enter the palanquin. Without
further ado, the bearers rose to their feet. The guard
immediately closed round and the procession started,
Yazathingyan riding behind the guard. The route taken
was not into the hunting palace. At first Thihathu
thought that the intention was to parade him through
the town, but when they turned aside towards the open
country, he began to wonder what was his destination.
Beckoning to a mandarin, he asked for information.
The official approached with every sign of respect and
stated that they were proceeding to an enclosure near
by, where the white elephant was lodged. This answer
entirely satisfied Thihathu, who during the long journey down stream had been counting the hours until
he should see the animal.

As the mandarin had said, it was not long before
they arrived at an enclosure. The heads and backs of
elephants could be seen above it. But few people were
in evidence; the place was deserted. It did not look

like the abode of a sacred elephant. Where was the gilded spire of its stable, where its attendants, its band of musicians? Thihathu stepped from the palanquin and looked round, a faint uneasiness creeping over him. The guard was on all sides; he could see none of his own staff.

Then between the soldiers he perceived Yazathing-yan approaching. He was dressed in an embroidered robe. As he drew nearer, Thihathu noticed that one of his sleeves was stained with a dull red stain. He did not immediately understand; for an instant he failed to connect the stain with what had happened four months earlier in the audience hall. Then suddenly the truth flashed on him and he knew that he had fallen into a trap.

Yazathingyan came up close, still preserving some form of respect. He did not kneel, but he bowed. On his face, however, was an insulting expression. Raising his sleeve, he looked at the stain and then, smiling crookedly, said:

'The lord Thihathu will remember how I received this blotch of red.'

Feeling that he might as well speak to a serpent as to this man, Thihathu did not reply. He looked round him again hastily, but there was no escape. He knew it was death; what kind of death was the only doubt. When he thought it might be prolonged, he fell on his knees.

'Your Excellency,' he said humbly, 'if I spat on your sleeve, it was just a burst of irritation. I was only heir-apparent then. Now I am King and can amply compensate you.'

'You are not King,' replied Yazathingyan insolently,

'because I have not chosen you to be King. No one shall be King who spits at me.'

Thihathu now prostrated himself before the minister. He was very young. Alone, facing some death, his nerve failed.

'Spare me, your Excellency,' he begged. 'You are a grandee of Burma, that I know. It was wrong of me to have insulted you.'

'You should have thought of all that before you spewed your betel,' harshly said the other.

'Spare me this once! I will go into exile! Take my possessions!' stammered the youth.

But Yazathingyan made a sign and four of his minions laid their hands on him. For an instant he struggled violently, but they overpowered him. Calling out dismally, he cried:

'I have done nothing, I never harmed him—oh, let me go!' They led him towards the enclosure.

Inside were elephants taught to execute criminals. The soldiers dragged him, screaming for mercy, towards one of these. The brute, with a peculiar expression in its eye—for it was a tame elephant trained to kill men—reached out its trunk and held the prince in a vice. For an instant he drummed frantically on the trunk with his fists. Then, at a word of command, the elephant flung him high into the air, catching him as he fell on the flat of his tusks. Again it flung him up and again. Each time he fell on the ivory his bones were fractured. A fourth time he was thrown and caught, and then, still living, bleeding, palpitating, the elephant laid him on the ground and, placing a foot firmly on his chest, pulled off his arms and legs and, at last, his head.

Yazathingyan, who had superintended the execution, now put aside the embroidered robe and entering a palanquin, ordered them to carry him to the hunting palace. As he was borne along, a vast content enveloped him. He was safe; not only was he safe, he was master. King Narathihāpaté and Queen Saw, they were hardly more than children.

'If I cannot mould those two to my wishes', he thought, 'I am good for nothing. Besides, the girl has sense, her inclination is to back me.' A vista of power stretched in front of him. There was no limit to what he might do. So he was carried along. It was a neat day's work, interesting, too, for he recalled, what he had forgotten, how just after Thihathu had spat on him that morning in the palace hall, he had seen the pillars writhing and twirling like elephants' trunks. Yes, that was very interesting. He had never had a psychic experience before.

On reaching the hunting palace he presented himself at once before Narathihāpaté. Queen Saw was there.

'A fatal accident has overtaken Thihathu,' he said. 'Like his father, he has been killed by an elephant.'

Narathihāpaté said nothing. He was profoundly relieved.

'He is quite dead, I suppose?' he enquired at length. On hearing that this was so, he asked no more questions. Nor did Queen Saw speak, but she gave Yazathingyan a piercing glance. As he caught it, he felt the presence of a spirit more powerful than he had believed possessed her.

xii

The White Elephant

Yazathingyan's luck was in. The very next morning his servants told him that a countryman was waiting downstairs to see him on a matter of importance. The man was shown up; he appeared just a poor cultivator.

'I have a field on the edge of the jungle, your Honour,' he began. 'In the middle of it is a deep buffalo-wallow. This morning when I went out at dawn I noticed something in the wallow. Going up I saw it was an elephant calf a few weeks old. It had evidently become separated from its mother in the night and had stuck in the wallow. I took it to my house. It was covered with mud. When I looked closely at it, I saw that its eyes were light blue, surrounded by a salmon colour. That made me wash it. When the mud was off, its skin was a pinkish white, its toe-nails white.'

Yazathingyan listened to this with a good deal of scepticism. He had invented a story of a white elephant to entice Thihathu to his death, and now he was told that a real white elephant had been found. It seemed most unlikely. White elephants were rare beasts. The annals made it clear that sometimes two or three reigns would pass without sight of one. He began to cross-examine the cultivator. The man stuck to his story. If it was true, then fate was making him a present of what in popular opinion would go far to turn the usurpation into a legitimate succession. He told the man to bring in the calf at once.

Later in the day the creature was produced. Experts were sent for and they found after careful examination that beyond any vestige of doubt it was an authentic white elephant.

Yazathingyan immediately waited on Narathihāpaté. Telling him the story, he said: 'Our anxieties are at an end. An excellent reception at Pagān is now certain. The sole problem is how to keep so young an animal alive.'

'Are no she-elephants in milk?' asked the King.

'I am informed', replied the minister, 'that there are risks attendant upon putting elephant calves to females other than their mothers.'

'What shall we do? It is so important.' Narathihāpaté was quite at a loss.

At this moment Queen Saw came from behind a screen. She had overheard the conversation and said: 'It should be suckled by women. There are plenty of wet-nurses to be had in the town. Offer a reward and send out for some.'

Yazathingyan, for all his resource, had not thought of this solution, and, withdrawing, at once made enquiries. He was told that Dalla was stocked with wet-nurses of exceptional development, the Burmese jovial and robust, the Indians even larger but more serious, while, if his Excellency so desired, there was a sprinkling of Cambodians, Javanese, even Chinese, each with the characteristics of their place of origin.

'What we want is milk,' said Yazathingyan, 'milk and plenty of it. But all things being equal, give preference to Buddhists.'

His men hurried away. The matter was urgent, for the elephant was hungry. It had had nothing to eat since it had lost its mother.

When the news spread in the town that a white elephant calf had been taken and that a reward was offered for wet-nurses, there was a rush to volunteer. Within a couple of hours a tolerable band of women assembled in the royal precincts. The calf was led up to them. It weighed about sixteen stone and was likely to require a good deal of refreshment. Queen Saw had sent word that she wished to be present at the feeding and now appeared. She herself selected the nurse who should begin, a fine woman of monumental figure. But the elephant was upset. It would not go near. They spoke of cow's milk then, but the woman, who was most anxious to get the reward, began coaxing. It grew less shy, but still would not suck.

On Queen Saw's staff was a girl called Veluvati, a gentle little thing who was fond of animals. She now suggested music and a song. They looked round for musicians. In no time a small orchestra was in position.

It played a soft accompaniment on the wood and strings, as Veluvati herself sang an old lullaby, a piece originally composed to send just such an infant white elephant to sleep. By cleverly changing the last stanza she adapted it to the present case.

'Little elephant, do not fret for your mother; forget your cousins, your baby friends; nor worry for your speckled forests, your mountains or tumbling streams: evil spirits dwell there, wild beasts haunt there, and cruel hunters there seek for quarry.

'In the woods you had no servants; plastered with mud you lay down to sleep; flies and mosquitoes buzzed after you: but here we will pet you and wash you and fan you.

'Sweet one, stay with us! What is freedom?—thorns and prickly bushes and marshes. Why should you wish to cross valleys and ranges, drink muddy water, your feet cut with stones?

'We will take you up to the heavenly city; at Pagān in your stable of gold we will feed you with cake and sugar-canes, while dancers amuse you.

'So do not fret: look at these women, your nurses, their breasts full of milk, their rich breasts for you, darling: drink, darling, drink.'

So she sang, posed by the elephant and twiddling its ears. Queen Saw found the words a trifle sugary for her robust temperament, but the little animal appeared soothed by them, for it began to respond at last to the blandishments of the women. Its repugnance finally overcome, it started to suck and, having once got into the way, continued successfully, draining twenty of the eager nurses.

In the course of the afternoon workmen were ordered to run up a temporary stable. Though Yazathing-yan was hastening the preparations for the return journey to Pagān, which was fixed to begin on a propitious day at the end of the following week, it was thought worth while to gild the stable walls and to make a little work of art of the roof. There, bedded in fresh rice-straw, the calf was made comfortable. Besides a regular service of wet-nurses, a domestic staff, a band and dancers were engaged.

On the morning of departure the elephant underwent a special toilette. Maids had given it an early bath. It had been soaped all over, carefully dried and then scented. A red cloth was put on its back and a triple string of pearls round its neck. Its trunk had been gilt. When being led to the wharf two girls held umbrellas over it, while its band played and dancers tripped alongside. A contortionist clown somersaulted ahead in an effort to amuse it, while his opposite fell heavily in the dust, making such innuendos about the wet-nurses as to cause the dancers to strike him playfully with their fans.

By the wharf was moored a raft, laid across two boats, on which was a pavilion with a seven-tiered roof. The roof was thatched with flowers woven in patterns representing the Eight Precious Symbols of the Buddha. The sides of the pavilion were hung with crimson velvet curtains. On the floor were mats of the finest texture. The elephant was embarked with its staff. Thereafter the King and the whole court embarked. To the stern of the elephant's raft a number of ropes of different kinds and lengths were attached. Those in the middle were made of fine silk. With his own hands Narathihāpaté tied one of these to his barge, while Yazathingyan followed his example with another. The mandarins did the same, as also the queens and principal concubines, longer ropes of ordinary material being provided for the vessels which carried the troops, the musicians and their servants. In all, five hundred craft were webbed together.

When the paddlers dipped their blades into the water and all the boats got under weigh, it was a remarkable spectacle. They covered an area of ten acres. The ropes were dyed red; the gilding of the barges glittered in the sun, each barge with a figured prow and stern, the King's in this case a scorpion, Yazathingyan's a dragon, the others' ducks, serpents or celestial spirits; and the band was playing exultantly, while countless girls posed and sang on what deck-space there was. It called for the utmost skill on the part of the steersmen. But these were experts; they had to be so, for the penalty exacted for a collision was extreme.

On the banks a vast concourse of people watched silently, but with profound satisfaction. It had been a glorious day for Dalla when Usana had come down. His hunting and his death, the acclamation of Narathihāpaté as his successor, the enticement and summary execution of Thihathu, and finally the unexpected appearance of the calf, a veritable white elephant, had provided the population with inexhaustible gossip. The entertainments, too, had been very lavish; open to the poorest, they had made the season one long gala. No wonder, then, that satisfaction was spread on every face, that every man and child rejoiced that it had been their lot to be born again under such a good government.

The flotilla made upstream slowly. There was a long journey before them against the current, three hundred and fifty miles. To start with, of course, they had the flood tide, but they overtopped that all too soon and day after day it was a steady push against falling water. However, they were in no hurry. There were the strongest reasons of policy to halt frequently and allow Narathihāpaté to show himself to his subjects in company with the white elephant.

Of all the sights and sounds of the voyage, the one which left, perhaps, the most indelible impression was the lights at Yenangyaung, the oil wells. There, the mandarin in administrative charge lit ten thousand oil lamps and, placing them on floats distributed over a wide area of the river, provided a spectacle, lovely and evocative. The floats were released some distance above the anchorage and, as they approached on the current, it seemed as if the hosts of fairyland were arriving. They rode up, ten thousand lights, but multiplied indefinitely by their reflections, and then passed away down the great river, seeming to gather together, as in one flame, until hardly seen in the far distance they were swallowed by a bend. So poignantly did their impermanent beauty affect the onlookers that many found themselves reciting, as they fingered their rosaries, the Three Subjects for Meditation—*Anissa*, transitoriness; *Dokha*, unhappiness; *Anatta*, illusion. The Cambodian dancer, now a member of the concubinate, was greatly impressed. In spite of the natural exuberance of her character, she was heard to murmur subduedly: 'We have

King Suryavarman at Angkor Thom, but not even on the festival of Hari is the embattled moat ablaze with such a tide of fire.'

The next day but one they arrived at Pagān and entered the palace. The usurpation was complete.

King Suryavarman of Cambodia standing on his
Elephant, with Fans, Umbrellas and Yak-Tail
Whisks carried beside him
From the reliefs at Angkor

xiii

Appointments and Transfers

Like every new reign, Narathihāpaté's began with a series of appointments and transfers at court and in the services. These may seem dull to us, but for the persons concerned and their rivals they had more interest than the rope trick or the capture of the white elephant. A reference must be made to them, for some of those moved up were destined to play a part in events of importance.

The matter of Usana's five queens first engaged attention. The Chief Queen, who was Thihathu's mother, was sent to a nunnery. Of the remaining four there was one called Sawlon, a handsome girl of about Narathihāpaté's age. She had royal blood in her veins and let no one forget it. He decided to make her his queen. Alliance with at least one of his father's queens was considered necessary to stabilise his position. The other three were retired to their estates. That left him with Queen Saw as his Chief Queen and Sawlon as his second. For his third he made an appointment which shocked everybody at the time. The Cambodian dancer was elevated under the title of Shinshwé. She owed this promotion to her ability to sing songs, indescribably broad, with delicate effect, a trick which invariably convulsed the King. When she heard of her promotion she said: 'To think that I might now be dancing in some provincial town with the old men leering at me from the front seats, if I hadn't been quicker than the other girls up the trunk!' There was no love lost between her and Sawlon, who had called her a tart on the river trip. This was grossly untrue for, if not exactly a virgin, she was a good girl, and her maids adored her because she was so generous.

The remaining two appointments in the cadre of queens were filled by well-born women of undistinguished character, but who within the year produced sons, Narathihāpaté's only sons, one of whom was destined eventually to play a fatal rôle.

The King made another promotion which was notable. His uncle, the ex-monk, was created a member of council with the title of Theimmazi. There was no one more good-hearted, but he had a failing which interfered with his usefulness, being rarely sober after the sun was down. It was he who suggested to the King that the latter's mother might now be recalled to the palace from Myit-tha village, where she had been vegetating ever since Usana's accession. But Narathihāpaté refused to do this. His mother had been frozen out of court because she was so common, and he had no desire to be embarrassed with her now. He sent her a small present, which was delivered to her one morning as she sat on her verandah expecting a letter inviting her back. This coldness of her only son outraged her to such a point that she returned the present and threw herself off a bridge. She had never been able to adapt herself like her brother Theimmazi.

Queen Saw, on the contrary, invited her father and mother to court. But after a week the farmer became uneasy about his fields. Moreover, he missed his flute and the presence of the mountain. The palace way of life confused him, the grandees alarmed his gentle spirit. He took leave of his daughter and returned to Kanbyu with his wife, who had tried unsuccessfully to induce him to accept the appointment which was offered. But he had said: 'I have everything I want at Kanbyu, a house, a garden, and enough land to provide me with rice. I am a free man there, I need grovel to nobody. I can play my own tunes and dream my own dreams.'

Yazathingyan brought forward three names. He wanted firstly to mark his appreciation of the conduct of the Mayor of the Palace, who had been of great assistance to Mahabo in helping him to convince Thihathu that a white elephant had been caught. The Mayor accordingly on his recommendation was given the grandiloquent title of Tharepyissapaté with the rank of General, while continuing to hold his office at court. There was no one to beat him at organising a party, but people found it difficult to imagine him commanding in the field. He was very stout. The other two names Yazathingyan had in mind were those of his sons, generally called the Ophla brothers. They were splendid young men, if rather dull—decidedly dull—but he must do something for them. For the elder he got the appointment of Comptroller of the White Elephant. No intelligence was required there. So long as he saw that the brute was fed and not overfed, he could leave the rest to his Brahman secretary. There were pickings, too, for all notabilities visiting the capital had to make a present in gold to the sacred beast. For the younger he obtained the captaincy of the bodyguard. The uniform was becoming and he was the handsomer of the two.

It is worthy of note that in this distribution of honours the Royal Chaplain was not forgotten. The King offered him the title of Aggamahapandita or Supreme Scholar, which he refused.

So much for rewards, but a matter of punishment, also, came up, which, as it throws a peculiar light on what follows, must be mentioned. Narathihāpaté had not forgotten how he had been caused to trip by a Tartar when leaving the pavilion in front of his father's mausoleum. The man was arrested and brought to Pagān, when the Royal Chaplain was asked to interpret the occurrence. His answer was vague; it spoke of danger from the north, but what danger or when it might arise was not stated. When pressed to be more particular, he repeated that the episode as such indicated danger from the north and no more. It was impossible for him therefore to particularise further.

The King then consulted Yazathingyan. Was it necessary to take any action to ward away the danger? The minister replied in substance as follows: If the Tartar was a symbol of danger, it would be logical to destroy him, for by analogy his death must abate the danger for which he stood.

Narathihāpaté was not sure whether he understood this argument, but he enquired what sort of death the Tartar should die in the circumstances.

'The execution should not be an ordinary one.' The minister continued his exegesis. 'As the Tartar symbolises danger, his soul should be chained to guard the city against that very danger. What if he be immured in the Tharaba gate and act as colleague to the existing guardian, Tepathin?'

Narathihāpaté thought this proposal very neat, but suggested that the Royal Chaplain be consulted, as Tepathin was accustomed to attend on the prelate. There might be arcane objection.

While they were waiting for the Chaplain's arrival, Yazathingyan enlarged on his theme. This danger from the north, what could it be? Burma was marvellously protected against danger from every quarter. Westwards and eastwards a jumble of ranges and forests warded away Bengal and Cambodia. Southwards was the perilous sea, an everlasting ditch. The north was as embattled with its peaks and gorges and, though report had it that the Tartar clans under Genghis Khan had destroyed the whole upper world and now, ruled by Kublai Khan in China, had a veteran army, incomparable bowmen, they had never attempted to force the mountains and attack the country chosen by the Blessed One as the safe repository of the faith. Yet if they sought at any time to do so, it would be of value to have one of them as a spirit, bound by astrological formulas for ever to protect Pagān.

★ *Appointments and Transfers* ★

The Chaplain arrived at this point and was asked whether it would be tampering in any way with his arrangements if an additional spirit was chained to Tharaba. On being more fully informed of the circumstances, he replied that as head of the Religion, he did not countenance such practices.

'But', urged Narathihāpaté, 'it is upon you that Tepathin waits. When he has anything of substance to report he goes to you. How then can you disclaim him and the art which binds him?'

'Tepathin was chained at a time when our knowledge of the pure faith was not what it is now. I inherited Tepathin, but I have never felt that he consorted well with my real beliefs. Therefore, I shall not accept for him a coadjutor. Moreover, to put the Tartar to death, an innocent man, guilty at most of rudeness, is no way to avert evil. Such deeds cause the doer to wander interminably in *Samsara's* glassy maze.'

Saying these words solemnly, he left the room. Before the others came to any decision, the Tartar escaped. He was never recaptured.

xiv
The Coronation

In due course Yazathingyan caused Narathihāpaté to be crowned. It was a great ceremonial occasion, which began at dawn one day when the King emerged from the apartments of the bed-chamber and passed in procession across the inner audience hall to an ablution pavilion, which had been erected for the occasion. He was dressed in a simple robe of white. Taking his seat in the pavilion, round which the whole court was arranged in prostrate attitudes, he poured over his head water from the five rivers of the kingdom, which was handed to him in conch-shells by the Brahmanic acolytes, who officiated at coronations, for as the pure faith did not provide a suitable liturgy, resort was had to precedents of Hindu origin. The water was scented, and he poured it again and again, while the Brahmans played ritual music and a fanfare of trumpets sounded.

Purified by this water baptism, he returned to the
bed-chamber and shortly reappeared dressed in a tight
jacket of white silk, which flared up like two half-open
wings at the waist-line. Below this was a skirt of coloured brocade, wherein red and gold predominated.
His head and his feet were bare. Another procession
was formed, which moved towards the west of the
hall, where an octagonal throne of figwood had been
placed. In front walked Brahmans beating drums
shaped like hour-glasses, other priests blowing conchs
and scattering roasted grains. Behind were pages and
chamberlains, bearing the regalia, namely the great
White Umbrella, the Whisk of the Yak's Tail, the Slippers, the Crown of Victory and the Victorious Sword.
The rear was brought up by the White Elephant, the
elder Ophla leading it in.

On reaching the octagonal throne, Narathihāpaté
seated himself on the side facing due east, the rising
sun. Eight girls now advanced and stationed themselves opposite the eight sides of the throne. Each of
them held a conch of oil in her clasped hands. As the
drums gave a burst of sound, the girl standing east of
the King approached to his feet and making a profound
obeisance said this verse:

> *I invoke for the King victory in the eastern quarter.*
> *May he rule justly, holding to the Three Gems,*
> *The Buddha, the Sacred Law, the Sacred Church.*
> *So shall the Celestial Guardian of this quarter*
> *Protect him against the evil which comes unseen.*

So intoning, she handed him her conch of oil, with
which Narathihāpaté anointed himself, saying:

'I shall protect this kingdom and her religion and her people.'

In like manner he faced the seven other girls, each of whom chanted a similar verse and handed him a conch.

Thereafter five Brahmans approached with the five regalia. The White Umbrella, formed in nine tiers, was raised over his head. He was handed the Crown of Victory, shaped like a conical helmet, and this he put on. Sitting thus crowned under the White Umbrella, he was invested with the Sword and the Slippers, while in his hand he held the Yak-tail Whisk. At the conclusion of the rite, there was a fanfare and from chapels beyond the hall came the sound of monks of the Religion chanting a blessing.

Narathihāpaté had played his part without much dignity or conviction. His low forehead was corrugated and he wore an uneasy smile. But Yazathingyan had expected no better. For him the sole importance of the coronation was that it legalised his coup. The King he had placed on the throne was now consecrated, and with him the power which had set him up. It was the seal on a satisfactory piece of work. But like many another patron before and since he misinterpreted the character of his protégé. Narathihāpaté's uneasy expression arose from a conflict within him, a sense of his inferiority fighting with his desire to prove himself the superior of everyone else. The tension thus set up governed all his future actions. But Yazathingyan had no inkling of this.

Following the coronation was a review of the guard, four thousand men in dark quilted tunics and gilded helmets. There was also a march past of the elephants, of which two thousand paraded. Armoured themselves and carrying armoured towers from which archers and javelin men could discharge their missiles, they were moving forts, and constituted the contemporary solution of that everlasting problem of tactics—how to approach unhurt opposing infantry and destroy them.

It was during this review that Queen Shinshwé, the Cambodian, called out in her usual impulsive manner to Queen Sawlon, who was trying not to see her: 'Our elephants at Angkor Thom may not be as fierce as the ones here, but they have more expensive armour.'

To this Sawlon made no reply, and Shinshwé, turning to her maids, said: 'They don't like to think that Angkor is grander. It's real stone there, girls, not the brick and teak of this place. Still, the elephants here I must admit are spanking brutes. I hope the day will never dawn when they show their tails in a bloody rout.'

This chance remark, spoken lightly by a woman of ebullient character, was overheard by two of Yaza-thingyan's agents. Trained as they were to look for signs, it struck them as having an ominous significance. They made a careful summary of all the circumstances and submitted a report.

XV

The Banishment of Yazathingyan

Narathihāpaté's complex drove him first to try and prove himself superior to his father. The late King had been very easy-going. He had interfered very little with the establishments of the queens and concubines; he rarely called for the accounts of the palace mayor; the expenditure on the kitchens, the stables, on uniforms, went unchecked. Moreover, the rules relating to discipline were lightly enforced; people were allowed to come and go as they liked; the concubines used to give parties in each other's rooms; even love affairs were carried on without very much risk.

Narathihāpaté decided to change all this. He appointed a number of Indian accountants, whose duty it was to examine daily the expenditure of all departments. He also instituted a corps of proctors who had instructions to enforce the palace rules. At the end of twelve months he was able to congratulate himself on small savings and was pleased by the nervousness of some of the courtiers, a number of whom had been punished for petty offences.

This success in the palace tempted him to try his hand outside. He conceived the idea of baiting Yazathingyan. The Chief Minister was, indeed, offensively powerful. He had piled up a large fortune and by putting his men into key positions had organised a strong body of supporters. But he was very competent also, keeping the country quiet and seeing that the revenue was paid in punctually. Narathihāpaté did not dare to attack him openly, but thought that if he could annoy him by a series of pinpricks he would make him feel that there was a king. His discomfiture would be amusing to watch. Perhaps he might do something rash, something that would give a handle against him.

For some months Narathihāpaté tried with small result to provoke his minister, but during a tour to Pōpa, undertaken fourteen months after his coronation, he was more successful. They had reached a village halfway between the capital and the mountain, where he intended to stay the night. As usual, the local elders were waiting to receive him.

'Who is that fellow there?' he asked Yazathingyan.

'That is the headman,' replied the veteran minister.

'How long have you been in charge?' the King asked the man roughly.

'I was recently appointed by the Honourable the Chief Minister,' replied the headman with respectful sturdiness.

'I remember nothing about this,' said Narathihāpaté

with an assumed air of surprise. 'Was the appointment order countersigned by me?'

'It is not customary to disturb Your Majesty with routine matters of such a kind,' interrupted Yazathingyan.

'Quite so,' agreed Narathihāpaté, 'but let me see if the fellow knows his work. You there!' and he turned round with an ugly look, 'what are the five duties of a headman?'

The man, much disturbed by the King's tone and by an instinctive feeling that the Chief Minister was displeased, flattened himself right out on the floor, his whiskers in the dust. He found himself tongue-tied.

'Speak up,' bullied the King in a raised voice. 'What are your five duties? Don't you know them?'

The headman tried to reply twice, but could not articulate.

'He seems fairly useless,' observed the King.

'It's only fright, he's flustered,' put in Yazathingyan, who began to prompt him with, 'Come, my man, the five duties—night-watchmen, the stockade—you know the rest?'

But the unfortunate creature's mind was a complete blank. All he could say was: 'I place your Honour's orders on the top of my head.'

'I'm afraid I can't have headmen of that kind, certainly not for appointments so near the capital,' pronounced the King. 'You will have to get somebody else. And, before you make the selection, put the papers up to me.'

The elders were dismissed in a state of collapse.

Somehow Yazathingyan could not take this lightly. It is only fair to add that he was liverish at the time. As

soon as he was free, he went to a pavilion where Queen
Saw was seated, listening to music. He told her the
whole story.

'What is happening?' he asked in conclusion.

The Queen turned her great eyes upon him. It
seemed impossible that a girl of her age could have
such a presence, he thought.

'Do not worry about trivial matters,' said she. 'The
more you show your annoyance, the more delighted he
will be.'

Next morning they were on the march again early
and arrived without fatigue at the old camp by Pōpa's
foot. The villagers who had welcomed Usana were
waiting under the same headman who had spoken of
the triple flowering of little Ma Saw's bush. As the
Queen was carried to her pavilion, it seemed to her a
great age since the night she had entered the village in a
cart with her father. But if circumstances had changed,
she was essentially the same, calm but full of fire, humorous and high spirited. While aware that her qualities must elevate her eventually to a dominating position in the state, as a woman she also knew that her
nature demanded more than that. The full realisation
of this want came over her as she sat in the pavilion
during the quiet of the afternoon. Everybody was resting; she had dismissed her ladies—even the girls who
fanned her had been dismissed. Alone by a window,
through which blew a wind from the wide fields, warm
and scented, she looked up in the direction of Kanbyu
village, her home, and fell into a reverie. Had she remained there, she thought, some man or other would
have come, courted her in the village way, speaking to

her after nightfall through the floor of her room or, permitted to sit at the end of it in her mother's presence, have urged his suit during weeks and months. But could she have loved such a man? Only if she had been other than she was, only if she had been just a country girl. The lovemaking, yes, the kisses, the fun of embraces, all that, yes, but love, the adoration a woman of her character could give to a man of equal or greater depths, no, that could not have been at Kanbyu; there was no man in Kanbyu whom she could have loved with the power latent in her. But if the abandonment of that life was right, indeed inevitable, fortunate, did it bring her any closer to the realisation of herself as a woman? It had not, she reflected, it could not. What had Usana been?—an agreeable man, with whom she had spent amusing hours, teasing, laughing, tempting, satisfying, all in the luxury of a rich old palace, glorious food, faithful servants, every conceivable comfort and flattery. No wonder she had felt a certain pang when the news came in that the elephant had killed her boon companion. Boon companion, that was the phrase; it was as that she had missed him. It had gone no deeper; he had never moved her. Looking back, the affair seemed a mere episode, a brilliant introduction to metropolitan life. And now Narathihāpaté —what a man! She had faced facts and married him. At Usana's death there had been a moment of weakness, thought of returning to Kanbyu with her jewels and gold. But she had overcome the inclination, seen it was nonsense. She had grown clean out of Kanbyu, could not have lived there. And her family, what would they have thought of such a move? Her father, dreamer

though he was, would have found it craven, for she
knew well the bravery of his hopes for her. She repre-
sented for him the personification of his fancy, when as
a poet he travelled immense realms, battling with any
that barred his way. The daughter of such a man, she
could not have returned to Kanbyu with just a box of
jewels or an estate with slaves. With the world at her
feet, such a course would have seemed to him a flight,
a rout of the spirit. And she knew that she would have
agreed with him. So it had had to be Narathihāpaté.
With him, of course, she had far less in common than
with Usana. There was something frigid about him,
something low, ungenerous. He was unbalanced, she
felt, without intellect, without courage. Not that she
was fearful for herself, she knew how to manage him.
He had conceived a respect for her that was almost
superstitious; she was always right, he had once said
unguardedly. If things turned ill, he would certainly
lean on her. And they would turn ill, of that she was
certain. But was this a woman's life—power? Was this
her lot then, to watch over the state, was she to find
satisfaction for her nature in politics? In politics! She
sighed. Softly blew the wind through the palm fronds,
the laced greenery of the tamarinds shook. So she was
never to meet a man upon whom she could pour out
a wealth of love, a great man, a man of heart and mind,
never to feel the madness of love burst up, never, when
there was such a fire in her, never, never! And as she
looked over the land of Burma, she wept.

But her sense of the actual returned very soon. She
sent for her ladies and made a grand toilette. When it
was finished, she had a dazzling appearance. Her hair

was done in a high looped knot, scented and jewelled, her eyebrows plucked, her whole face carefully powdered. She wore a jacket of Indian lawn, as fine as gossamer, white and peaked out at the shoulders and hips, cut with a lively rhythm, admirably fitted. Her arms showed through it and her breast, a golden colour. The old rose of her skirt was soft as sleep. Sitting sideways on a carpet, one arm supporting her weight, the elbow bent in against the joint like a bow, the other hand on her thigh, a large emerald on a tiny finger, she was so striking with her gracious face that the women fell back to admire her and, apt though they were at easy flattery, spoke from the heart when they uttered, 'Lovely lady, we worship you.'

At this conjuncture a maid announced that the Chief Minister sought audience. He came in, his face drawn, but such beauty flowed from the Queen that it seemed for a moment to wash away his agitation. He sat down and began at once:

'I had to trouble you yesterday about a trivial matter. To-day I have had to support something more tart. We had hardly arrived when His Majesty started to make enquiries. Unacquainted as he is with the details of administration, he asked a number of meaningless questions. No one could understand what he desired to know, but I surmise that what he sought was any matter with which he could find fault. At last, however, he asked the headman:

' "Have you credited yet your percentage of the rice crop?"

' "Not yet," said the man; "the grain is hardly in the granary."

' "I want it lodged at once," said he.

' "The Chief Minister has fixed the end of next month," replied the headman, foolishly, I fear.

' "But I have given you an order," said he.

'What followed was most unfortunate. All the headman had to do was to keep silent. Instead, he said that he did not understand, that the village belonged to the Chief Minister. I had to interpose. As you may know, the late King gave me the village as an estate and I settled the rents on my second son, now Captain of the Bodyguard. I explained this to His Majesty, but he replied:

' "I do not recognise grants made before my time. The lands will now revert to the crown." '

As Yazathingyan said this, there was deep anger in his voice. He went on:

'To think that I gave him the throne less than two years ago! What does he mean, what is he aiming at by taking from me my lawful property?'

The explanation was clear enough and both of them knew what it was, but that day Yazathingyan seemed to have lost his usual phlegm. He was liverish, of course.

'I can't stand it,' he went on. 'Where will it end?' She tried to soothe him:

'As long as you take no notice of his slights, your position is impregnable. Go on with your work as if nothing had happened; always present a smiling and respectful face; bow to annoyances and they will blow over your head without hurting you!'

'But where will it all stop; may not annoyance become insult, insult menace?'

'If you have the support of influential people, and if by considered conduct you give no handle to those who range themselves with the King, the annoyances you will have to bear will always be supportable. Narathihāpaté will not dare, certainly at present, to break with you.'

'But consider the prestige of the monarchy, its power of patronage. The King inevitably has the support of many, sycophants, place-hunters and adventurers. One day they will try a stroke at me. When a minister falls out of favour, advantage is quickly taken.'

The way his plans were rebounding seemed to have shaken him. Narathihāpaté was so different to what he had supposed.

The Queen, however, felt that her advice was correct, and she repeated:

'You must adapt yourself to present developments. The right line, I feel sure, is pliancy. Watch from the shade and, maybe, an opportunity will offer which, if taken promptly, will reverse the position. But whatever you do, avoid a clash. It does not pay in a case like this. You would lose support at once. I, for one, could do nothing to help you.'

Yazathingyan bowed, but did not reply. Instinct told him that the Queen's advice was profoundly sane. He had never heard her speak better. His earlier recognition of her immense talent was more than confirmed. But he was not sure whether he was capable of taking her advice. He asked leave to withdraw and returned to his quarters.

Hardly had he entered when a message arrived to say the King wished to see him again. After a hurried drink, he set off and found Narathihāpaté looking through papers with his Hindu secretaries. Though he knew his minister was there, he pretended not to see him and continued to work on for some time. At last he looked up and said:

'Ah, the Chief Minister, what does he want?'

'Your Majesty sent for me.'

'Yes, so I did. I was wondering whether the cost of erecting this camp has been debited against my revenues.'

'That is so.'

'But the camp is on property which till this morning was your estate. I think you should have funded it. I have directed the clerks here to make the necessary alterations in the accounts. That will do.'

Coming so soon after the other, this profoundly shook Yazathingyan. He went back to his rooms in a state of mental confusion. Mahabo, his ingenious secretary, was in Pagān or he might have been saved. As it was, there were only servants and women, with his outdoor gang under Tit and 'Nit.

When their master came in, they saw at once that he was upset. Taking his uniform off, they washed his feet, while two girls massaged him with bright competence. But he had a wild look in his eye which they did not understand. At five o'clock they brought in his dinner.

'The propitiatory dancing begins at dusk,' he observed generally. 'Give me plenty to drink. I shall want all I can take when I attend at the Golden Feet.'

The girls hastened to fill his cup. He drank off two or three.

'What's the brand?' he asked.

'The usual kind, your Honour,' they chorused, 'with stewed stork in it.'

'Give me another,' he said, 'but see if you can find any with rhinoceros horn. I want sustaining.'

They hastened to obey and soon returned with the variety he wanted. One of the maids, a plump girl called Ma Than, whom he sometimes noticed more particularly, poured it out for him with frank goodwill.

'That's better,' he said when he had finished the draught. 'Fill up. I'm not going to be quite sober to-night. You people have no idea what I have to put up with now. I've been Chief Minister of Burma for I don't know how many years, but I've never been robbed before. If this goes on, we end up paupers.'

They didn't exactly know what he was talking about, but they liked his manner. He seldom unbent in this way, but when he did, he would give them something or have fun with one of the girls. They refilled his cup, a jade cup with carved handles. He raised it with both hands. The rhinoceros horn was doing him good.

'Yes, paupers,' he went on. 'How would you like it if your estates were sequestered?'

No one knew what 'sequestered' meant, so they filled the cup again and Ma Than beamed on him.

'They tell me I am not diplomatic enough!' he laughed. 'Some advice was given me to-day. I won't tell you who gave it—a beautiful lady, very high placed. She spoke of pliancy.'

The plump girl dared to say that all the ladies were in love with his Honour. This obviously pleased him. He smiled at her and proceeded:

'Pliancy, if you please! In reason, certainly; a polite conciliatory manner, an obliging way, and, of course, all respect; right down on the ground every time; there's no harm in that. But when you *are* paying respect, to be insulted, that's too much. I've never stood it. You remember the prince; he was sorry he spat at me.'

They all laughed heartily at this. Tit and 'Nit, who had moved up on their hands and knees, though they really had no business in the house, chimed:

'Your Honour was wonderful on that day. It was the funniest thing to see his Highness plead for mercy. And the elephant,' they tittered, 'how the prince screamed when it tossed him. He was sorry then, as your Honour says.'

Ma Than wriggled slightly when she heard this, exclaiming:

'How I wish I'd been there. His Honour is marvellous.' She became so excited that she asked leave to show him a dance she had seen, through a crack in the panelling, one night when the Cambodian queen was performing for an inner circle in the bed-chamber. That lady had claimed dancing could go no further. She was probably correct. At any rate the abandon of the girl's gestures seemed to remove what remained of the minister's restraint, and after another cup he began boasting:

'No, he's mistaken if he thinks I'm taking that. I know better things! A turner's grandson, his mother the commonest of the common! His father saw her first at a well, you know, washing her bottom. Besides, he's only half-witted. Where would he be, I'd like to know, if I hadn't put him up? Under the sod, Thihathu'd have murdered him!'

His audience, who had been drinking surreptitiously behind his back and now were as drunk as he, began to second these sentiments hilariously, when he rose to his feet and said:

'Come on! I'm going to see him now, and I know what I shall say. Give me that bronze bowl there. We'll all go, just as we are.'

They staggered out of the mat house, Yazathingyan carrying a broken bowl full of rice, his men laughing and disorderly, some of the women behind, including the plump girl, who had not put on her clothes again after the dance. There was a splendid sunset. So aflame was the sky that the very dust of the road was tinged with red. It tinged also the saffron limbs of the girl, till she looked like the fabled pink women of the north.

Narathihāpaté was in the act of taking his seat before the open space where the ritual dances were staged to take place, when he saw approaching his Chief Minister in a raggle-taggle of followers. After a momentary surprise, he was not altogether dissatisfied. Queen Saw also caught sight of him, and, taking in the situation at a glance, sent a man to draw him aside. But she was too late. He came before the King, sat down and began to eat the rice out of the broken bowl, holding up the same and studying it, his head on one side, leering and chewing.

'What are you doing there with that broken bowl?' asked the King, in the very sober tone of a drinker who had not yet begun to drink.

'Eating my dinner out of it, Lord,' said Yazathingyan. 'I'm obliged to—there's not a whole one in the house; can't get them mended now that the turners and tinkers have all become so great,' and with an excess of drunken folly he held out the bowl to the King, as if asking him to mend it.

At these words, at the effrontery of his action, there was a dead silence. It was evident that his supporters in the court circle considered he had gone too far. Friends tried to slip off, enemies glanced furiously and leaned towards Narathihāpaté. The King saw his chance. In a voice which he was able to make toneless, he said:

'I know that your Excellency is versed in the arts, particularly in building. Tell me now, when they want to put the finial on the summit of a new temple, what do they do?'

The question disconcerted Yazathingyan. Through the fog of his mind he perceived a threat. The King had not crumpled up as he had expected. Assurance half gone, he replied:

'They put up scaffolding.'

'And when the finial is in position,' continued the King, 'do they leave the scaffolding?'

Unable to see what was coming, but sure that he was being led on to a climax, Yazathingyan wanted to avoid a reply. But everyone was looking at him, and too fuddled to devise any sort of an exit from what he began to perceive was an impossible situation, he was obliged to say tamely:

'When the building is finished, the scaffolding, of course, must be removed.'

'Quite so,' said Narathihāpaté, 'removed. Well, need I labour the point? But perhaps for a person in your

condition it is necessary to do so. You were the extremely efficient scaffolding upon which I was raised to
the summit of the kingdom. I am, and must always be,
much obliged to you for your efforts on my behalf. But
I feel that the time has come to take down the scaffolding. It now serves no useful purpose; indeed, it ob-
scures the splendour of the main structure. In the circumstances, I propose to relieve you of your office and
send you to Dalla. I choose Dalla because I cannot
think of any place further away. You will go under escort in case, when your sobriety is fully restored, mortification should tempt you to self-violence. All your
effects—that is to say your palace, your estates, your
elephants and your staff—lapse to my keeping. They
would be useless to you in Dalla.'

When he had spoken—and there were many present
who considered that he had acted with excessive moderation, while even Yazathingyan's friends felt that the
old man had courted punishment—a squad of the
guard took the delinquent back to his quarters. He
thanked his foresight in having appointed his son captain of that force. It meant that he was treated with
greater consideration than would normally have been
extended to a fallen minister. Now wholly sobered and
miserable, he collected a few valuables and mounted
the elephant led in by the soldiers. They started at once
for Pagān, though night had fallen. At a distance behind, three members of his household followed with
furtive steps. They were Tit and 'Nit and Ma Than, who
was weeping.

As the violent sunset had presaged, a storm gathered. It began blowing very hard from the north-east.

The full moon was a quarter up the sky, and it appeared to be racing in the wrack of cloud. Yazathingyan, huddled on the elephant, wrapped himself in a cloak. They were passing along the reedy shore of a lake with woods on their right hand. The velocity of the wind increased, tearing through the branches and whipping away the surface of the water. It was difficult to make headway, and those on foot sought shelter under the lea of the elephant. When the storm reached its maximum, great trees began to be thrown down before and behind them. Yazathingyan was past caring whether he was struck or not, but the elephant retained its wits and waded a short distance into the lake, coming to a halt among some tall water-plants where it was beyond range of the falling trees. These grasses were bending under the wind, pliant as whips. They stooped and righted themselves again as the gusts passed over them. Yazathingyan sat there watching the raging wind. He remarked its power over the trees; the greater they were, the more frequent their fall. But the grasses did not suffer; they bent and the wind was impotent to harm them. He saw in this a symbol of what had just happened to him. Queen Saw's word, pliancy, recurred to his mind. Had he been pliant as a water-plant, the King's malevolence could have done him no harm. What a fool he had been not to follow her advice! With all his experience, he had no sense, not as much sense as a water-plant, which knew how to preserve itself by leaning from the gale. Like the big trees, he had been uprooted, split and flung down.

The storm passed over, a deluge of rain in its tail. They continued their journey. At dawn they entered the outskirts of Pagān, tired and haggard. The escort had orders to use all haste, for the King wished to get Yazathingyan away as quickly as possible. Sympathy might veer, he was so influential a man. The instructions were to take him straight to the river and there embark. He was not even to be allowed to enter his residence.

As they went under the shadow of the Tharaba gate, they noticed a yellow-robed figure approaching in the centre of the road, his eyes cast down and a black lacquer begging bowl clasped in his hands. They drew aside respectfully to let him pass. When he was abreast, he halted and raised his head. It was the Royal Chaplain. His face was thinner; a long meditation in a cave, made without food or drink for fifty days, from which he had recently emerged, had wasted his body, but an extraordinary authority glowed in his eyes. Yazathingyan dismounted at once from the elephant and threw himself on the ground, as did the whole of his escort. Tit and 'Nit with the maid, who had followed doggedly throughout the night, while preserving their distance, did the same.

'Master,' said Yazathingyan, 'if I am permitted to obtrude my personal woes at the moment when you are in the act of observing the practice of the first disciples, may I draw attention to this escort and to my attenuated train and announce that I have fallen from power and am to be exiled?'

The Chaplain remained for some moments without speaking, and then he said slowly, quoting a stanza of the sacred Law:

'Whatsoever tends to rise, is like to fall. Whatsoever

tends to fall is like to rise. Nirvana only abideth, the calming of this Law of rise and fall.'

With that statement, at once an explanation of the ultimate nature of what had happened and an announcement of what might be expected to occur in the future, he turned his head, lowered his eyes and proceeded on his way. Yazathingyan remained in the dust till he had disappeared beyond the gate and then, strengthened and with hope, remounted his elephant and went forward with the escort. They traversed the capital without attracting attention, for he muffled his face from the gaze of the inquisitive, having no desire to be recognised in his disgrace. On reaching one of the wharves they embarked shortly afterwards for the south. Tit, 'Nit and the maid were allowed on board. As the boat put off, the girl began to prepare a meal for her master from provisions she had bought as they passed through the bazaar. She was strangely happy.

xvi
The Recall of Yazathingyan

There followed a happy time for Narathihāpaté. The tension from which he suffered was eased. He felt a great man. On his return from Pōpa, where the séance had been colourless, he appointed his uncle, Theimmazi, Chief Minister. That Theimmazi was incompetent was a point in his favour. The King knew he could work more comfortably with a person of that kind. He then proceeded to make himself felt all round. By listening to anonymous petitions he bullied the provincial governors. During his tours he exacted services from the people which they were not obliged to give by law. He took women for the concubinate against the wishes of their parents or husbands. Rasher still, he interfered with the tenure under which the Church held certain estates, insisting that the land was crown property. In all this he was actuated by his pressing desire to prove that he was a high and puissant lord of men. He proved it to himself, but his subjects were not deceived. Those directly in his power cordially detested him; they felt not an atom of admiration for his rule; while certain others, whose situation was more independent, summed him up and decided it was safe to rebel.

One morning, after Yazathingyan had been in Dalla about two years, news reached the palace that the Duke of Martaban had refused to pay revenue and was collecting an army. Martaban was at the extreme southeast of the kingdom, four hundred miles from Pagān. Its duke was a feudatory, one of the few remaining feudatories in Burma, the country as a whole being administered by official governors.

This news of the defection of Martaban was immediately followed by the further news that the hill tribes resident west of the Irrawaddy had descended from their mountain villages and were raiding the plain up to the river.

The effect of this intelligence upon Narathihāpaté was devastating. After an initial reaction, when he refused to believe that anyone would dare to flout him, he became much alarmed and summoned the Council. In a manner which he tried to make haughty and collected, he desired his ministers to advise him. The discussion which followed revealed the strategical position to be of special difficulty. To attack the Duke meant exposing flank and communications to the hill tribes; to operate first against the latter would lead the former to believe that with the army engaged elsewhere, it was his opportunity to break out; and to operate simultaneously against both would deplete the guard and leave the King exposed to a rising nearer home, a possible contingency in the state of public feeling. Theimmazi, perspiring profusely, found himself at the conclusion of the debate unable to submit concrete proposals. The Council broke up with nothing decided.

Next day messengers arrived to report that the Duke had declared himself king of the whole south, and that the hill tribes had crossed the river, thereby blocking an advance upon Martaban.

Narathihāpaté heard the news while he was still in the bed-chamber. He was seized with panic and instead of again summoning the Council, traversed the galleries leading to Queen Saw's apartments. Entering her room brusquely, he said: 'We are attacked.' His manner was abject.

Queen Saw, who had heard the news already, enquired what he proposed to do. When he replied that he had no plan, she asked why he did not consult his advisers.

'My advisers,' he cried, 'they are useless! I asked Theimmazi to submit a scheme, but he was unable to do so. Nor had anyone else proposals to put forward.'

'In that case', replied Queen Saw, 'I suppose that the rebels will do what they like.'

'You are very calm,' he whined. 'Do you realise that this is a serious matter?'

'I am only a woman,' she replied. 'Surely it would be better to take some competent person's advice.'

This only made Narathihāpaté more distracted; 'I have no one to turn to but yourself. Can you recommend nothing?'

'I can recommend nothing,' replied the Queen; 'but if you find Theimmazi is stupid and the rest half-witted, why do you not send for the one man in your kingdom who over a long course of years kept the frontier inviolate?'

'You think I ought to recall Yazathingyan?'

'It seems the only thing to be done, if your present councillors are useless. Let the situation develop and the rebels may overwhelm you.' There was a pause. The King seemed thoroughly intimidated.

'I had to exile him,' he said at last. 'You don't think I was wrong?'

Queen Saw, remembering the actual circumstances —that the King had deliberately baited him—made no reply.

'His behaviour was outrageous,' continued Narathihāpaté.

'Even a man of long experience, eminent in council, will sometimes make a mistake,' she observed. 'He was a faithful servant of the state. He can save it now.'

Narathihāpaté was already feeling much the better for the psychic support which a talk with Queen Saw invariably afforded him. He replied: 'You are right. We must recall him. As you say, procrastination or a false move may be disastrous. If the rebels were to establish themselves firmly in the lower country, the upper might join them.'

Queen Saw, who had always found silence and a certain expression of face a powerful clinching argument, said no more. The King left her room shortly afterwards, his step quite springy. He sent for General

Tharepyissapaté, Mayor of the Palace and a Member of Council. That stout personage arrived out of breath. He had been desperately thinking of a plan of campaign. Without waiting for the King to speak, he now blurted out a suggestion. 'We could buy off the Duke,' said he.

Narathihāpaté, having found his aplomb, was able to be quite brisk with him. 'I have considered the whole matter,' he said, 'and have decided to recall Yazathingyan. You will take the fastest boat at anchor in the road. Using relays of oarsmen and with the wind and stream, you will make Dalla on the fifth day. There embark the former Chief Minister within the time taken to boil a pot of rice. Double the relays coming up and be back here by the twelfth day. You will have to be careful when traversing that part of the river dominated by the hill tribes.'

Tharepyissapaté was much relieved to receive these orders. Gladly he set out and in a short time was speeding south in a boat of racing cut, propelled by twenty men of muscular development. The relays were regularly picked up; they glided at night past Thek hill, which was said to be the headquarters of the hill rebels, and reached Dalla without incident on the fifth day.

Tharepyissapaté hurried at once to the house which Yazathingyan was occupying in the town. It stood in a pleasant garden of fruit trees and flowering shrubs. At the foot of the stairs leading to the main front room was a girl.

'I wish to see his Excellency on the most urgent business,' said the general, as he wiped his forehead.

He was ushered upstairs without delay. The ex-minister was seated on a carpet before a low table. Piles of manuscript lay everywhere. He was writing busily.

'Ah, Tharepyissapaté,' he said, hiding his surprise, 'you arrive at an interesting moment. I have just completed my book on signs. It is a life work. I feel sure I shall be remembered by it long after my efforts in council are forgotten. Please sit down. Bring his lordship refreshment,' he called. 'You must excuse an author's vanity, and let me read you one or two of the more striking passages.'

'Your Excellency,' interposed Tharepyissapaté, 'I have a pressing communication from the Lord of Life.'

Yazathingyan put down his manuscript with apparent reluctance, but there was a glitter in his ancient eye.

'I left the Golden Palace less than five days ago,' continued the general, 'so you can imagine the urgency of my present news.' He then gave as full an account as his haste permitted of the circumstances leading to his sudden mission. 'Your Excellency is recalled,' he said in conclusion. 'I trust that you will embark without delay and proceed with me upstream.'

Yazathingyan was swept by the excitement which men of action in forced retirement always feel when there opens for them a new field of adventure. 'So they couldn't do without me,' he thought to himself. With animation he wrapped up his manuscript, remarking: 'I may as well take this with me; it has the value of a state document.' Then summoning his household he told them of his recall. 'Great events are portending,' he announced. 'Pack my things at once. I leave within the hour.'

The girl, Ma Than, undertook this office. During

the poverty and disappointment of his exile, she had devoted herself body and soul to his comfort, having acted as his mistress, his cook and his secretary. She had encouraged him with his writing, danced for him, sang to him, enveloped him in a devotion which was some solace to him. Now she packed, blinded with tears. It was all over, this happy time. For a whole year, a humble girl, she had been the close associate of a great man. It had been marvellous to bathe in his mellow spirit, to look into his eyes and see mystery and strength. Now he was going back to his high position, his grand family was waiting to welcome him. No doubt she would still be retained in his household, would follow in due course to the capital. But it could never be the same again, as when she had had his Honour all to herself.

Almost within the boiling of a pot of rice, the time specified, the two ministers reached the wharf. There was little room on the racing boat, and Yazathingyan took nobody with him. They embarked at once. The old minister's household knelt on the jetty. His girl had drawn a scarf over her face. With a shout the crew plunged in their paddles. Yazathingyan in the prow did not look back.

xvii
The First Campaign

little episode occurred as they went upstream which suggested to Yazathingyan, always on the look out for that whisper in the phenomenal world which signifies an event on the way, that his luck had turned. Not far from Minbu they met some fishermen who were returning from a monastery, where they had made an offering of part of their catch. Yazathingyan called on them to stop, as fish was wanted for supper. While the purchase was being made, he noticed a green spoon in their boat.

'What's that?' he asked the steersman, a grizzled and sheepish man of sixty.

'We got it out of the river, your Honour,' he replied. 'It came up in the net. I'm taking it home for the children to play with.'

They handed it up to the minister. He examined it carefully. As far as could be made out, the bowl of the spoon was carved from a huge emerald, the handle being of mother-of-pearl. It was an antique and had evidently been at the bottom of the river for centuries, for it was scratched and dull. But when he rubbed it on his sleeve, it began to glow with a lovely colour.

'I'll buy this from you,' said he to the steersman. 'How much do you want for it?'

'It's only a trifle,' said the old fellow. 'If his Honour likes it, he's welcome. Spoons are not used by folks like us.'

Yazathingyan saw that not only was it valuable as an emerald, but that as an antique it had great interest. He concluded that very probably it had belonged to the treasure of the kings of Thaton, whose valuables had been taken in the campaign of two hundred years earlier and brought up river. No doubt it had fallen overboard at that time. That an old piece of loot should, as it were, rise out of the river for him at this juncture struck him as a hint that the campaign he knew he would have to undertake against Martaban would provide him with similar spoils. Delighted at his interpretation, he pressed a piece of gold upon the dazzled fisherman and hurried on his way. By dint of hard paddling and constant relays they reached Pagān within the twelve days.

As they disembarked a footman came up in the gold livery of the palace and reported that the King had sent down an elephant from the royal stables to carry his Honour into the city. The beast was brought forward. On its gilded dais Yazathingyan mounted with Tharepyissapaté.

It was five o'clock on a December afternoon. The

sun, which had shone all day, was hanging now on the crest of the palm-trees, throwing immense shadows across the road. Its slanting rays struck the gates and towers of Pagān, the pinnacles of hundreds of shrines, pagodas and monasteries. The gold leaf with which most of them were covered flashed back the light, until it seemed that the title, the Golden City, was but a plain statement of fact. Though Yazathingyan had lived there from infancy, it had never seemed to him more beautiful, it had never seemed so imposing, such an august capital. He was deeply thankful to be back.

His interview with Narathihāpaté, which followed at once, took place in one of the private rooms. The King was in a peculiar state of mind. Still very anxious about what the rebels might do, he was impatient to see Yazathingyan, though he dreaded the humiliation which the interview implied. The fact was that he had received a grave mental wound. To protect himself against an aggravation of that wound, he received his minister as if he had returned from an official tour of inspection on the southern frontiers. The exile was not alluded to; he was asked for a report on the Duke of Martaban's preparations. The military dilemma was sketched and his advice solicited. Yazathingyan observed the comedy and gave his solution. He was asked to put it into execution, being invested, in addition to the restored office of Chief Minister, which he was assumed not to have vacated, with the command-in-chief of the whole army. No reference was made to the seizure of his estates, it being insinuated that they had never been confiscated.

Yazathingyan left the palace very satisfied with his

Part of a Tai Regiment
From the reliefs at Angkor

prospects. If he could make a success of the two campaigns that lay ahead he would be more powerful than
he had ever been. The only question was his age. He
was over sixty. Lean and tough though he was, could
he stand long campaigns? He dismissed the thought.
He had never felt better in his life. Action was what he
wanted after that book—action would be his tonic
against advancing years.

What followed was a demonstration that the royal
forces under competent leadership were strong enough
to maintain the King's supremacy within the frontiers.
Yazathingyan elaborated his strategical plan. With the
main army he would attack the Duke, while Tharepyissapaté with country levies and the Tai guard, a
highland regiment from the eastern plateau, would in-
vest the hillmen, the main assault against them not to
be launched until Yazathingyan returned with his
troops from Martaban.

The stroke at the Duke was a brilliant affair. Yazathingyan, who was determined to have at him before
the rains in May made troop movements impossible,
dropped down river in February, only six weeks after
his return, with five hundred elephants, half the foot
and the whole cavalry of the guard. Disembarking
some fifty miles north of Dalla, he made for Martaban
south-east along a road parallel with the coast, and was
on the Duke before he realised what was happening.
That feudatory, much alarmed when he heard that it
was the great Yazathingyan who was marching at him,
threw himself behind his walls and prepared to stand a
siege. But as he had neglected to provision the place in
advance and had allowed refugees to crowd in, he was

immediately in great straits, particularly as the water-supply was inadequate. Ophla, Yazathingyan's younger son, who was serving under him as Captain of the Guard, wanted to deliver an assault at once, but Yaza-thingyan by waiting a week gained a bloodless victory, for the Duke surrendered. In short, it was a very neat piece of work from first to last.

As Yazathingyan entered Martaban city in triumph at the head of his elephants, he found it difficult to real-ise that only three months before he had been sitting in Dalla writing a text-book, stuck in a little house and trying to kill time. This was real life again. What a magnificent procession it was, his elephants curling their trunks, noble beasts; his cavalry prancing, his ar-moured footmen; and that music, how it mounted up, exultant and gay! He remembered the way Queen Shinshwé used to boast of Angkor, but, by the Holy Foot Print, this was as fine a cavalcade as ever depicted on the walls of King Suryavarman.

The Duke's surrender did not save him. His fief was abolished, the administration being placed under a Burmese mandarin. He himself, wives, children, ele-phants, countless dancing girls, innumerable concu-bines, were carried back prisoners to the river in April and embarked for the capital.

The victorious army made its slow way home upstream and in due course reached Minbu, the base from which Tharepyissapaté had been instructed to operate against the hillmen. As they put into the road, it was evident that something untoward had happened, for instead of an orderly camp, boats plying, an army bazaar, they saw that Minbu town had been burnt to the ground.

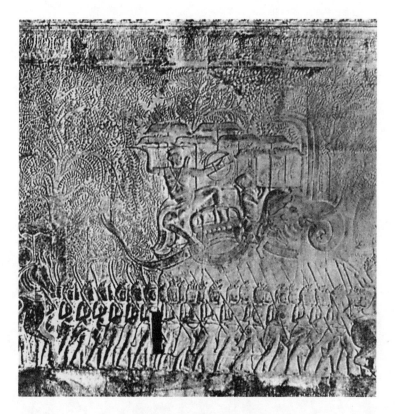

A General in a Procession of Troops
From the reliefs at Angkor

No troops were in sight. A small stockade on the bank was the only sign of habitation.

They anchored offshore. In a little while a boat put out from the stockade and came alongside Yazathing-yan's barge. From it stepped Tharepyissapaté, looking very much thinner, the big ears for which he was noted almost flapping on his neck. He sought the Chief Minister's cabin at once and threw himself down on a carpet with a miserable gesture. He smelt of drink.

'My poor Tharepyissapaté, what has happened to you?' asked Yazathingyan, for he had almost an affection for the Mayor of the Palace.

'You ought never to have made me a general,' groaned his subordinate. 'No one could fix a party like me; I was wonderful at that. Why didn't I stick to illuminations and fancy menus? Campaigning is so different. Do you believe in ghosts?' he added with apparent inconsequence.

'Not just like that,' said the minister.

'Nor do I, of course, but there was something very funny up on the hills. To look at, the tribesmen are just bandy-legged little fellows, but in their own haunts they can be downright creepy.'

'What's all this leading to?' interrupted Yazathing-yan. 'You don't mean to tell me you've had a reverse?'

'I like to hear you call it that—just a reverse.'

'You'd better give me the whole story, I think.'

'My army's gone!' now burst out the general. 'You see that stockade on the bank? There are five hundred men in it, a remnant, just the Tai guard. All the rest, all the country levies, ran one night we were in the hills, ran without seeing the enemy. It was what they heard

that frightened them. I had to retreat and stockade myself here. The hillmen followed and burnt the town at
leisure.'

'If I am to help you,' suggested his chief, 'I must have
the full facts. What did your men hear in the hills?'

'We were marching to a night attack on a stockade,'
explained Tharepyissapaté. 'I really don't know how
to tell you, but there was a girl with me in my palanquin—little Veluvati, you remember the Queen's lady-
in-waiting. When I left for the front, she would come
with me. Said she loved my ears, the stupid little
thing.'

'Go on!'

'Well, the curtains of the palanquin were drawn, we
had made ourselves comfortable, when suddenly the
bearers plumped the thing on the ground. Veluvati put
her head out.

' "They've bolted!" she cried.

'I sat up and pulled back the curtain. There was a
fine moon; you could see the hills cut out like velvet,
though the forest where we marched was in deep
shadow. The whole column had come to a halt.'

'What a story! Sleeping with a girl when you were
marching to the attack. Go on!'

'I don't know how to go on. It sounds nonsense.
My brigade-major came tearing down the path.
"What's up?" I called. "The men say they hear whispering in the trees," he panted. "They won't move another step." At that moment Veluvati screamed: "I can
hear it myself!" and threw her arms round my neck.'

'Did *you* hear anything?'

'I didn't panic, if that's what you mean. I calmly told

the major to sound the retreat. It had, in fact, already begun. There was rather a scramble out of the wood. A good deal of equipment was dropped, I'm afraid. I haven't seen the levies since.'

'But did you yourself hear anything?'

'As you insist, I confess I did. After all, a little breeze in the tree-tops wouldn't have taken in country levies, mostly men used to the jungle. Ten of them, mind you, died in convulsions. Something was there, sure enough. "Whispering" is a good description, but it was suffocating too.'

Yazathingyan stopped his cross-examination. He could not doubt that what he had been told was a genuine experience. Like everyone else, he knew the tribes made a speciality of the occult. They were not Buddhists. It was disconcerting enough, for the duty of bringing the campaign to a successful issue now devolved on him. Finally he asked:

'Did you send the King a despatch to this effect?'

'I was afraid to, but he may have heard.'

'Well, my advice is to keep quiet for the moment. We have been so occupied attending to your misfortunes that you have not heard the story of my success, but look out of the cabin there at all those boats. They contain captives, treasure, every sort of girl; Martaban had an interesting collection, white girls, black girls, yellow girls, and all the intermediate shades. Let me tell His Majesty my story first. When I have produced the treasure and the girls, it will be time enough for you to show your empty hands.'

Tharepyissapaté thanked him profusely. The minister weighed anchor shortly afterwards and began to battle again with the stream, greatly swollen by the melting of the far northern snows. A few evenings later they reached a town called The Crossing by the Little Bank. They moored and Yazathingyan was surprised to see his elder son, the Comptroller of the White Elephant, waiting in the crowd. The young man came aboard at once.

'What are you doing in this forsaken place?' asked his father.

'I'm on duty, on my way downstream; an unpleasant duty. You've heard, of course, about Tharepyissapaté. So has the King. He was very angry. "I wouldn't have minded so much if he had been beaten in a hard-fought day, but to lose an entire army without a blow struck, without a manœuvre, that is too much. A general like that cannot expect to live." I was the senior officer present. "Go and make sure he hangs himself," he said to me. Not a very pleasant mission, I'm afraid.'

'My son,' said Yazathingyan, 'in this world more has been lost by precipitate action than by any other cause. If I were you, I should not hurry. I have had a tremendous success. I've got things in my luggage which will make the King see the world in rose colour. Tharepyissapaté is not a good general, but he is an old friend of mine. Until you get a messenger from me, "let not your hand exceed", as they say in the classics.'

Two days later the flotilla came to anchor at Pagān. It was the height of the hot season, May, when a burning wind blows all day from the north-east. They landed at dusk and marched towards the moat, on which the lotus flowers lay in profusion, red and white. The wind had fallen and a cloud of dust billowed over the procession. Martaban was there walking, his hands bound, a board round his neck. He was naked save for a loin-cloth; soldiers beat him on. As he had surrendered at discretion and there had been no bloodshed, he hoped that his life might be spared. That aspiration helped him to bear his ordeal. He was a tall man with a dark skin. Even in humiliation his face was proud. After him came a great host of captive soldiers. Their fate, they knew, was slavery, service in perpetuity at some of the temples, which they would have to keep swept and in repair, the lands of which they would have to cultivate. Behind came the women. Here a reasonable distinction had been made. The elder were on foot and looked wretched enough. Domestic service loomed before them, and as some of them were ladies, it was a gloomy prospect. The Duchess was among these, a weeping woman, for her last infant had been lost in the confusion. But of the younger girls, many were in litters. Among these was a noted beauty, afterwards called the Lady Uhsauppan. She had been bought by the Duke's agents in Persia and it was said that in the world no one had a slenderer waist. Sitting upright in an open palanquin, she viewed the scene with the utmost composure. Her value she knew; a precious gem was as likely to be neglected. In this guise she came on to the moat side, where gold-mohur trees, thickly covered with red blossoms, lined the way. So red were these against the dusty air, that they seemed to reach forward and to touch her. The people who saw her in that setting never forgot it, longed for it again. To all of them she scattered her largess of beauty; then was carried over a white bridge and into the city.

That very evening Yazathingyan waited on Queen Saw.

'The least I can do to show my gratitude for all you have done for me', he said, 'is to give Your Majesty first pick of the loot.' He spread out a quantity of jewels before her.

The Queen made her selection, observing: 'I shall just take a few things. To-morrow is fixed, I hear, for you to show the King what you have brought back. Be careful to flatter him. He is trying to suppress the thought that he was unable to manage without you. But it is festering inside him. His order for Tharepyissapaté's execution shows what is passing in his mind. You follow me?'

The Queen's words were plain enough. Though Tharepyissapaté was acting under Yazathingyan's orders, the King had stepped in over the latter's head, as if he, not Yazathingyan, was directing the campaign. He sought that way of re-establishing his self-confidence.

'In point of fact,' said the minister, 'Tharepyissapaté is not dead yet, and I want to get him off.'

The Queen exhibited no surprise.

'Try after you have shown the treasure,' said she, 'and if I can, I shall interpose to help you.'

He was turning to go, when she asked: 'By the way, how are you after your labours?'

'I am rather tired. The heat is overpowering. Fortunately the campaign was short.'

'Take care of yourself and rest. There is still the hill trouble to settle.'

Through the next day a feeling of expectation increased in the palace. At dusk those of the court officials, queens and ladies, who had been invited to be present when the loot was exhibited, assembled in one of the larger rooms off the bed-chamber.

All being ready, Yazathingyan entered, spare, in a thin silk robe, followed by chamberlains carrying small boxes. Most of these contained jewels of various kinds, rubies, emeralds, pearls and diamonds, some made up into rings and bracelets, necklaces or pendants. Other boxes were opened, in which was gold plate. The King fingered the objects and passed them to the queens.

After a time Yazathingyan caused a chamberlain to approach with a basket. 'I have here', said he, 'something which I think is rather unusual.' He took up a large dish covered with a thick glaze, the colour of which was between green and blue. In the centre a lotus was incised. 'This Chinese dish', he continued, 'is one of the kind which are reputed to change colour if poisoned food is put in them. I have made some enquiry into the matter, and it appears that their normal colour is more green than blue, but that in the circumstances I have mentioned they become more blue than green. Far be it from me to suggest that there is any probability of poison being put into Your Majesty's food, but such dangers sometimes arrive unexpectedly, and from a quarter least suspect. To use a dish of this variety is to employ a reasonable precaution, and as, besides being a useful, it is an ornamental object, I trust Your Majesty will allow me to suggest that it be always laid for the royal repast.'

Everyone had heard of these dishes, but they had never been imported into Pagān. The sight of this one set the queens wondering. China—what a land of secrets that must be! The jewels they had just seen were haunting in their way, but this dish spoke more directly of life and death.

'By placing poison in it now, would it be possible to observe the change of colour?' asked Narathihāpaté.

'I gather not,' replied Yazathingyan. 'The change arises not on account of the presence of the poison, but of the presence of a motive to poison. Such a motive becomes visible to the intended victim if he looks at the dish.'

'How can that be so?'

'The dish may give a momentary clairvoyance, symbolised by the change of colour. Art is such a mystery.'

The King was impressed, but Queen Saw remarked, smiling: 'I can understand the Chief Minister's explanation, but I cannot believe it, for I would never receive a warning in that fashion. If I were to depend on a dish turning colour for me, I should be poisoned ten times over. I prefer to have servants on whom I can rely.'

There was some laughter, and Queen Sawlon said with a sniff: 'The story sounds to me like a merchant's puff. Since its invention, no doubt the price of these dishes has gone up. The Chinese have great gifts for trade. A dish of first-class quality and appearance which also has magical properties—what a clever notion!'

But Queen Shinshwé burst out: 'Well, I can tell you something! When I was very young I lived in a small village outside Angkor. One night my father woke up. "I've had a dream," says he; "saw a figure pointing to a spot in the garden." We went out in the morning and dug. A plate like this one was unearthed. Unfortunately it was broken soon afterwards. One of the buffaloes trod on it. But that shows what sort of stuff it is—gives you visions.'

Yazathingyan's next item was to introduce the lady who had made such an impression the day before on the populace. At his sign she was led in. If at dusk she had looked a beauty under the red blossoms, she was no less so in the subdued light of the oil lamps of that inner room. Her life had been adventurous. As a child taken from her home in Persia, they had bought and sold her at increasing prices while her beauty developed, until now she had no feelings beyond presents and a rich protector. Narathihāpaté seemed to her an improvement on the Duke of Martaban. Her manner showed that she thought the company first-rate. But if she had the outlook of a courtesan, her beauty was so extraordinary that she appeared everything that the poets have imagined. There was not a sign in those wide eyes, that parted mouth, of a common mind, in those hands, full and dimpled, of rapacity. Expression, sumptuous breast, sumptuous loins, told only of longing and ample reward, of soft dreams, sweetness and the last mystery of love.

'Anyway,' thought Shinshwé, 'she doesn't know Burmese—can't sing him the song that made my fortune.'

Sawlon took a deep dislike to her on the spot.

'Pretty,' she muttered, 'but dirty like all foreigners.'

'She can start work by fanning me now,' said Narathihāpaté.

Refreshments were brought in, and as Yazathingyan, answering the King's questions, began to render an account of the campaign, giving the total of the loot in elephants, gold and slaves, much animation prevailed.

When an hour or so had passed in this way, the King remarked to his minister: 'What you said just now about the green dish makes me wish that our information about China was more detailed than it is. From all accounts much has happened there lately. Did you hear anything new at Martaban?'

Yazathingyan had produced such a number of objects during the course of the evening that no one was surprised when he replied: 'Among the prisoners taken was a Chinaman from Hangchao, the capital of the Sung. I had several conversations with him on the way up. He is a very intelligent man. May I call him in?'

The Chinaman was not difficult to find and only a short time elapsed before he made his appearance, a

man of forty, bland and self-possessed. He wore a brocade gown and a black cap with points like bamboo
shoots. The kow-tow he performed differed little from
the Burmese prostration, but it was executed with a
more finished art, a mellower respect. He attracted
Queen Saw's attention at once. He seemed to her a person to whom one could talk, and she regretted that conversation would involve an interpreter. Meanwhile
Yazathingyan was saying: 'He told me his name was
the Elder Chang. He seems at one time to have been
Grand Secretary to the Emperor. His description of
Hangchao was very arresting.'

Narathihāpaté looked at this mandarin of China a
little uneasily. 'How does Hangchao compare with
Pagān?' he asked, for want of a less obvious gambit.

The Elder Chang, with a look round the room which,
had he had less control of his features, might have been
called supercilious, replied through an interpreter:
'Comparisons are invidious and in this case unnecessary. I find Pagān an art-integration. Your Majesty will
follow me when I say that it is unprofitable to assess
one art-integration against another. Integrity, the in-
tegral, is what matters. When a culture has that whole-
ness, it is absolutely the same and yet fundamentally
different to every other.'

The interpreter, though a southern Brahman of the
most brilliant attainments as linguist and scholar, had
difficulty in rendering the Chinaman's thought. He
paraphrased it with virtuosity, but was by no means
satisfied that he had expressed its essence.

Narathihāpaté did not understand what was meant,
but he was careful not to show it. 'Very true,' he ob-

served, wondering how he could change the subject
and quite unaware that the mandarin had spoken in
this high-brow style to amuse himself at the expense of
his captors, whom he regarded as dreadfully provincial. But Queen Saw was annoyed. No high-brow was
going to make a fool of her. She recognised the patter
of an intellectual clique and was not in the least impressed by its artificial sophistication.

'Tell the gentleman', she said to the interpreter, 'that
neither the occasion of a triumph nor the temperature
of the evening accords with so frigid an approach to
our problem. Let me put the question again in a more
topical form. Suppose it was a matter of sacking Hangchao or Pagān, which of the two cities would provide
the greater loot?'

When this was conveyed to the Elder Chang, he
glanced at the Queen in a startled manner. He was observed to sigh and to make a movement of respect. He
could not suppose that she spoke from information,
yet in her trenchant manner she had hinted at what in
Hangchao was the most discussed topic of the moment.
How had she divined this? Was it only a chance hit? Or
had he misjudged this court? Did it contain at least one
person of marked intelligence? Disregarding his former manner completely, he said: 'The Queen has favoured me with a hypothetical question, which, indeed,
is extremely topical. I left the Clouds of Heaven two
years ago—a verse composition, a favourite's annoyance, you know the sort of thing, a word taken in its
other meaning. . . . I visited Cambodia, I desired to see
India. But I have kept myself informed. A situation is
developing. The Tartars are already masters of all land

Portrait of the Emperor Kublai Khan, believed
contemporary

north of the great Kiang river. Their Khan, Kublai, reigns at Peking. When I was Grand Secretary I memorialised the throne on five occasions, advocating a larger army, better fortifications. The present Emperor, however, is a confirmed pacifist. He believes the Tartars can be rendered innocuous by talk. Battle seems to him a stupid substitute for negotiation. My proposals were not accepted. That is one reason why I was glad to travel. Hangchao is enormously rich. Without disrespect for what I can see is also a wealthy and cultured city, I am obliged to say—and my fears suggest why it would be better if I could not say it—that Hangchao provides the richer bait.'

'These Tartars,' interposed Narathihāpaté, 'I understand they have penetrated to the furthest west. In my youth I remember speaking with one of them, a powerful squat man, who came here with a caravan. Ten years before, he said, he was with the army of one Batu. They reached a place within sound of the ultimate sea. There they met bearded white men clad in chain-mail and mounted upon horses armoured to the hocks. "What happened then?" said I. "With our buffalo-horn bows we shot them through; their greatest lords fell on that day," he replied. No doubt he was boasting. He was a filthy-looking fellow.'

'Your Majesty's informant was but stating a fact. As Grand Secretary I thought it my business to study their campaigns. The reference was probably to Liegnitz, a battle beyond journey's end. And I fear they contemplate other strokes of a like nature.'

'They cannot get in here,' pronounced Narathihāpaté. 'Our northern mountains are a great wall.

Moreover, they have no elephants. They could not stand the charge of our beasts.'

To this the Elder Chang made no reply. He had been Grand Secretary; he had heard his late master in as confident a mood.

The Chinaman's words had come as rather a shock to Yazathingyan. Danger from the north was evidently more real than he had supposed. But this was no time to go into such matters. He was looking for an opportunity to introduce the subject of Tharepyissapaté. Luckily the King now called for more wine. Shinshwé, glad of a break in such tall conversation, whispered as she filled his cup: 'At Hangchao the Emperor has marvellous girls.' This started the talk in a new direction. Chang was induced to describe the Emperor's lake, where beauties bathed for his amusement. 'He found more distraction in the sight of their rolling limbs than in the odes of the T'ang', was one of his phrases. Something was said also of the girls who coursed hares in the park, and of the actresses who performed on horseback. Chang realised that he was making an excellent impression, and to improve it said: 'But no doubt Your Majesty has entertainments of a similar kind. If not, it would be a great honour should I be allowed to advise.'

A good deal of wine had been drunk by this, and Narathihāpaté, delighted with the idea of emulating the Sung, conferred on Chang the appointment of Superintendent of Fêtes. At this the ex-Grand Secretary kowtowed three times, reflecting that the court of Pagān was not after all so provincial and that a place in it was certainly preferable to sweeping rubbish in a temple yard.

A Chinese Actress on Horseback

From a wooden statuette of uncertain date presented by Mr. and Mrs. Manley to the Victoria and Albert Museum

Yazathingyan now saw that the moment had arrived to bring up Tharepyissapaté's case. But it must be done cleverly. The King at the moment had a picture of himself as a cultured monarch, like the Sung Emperor. He therefore put the matter in this way:

'The enormous success which has attended Your Majesty's operations against Martaban insures for the reign peace at home and reputation abroad. The small affair of the hill-tribes is outstanding, but if I am instructed to take on the operations from the point where your able general Tharepyissapaté has left them, I feel confident of returning a second time to Pagān with notable loot.'

'Able?' enquired the King. 'You say Tharepyissapaté is able! I had to send him a rope.'

'Your Majesty refers to his temporary reverse. That reminds me of what the Royal Chaplain said the other day. He was quoting an old dictum from the philosophers. "Equilibrium does not exist except in the absolute; only therein is pause in the tide of rise and fall." It is therefore in the nature of battles that a reverse should be followed by a victory. Tharepyissapaté, to ensure the final victory of his soldiers reinforced by my troops, allowed the hillmen to claim a preliminary success.'

From the time when the Royal Chaplain had failed to instil into his mind the subtleties of the *Abhidhama,* Narathihāpaté, though detesting metaphysics, had regarded them with awe. He did not follow now Yazathingyan's argument; he did not know whether it was valid; but he was afraid that it might be valid. His eyes sought the faces of the court. But Tharepyissapaté had been a popular mayor of the inner palace. All the women had a coaxing air. He glanced at Queen Saw.

'I can remember the rest of the quotation about the impermanence of the phenomenal world. Shall I repeat it?' she asked.

'That is unnecessary,' replied the King sharply. 'I know it quite well myself. For a matter of fact I was aware that Tharepyissapaté was employing the very method of victory the Chief Minister has mentioned. If I sent him a rope, it was merely to fit in with the fall and make the rise all the more inevitable. My orders will now, of course, be countermanded.'

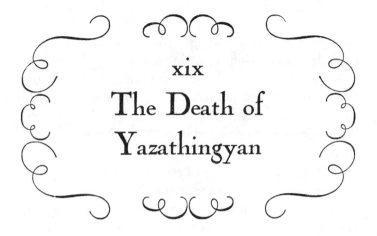

xix
The Death of Yazathingyan

It remained for Yazathingyan to subdue the hillmen.
Then as victor in two wars he felt that his position
would be unassailable. The King's character was
clearer now. If one could flatter his self-esteem, convince him that he was a great man, all would go comfortably. The mistake before had been to stimulate in
him a tension. Chang was a lucky find. Let him dress
up Narathihāpaté as the Sung Emperor. That reminded
him of what the Chinaman had said about the Tartars.
He would consult the Royal Chaplain.

A brilliant morning a few days later he set out for the
monastery. Some showers of the early monsoon had
fallen, laying the dust. The flowers on tree and bush
were fresh and bright as birds. But he was feeling his
age. Dandled in his palanquin, he sniffed the warm
scented air and wished he were younger. The late campaign had left him more tired than he had expected. He

leant back and, half dozing, vowed that on his return from the hills he would take life easily.

When he was seated with the Chaplain in the room behind the circumambulatory and had exchanged the usual civilities of meeting, he recounted Chang's view of the foreign situation, adding: 'Your Reverence once spoke of danger from the north.'

'That is so,' replied the Chaplain.

'Can you be a little more explicit?'

'All I can say is that, astrologically speaking, the kingdom is entering a period of danger and that the direction of the danger is from the north. It is impossible for me to tell you whether the Tartars are that danger. But I can reassure you on one point. The danger is not imminent. Years may elapse. But it is grave.'

It was clear that the Chaplain was not disposed to say any more. The Chief Minister now took him on to another point about which he had been thinking.

'Your Reverence', he said, 'is reputed to have certain powers. I do not refer to astrology, which is, after all, more an intellectual study, nor to the power of vision, vision of the truth, which I know meditation has given you, but to certain other aspects of thought which some of the Hindu masters have not considered unworthy of attention. But allow me to be more precise. There are currently supposed to be guardian spirits of the realm. Tepathin of Tharaba is one and your Reverence knows of many others. Would you be prepared to use your power over those spirits to assist me in the hill war? You have heard, no doubt, how Tharepyissapaté was driven back. I want appropriately to counter what routed him.'

'I had made it plain, I thought,' replied the Chaplain, 'that I never meddle now with such practices. They do not consort with the Eightfold Path. When I was younger, I gave some thought to them; I developed powers, I indulged in marvels. But they clouded for me the real light; when I entered meditation, shapes thronged round me. I was as far from the Knowledge as any man plunged in common living. You must fight the hillmen as you can. It is not a war of much importance.'

'With great respect, I have one last question to put to your Reverence. Supposing this country were to be threatened with instant peril from the north, would you employ what powers you possess?'

This question seemed slightly to offend the Royal Chaplain, for he dismissed his visitor.

During the rains, which were regular and sufficient, the court amused itself immensely, for Chang made a number of novel suggestions, improving the fireworks and enlivening the drama. Yazathingyan, however, devoted himself to the re-equipment of the army, but December came before he embarked his men. He desired the ground to be quite dry before he ventured into the hill valleys.

Landing at Minbu with a strong force of cavalry, elephants and foot, he advanced into the hill region to the westward. As he proceeded, he burnt villages and granaries. The inhabitants crowded for safety into a fort on the mount of Theks, to which their chieftain had retreated before the royal army could catch him. There, behind his spiked stockade, elephants or cavalry could not hurt him.

★ The Death of Yazathingyan ★

Yazathingyan drew a cordon round him, but failing to penetrate the fortification, was obliged to settle down to a regular siege. All through the cold season, drenched in fogs, his troops lay in their bivouacs. It was a tiresome check. He could not force a decision. More tiresome still, what with the indifferent food and the exposure, he contracted dysentery. But it was impossible to withdraw. He could not return to Pagān without a victory. The ridicule would be unbearable. Thus, in spite of his disease, he felt obliged to stay on. Every week he expected would finish the war. No provisions had entered the stockade for months. Its defenders must be starving, his own men were on short rations. But more months passed and still the hillmen held out. As for enchantments, nothing of the kind was observed, nor was any explanation offered of the previous episode. It was a siege of the most ordinary type, intolerably dull for both sides.

Yazathingyan's disease grew worse. He was now unable to walk, but carried on the work from his bed. At last, after a six months' siege, the hill chief surrendered. Sending the Captain of the Guard, his son Ophla, to announce the news at court, Yazathingyan caused himself to be carried slowly down to the river. He was very seriously ill. The dysentery had reduced him almost to a skeleton.

On arrival at Minbu he recalled that when in exile he had made the acquaintance of an Indian doctor who specialised in dysentery. He now decided to go to Dalla instead of to Pagān, where to his mind the doctors were not so good.

His men rowed him downstream as fast as possible.

They feared he was dying. On landing at Dalla wharf, where not so long ago he had marched Thihathu to his death, he was borne to the little house where he had written his book. It was his own property and he kept there some of his servants. Among these was the girl Ma Than, who had never been ordered back to the capital, for he had entirely forgotten all about her.

When she saw her master unexpectedly in the garden, looking so pale, so terribly emaciated, she hurried forward eagerly and knelt by his litter. Informed by a clerk of what had happened, for Yazathingyan himself was too tired to speak, she told them to carry him up to his bedroom. Everything was in its place; she had always kept it ready.

When he was comfortably in bed, she sent for the doctor and went to the kitchen to prepare soup. She was surprised to find herself humming a tune. Left behind at Dalla, she had suffered a good deal. But she had thought—he has left me here for some reason; perhaps he is coming back; I must always be ready for him. Great men have so much on their minds; I shall just wait. And now he had come back. She knew he was very ill, but she would have him for a bit; perhaps, even, she would be able to save him. So she hummed softly, her face humble and adoring, as she strained the soup and carried it upstairs.

With the rest, a good diet and the doctor's drugs, Yazathingyan seemed to rally. He was able to give some orders in a day or so and even dictated a few letters for despatch to the capital. But the disease was not arrested; it had gone too far. On the tenth day it was clear that he was sinking. Ma Than knelt beside his bed; the ten days had been to her both paradise and hell. She had given her heart rein; it was agony and bliss. As she knelt, he began to speak. He had worn the mask all his life, but with the approach of death it began to slip. Besides, with her he had never bothered.

'I have been very ambitious,' he said, more to himself than to her. 'When I guessed that my old chief, King Usana, was fated to die after a short reign, I was not altogether displeased, for I hoped to be master of the kingdom under his successor. These last two wars would have made me that, but though victorious I have been taken in the rear by another enemy. So I lie here. But if I must die,' he went on, speaking now directly to her, 'I am happier to die in this small house than in my residence at Pagān. One learns a little on the threshold of death. I know your grief has more value than would have my family's lamentations. I should be lonelier there than in the warmth of your heart.'

He paused and then, in a voice gentler than she had ever heard, said: 'Don't cry for me overmuch. You have been a good girl. Marry that clerk of mine who came down this time. He's a rising fellow, I know he admires you. And take this ring for your dowry. It's worth enough to set you both up.'

With that he seemed to drift away. She continued to kneel. The others had crowded in at the door. They all waited; perhaps he would speak again. After what seemed a long time, he opened his eyes very wide and, looking round abruptly, said: 'Bar the north!' They had no clue to his meaning, but their thoughts were distracted at once by a deep sigh. It was his last breath.

When the girl knew that he had gone, she rose to her

feet and stood looking down at the face. There was something alarming in her attitude, the abandon of utter grief. A young man crept forward and whispered anxiously: 'I overheard what he said about us; be calmer, don't do anything!'

She turned on him with dreadful passion. 'After my lord, do you think I'd touch you, you fool! Get out of my way! What do you know! There's nothing more for me!' And with her hands over her face she rushed from the room. They found her body afterwards at the bottom of the well.

XX

Queen Saw and
Chang Hsien Ch'ung

The death of Yazathingyan was a capital event. When all was said, his presence had insured the integrity of the country. Queen Saw realised how grave was the loss; she also perceived that the whole weight of government now rested on her shoulders. Her position, however, was extremely delicate. It was becoming gradually apparent that Narathihāpaté was a pathological case. His inner knowledge that he was unable to cope with the problems of his high station made him increasingly determined to prove that he was a big man, who could not be trifled with, of whom people were afraid, who knew what was best. How could she guide such a man, wondered the Queen. The very fact that he had a profound respect for her judgment made him paradoxically the more eager to assert himself. If events moved in a normal pattern, it might be possible to carry on, but if any sort of a serious crisis developed, her task would be hopeless.

Thanks to the thorough defeat inflicted by Yaza-thingyan on the forces of disorder, events did move normally for a time. Adventures went out of fashion, and for several years complete tranquillity reigned. During that period Narathihāpaté was often petty, mean, stupid and cruel. But that did not matter very much. Only a few individuals suffered; there were no wide repercussions. The Queen, moreover, had gradually worked people on whom she could rely into key positions. How she secured the appointment of Chang to the Chief Ministership is a case in point.

After Yazathingyan's death a number of persons occupied that post. Theimmazi was offered it again, but he refused this time. Tharepyissapaté held it for a year, but he could not get up in the mornings. The two Ophla brothers were then tried. In consideration of their father's services to the state, they had been raised to the first rank of the mandarinate and made councillors. The distinguished titles of Anantapyissi and Rantapyissi had been conferred upon them. But these honours failed to change their essential mediocrity. Each of them did his best for a time, but what with the book-work and the continual bother of serving a king like Narathihāpaté, they asked leave to return to their substantive appointments, Comptroller of the White Elephant and Captain of the Guard.

The vacancy caused by the retirement of the last was filled by Chang. His full name was Chang Hsien Ch'ung, as by this time they had discovered. He had long since ceased to be regarded as a prisoner. As Superintendent of Fêtes he had enjoyed much popularity. His talent was considerable and, of course, his experience of affairs was wide. He mastered the Burmese language and acquired a general familiarity with Burmese administration. But his chief claim to interest was his intimacy with Queen Saw. Her first impression, that he was a man one could talk to, was early confirmed; his, that she was a remarkable woman, was greatly amplified. In connection with his work on the Board of Entertainments he used to see her frequently. They held long conversations together. The interest she displayed in anything he could tell her of China and its history enchanted him. He found that her taste was exceptional, her feeling for a work of art intuitive and fresh, her literary instinct robust and classic. In short, they had a great deal to discuss, and it was clear enough that if he looked up to her, she looked up to him in a way she had never done to any other man.

His appointment as Chief Minister was effected in this way. After the retirement of the second Ophla, Rantapyissi, the King was at a loss whom to appoint. As was his practice, he decided to consult Queen Saw.

'The dearth of personalities is rather extraordinary,' he said. 'The rest of the council is composed of nonentities. I declare the women in this country have more ability than the men.'

'Has the name of Chang Hsien Ch'ung ever occurred to you?'

Narathihāpaté had clearly never thought of the Chinaman in such a connection. But the suggestion was attractive. There was a great deal to be said for a foreigner as Chief Minister. Without relations and backers round the country, he should be easy to control. And he liked Chang Hsien Ch'ung, who had helped him to copy the amusements of the court of China. Queen Saw clinched the matter by pointing out that to have as Chief Minister a man familiar with far-eastern politics might prove very advantageous at a time when so much was happening beyond the frontiers.

The day after Chang Hsien Ch'ung was invested with his new robes he called on the Queen. The gratitude he felt for the appointment caused his feelings, already brimming, to overflow.

'Gracious lady,' he murmured, and came to a stop. He looked up at her as she sat smiling from her low dais. Carefully dressed as usual, her appearance was intoxicating. The passage of time had increased her beauty by lending interest to her expression. In its intelligence was softness, in its humour a touch of melancholy. Chang felt himself swept by a cruel longing. If only he could talk Burmese as fluently, as elegantly, as he could Chinese! He ventured:

'I have come to offer my poor thanks for your infinite condescension, and to beg that you will command me in all things.'

The Queen seemed to hesitate a moment, and then she said: 'I am happy that the King fell in with my suggestion. These last times have shown me a glimpse of something I did not expect to see. You must have weighed this court. It balances against a little dust. But your conversation was real. For the first time I found myself with a companion.'

'You can imagine what your conversation has been to me,' answered Chang Hsien Ch'ung. 'When I was captured by the late Chief Minister, I thought it a calamity. As I was borne up river into the interior of this

unknown kingdom, Hangchao and my friends seemed
very dear. I remembered promenades there with scholars, of reciting by moonlight the poems of T'ang. That
life of the mind, of the emotions, seemed gone for ever.
And then, the evening they brought me in as part of
the spoils, I saw the lamplight falling on your cheek.
I dared to think that you inclined slightly, as if interested. Certainly you turned your face towards me. In
that beat of time, the whole chamber was filled with its
loveliness.' He paused and then smiling said: 'You
made me want to show off before the King. But when
you saw through me, I was delighted. And it made my
fortune.'

'Your Burmese has improved wonderfully since
then,' she interrupted softly.

'From that first meeting', he continued, 'I thought
less and less of Hangchao. After a time I would have
regarded it as exile to have been obliged to return there.'

Listening to these words, she had hidden at first her
emotion, but now she cried: 'You have found Burma a
happy land, and that I never did until you came. But
listen to me,' she went on more evenly, 'and forgive me
if I sound egotistical, for I am not really so. A strange
chance made me queen of this country, for I was not
born in the purple. When I left my village on Pōpa's
flank, I thought the adventure would satisfy my nature.
But as a woman I found that was not so. By the time I
had made the discovery I was committed to the affair.
It had become, too, more weighty than I had thought.
I stand, indeed, between the country and confusion. A
woman, I am cast for a man's part.' She spoke with increasing vehemence and emotion.

After Chang Hsien Ch'ung had pondered her words, he urged: 'I know that what you say is only too true. You are the government, without you it would collapse. But you cannot turn your back on love. Nor is it necessary; many great queens have had lovers. There is some leisure from affairs of state. What more profitable than to employ it so?'

But she said rapidly: 'I was not thinking of love like that. It is easy enough for a queen to find such distractions. A pretty youth, a midnight corridor, a screen withdrawn, a frothy embrace—that is nothing; I have tried that way. It was far other I had in mind, when a woman can say "my beloved", when she surrenders herself to love. Only that could satisfy me, but alas! it is incompatible with what I have undertaken. Were I to yield to it, the outward scene would vanish. Even if it could be kept secret, I should no longer be Queen Saw of Burma, but the girl, Ma Saw, of Kanbyu village. Perhaps I do not make myself clear, perhaps a man does not understand what love is for a woman. But at least it is not what you spoke of, a profitable method of employing leisure. I do not wish to love you in that manner, and I cannot love you in the way that my heart dictates.'

Saying these words she burst into tears and, signing to her maids, who were waiting out of earshot, allowed herself to be supported into her bed-chamber beyond.

xxi
The Sneeze

Some time after Chang's appointment the King's neurosis became alarmingly intensified. Without warning he issued orders that no one was to sneeze in his presence. It had never been considered in the past a breach of etiquette to sneeze in audience, and the prohibition had the effect of making even those without trace of a cold very conscious of their noses. Narathihāpaté himself never sneezed. Like many people of a certain mental deficiency, he was exceptionally robust.

Queen Sawlon, with whom he had never felt at ease —her blue blood and her freezing manner were the reasons—had engaged about this time a new lady-in-waiting, a country cousin of her sister's husband. The girl's attention was drawn to the prohibition of sneezing, the others telling her that there was really nothing to be afraid of, for if she felt a sneeze coming on, all she had to do was to press her lip against her sleeve. Al-

ready nervous at the prospect of this her first appearance in full court, the necessity of not sneezing made
her more nervous still, so that the moment she entered
the King's presence she felt her nose tingle and con-
tinually pressed her lip as she had been advised. But at
a certain point, seeing the King looking at her, she was
afraid to go on doing this, and a genuine sneeze suddenly overpowering her, she put her head into the
mouth of a large jar standing near by and sneezed un-
restrainedly. Far from damping down the sound, the
jar increased its volume. The reverberation was for-
midable.

The King looked round. 'What was that noise?' he
enquired in a nasty manner. 'I believe it was someone
sneezing. Who dares to disobey my direct orders,
deliberately, too, or the noise would not have been so
loud?'

A page, a sneaking boy with ambitions, pointed out
the culprit as she lay on the floor face downwards, her
utter confusion evidence of her guilt.

'Seize that girl!' said the King to members of the
guard, and working himself up into a mortal rage, he
began shouting: 'She sneezed as loud as she could on
purpose. You think you can laugh at my orders; you
think it doesn't matter when I tell you there is no
sneezing here. But you are making a mistake. You
shall see who is master.' Turning to the guard then, he
uttered with dreadful relish: 'Take the girl off! I do not
want to see her again—you understand, I do not want
to see her again.'

The men, who understood the formula perfectly,
dragged her away.

There was a hush. No one at court had believed the King would go so far. To order the death penalty for a breach of etiquette was unheard of, and where the breach was only sneezing, an involuntary natural reaction like a cough, it was ludicrously out of proportion. The condemnation had something maniacal about it.

Queen Sawlon, in spite of her pride, immediately flung herself down in front of Narathihāpaté and in tears begged him to reprieve her maid. It was such a slight to her dignity. She felt it as a personal affront. If her ladies were executed for bad manners, she would be the laughing-stock of the palace. She did not say this, of course, but it was clear from her rather inarticulate pleading that she was thinking more of herself than of the girl. She only succeeded, however, in irritating the King still further. He turned his face away and ordered the band to strike up a loud tune. Someone had slipped out and offered the guard a substantial reward if they would delay, and Theimmazi, than whom no one was more good-natured when sober, hurried to Queen Saw's apartments.

The Queen had not attended the levee because she was feeling slightly indisposed. Theimmazi, telling her maids that he had an information of great urgency to lay, followed on their heels and found Her Majesty in a state of undress, engaged in reading a pile of letters. Though he did not know it, these were from Chang Hsien Ch'ung. Some poems were among them in an exceptional calligraphy, with their Burmese translations. Queen Saw was too dignified to show surprise at the irruption, too self-possessed even to draw a scarf over her magnificent bosom. But she raised her eyebrows a fraction and motioned to Theimmazi to speak.

'My nephew has suddenly gone off his head,' he began at once. 'You know the ridiculous order about sneezing. This morning one of the maids of that cattish Sawlon sneezed. The idiot girl, in her attempt to stifle it, put her head into a jar. It was like an explosion. Narathihāpaté ordered her decapitation. Can you come and do something?'

Queen Saw slowly folded up the papers and placed them in a sandalwood box. 'Wait outside,' was all she said to him. When he was gone she ordered her ladies to dress her; she would put on her full court costume. As they busied themselves with her hair, powdered and scented her face and person, she wondered whether she was right in interfering. The girl was a nonentity and evidently stupid into the bargain. No principle of state was involved. If she took up so insignificant a case, might it not weaken her authority, give her less weight when obliged to make a stand over an important matter? But when she reflected on the gross injustice, she decided that it could not be allowed to pass without an effort on her part. She was far from sanguine of success. It was questionable whether she could deflect the King if his mood was very dark.

When she was ready, a pointed crown upon her head, she proceeded to the hall where the court was being held, Theimmazi having been sent ahead with instructions to introduce the subject of the maid at the first opportunity. There was a gracious sweetness in her expression, which can only be compared to the smile

of the Sung Boddhisattvas, and, indeed, Chang Hsien
Ch'ung had often made that comparison in his verses.
As she walked down the panelled corridors, her ladies
had the impression that they were gliding in the wake
of a heavenly presence.

As she entered, she noticed that Mahabo, formerly
Yazathingyan's secretary, but who on that minister's
death had been appointed Chief Secretary of the
Palace, was reading from a scroll a series of resounding
epithets. She recollected that some time previously the
King had ordered him to make out a list of his styles
and titles. He was rolling them out now in the classical
language—Master of the Opal, Lord of Life, Source of
Greatness, The Golden Foot. Narathihāpaté was
listening with evident satisfaction. There was no trace
in his eyes of the abyss. She took hope that something
might be done.

When the reading was over, he observed: 'You have
done well, Mahabo. Have these titles inscribed in gold.
And there may be some more. Make a further search
among the records.'

Theimmazi, who had greater licence than any other
man at court, now said: 'That ought to make people
think twice before they sneeze. The Golden Foot, the
Master of the Opal should not have to put up with
such low noises.'

This recalled, as it was meant to do, the affair of the
maid to the King's mind. He glanced at Queen Saw.
His inclination was always to obtain her approval of
everything he did.

'You were not present, I think,' he said, 'when I had
to sentence just now a lady-in-waiting. She deliberately

A Sung Boddhisattva
By courtesy of the Victoria and Albert Museum

sneezed in spite of my orders. I could hardly have done otherwise, could I?'

'I think you flattered her,' she replied.

'How do you mean?' he asked.

'Well, we have just listened to a list of titles. But Mahabo has omitted one of the most important. May I supply it?—Master of the Ninety-Six Diseases. Your Majesty has a remarkable immunity from ill health. If I may say so, more than anything else that divides you from the rest of mankind, sets you apart, as celestial spirits are apart, from the distempers of mortality. To make it a crime for your subjects to catch cold, to cough, or to sneeze, suggests, what is clearly not the case, that they can partake with you in your high distinction. Therefore, I said you flattered the girl. You made her by inference your equal in health, you supposed that her proper state was, like you, to be well.'

If there were any fallacies in this argument, Narathihāpaté did not see them. He replied: 'You think then that to punish her for not being like me was to lessen a style to which I am entitled?'

'Frankly, I do. I think it would be better to leave the commonality with their sneezes and thereby emphasise the gulf which divides you from them.'

'That never occurred to me,' said the King thoughtfully. 'But you are quite right. I should not be angry at what increases my state. Mahabo, you hear what Queen Saw has said. Add "Master of the Ninety-Six Diseases." It is a pity now that the girl has been beheaded.'

At this point it had been arranged that Rantapyissi, the Captain of the Guard, should say: 'Remembering one of the frequently expressed sayings of my late

father, Your Majesty's most devoted servant, that pre-
cipitation rarely pays, I listened to the maid's prayer
that she be allowed two hours in which to tell her
beads, and directed that the execution should not take
place until the expiration of that period. I am therefore
in the happy position to report that she is still alive and
awaits Your Majesty's permission to pay her respects.'

The girl was then led in and made a triple prostration. The episode was at an end.

But the King's condition remained far from normal.
He became subject at this time to a peculiar seizure
when he woke in the morning. By the usual routine
relays of ladies-in-waiting watched by him all night.
The practice of these women was to play dull music,
massage or fan him. If before he slept he desired to
amuse himself with a favourite, they had appropriate
airs, gestures and rhythms. When he was asleep, they
sat by his bed, so that should he stir there was someone
at hand to anticipate his wishes.

One morning when he opened his eyes, the girls
noticed in them a peculiar expression. At no time had
he been good-tempered when he awoke, but on this
occasion there was a sombre ferocity about him. According to custom, certain weapons like spears, javelins
or daggers, jewelled pieces, some of them connected
with the regalia, were ranged on a low table within his
reach. He now suddenly seized a spear and flung it.
Passing by his immediate attendants, it transfixed the
sleeve of a girl who was standing at the other end of
the room, pinning her to the woodwork. In a great
fright the others scattered, some creeping from the
room, some hiding behind pillars. The girl who was

pinned slipped out of her jacket and, her skirt falling
in the struggle to get free, ran naked towards the door.
As she did so, Narathihāpaté aimed a javelin at her. It
passed through the fat of her back, causing a deep
wound.

When he had flung all the weapons to hand, he
seemed to be much eased. The girls slunk back and
dressed him. He was a little distrait, that was all. He
made no reference to his actions, nor did he enquire for
the girl he had wounded.

The matter was reported to Queen Saw. Taken in
conjunction with the order about sneezing, it suggested
to her that the King's sanity was threatened. Indeed, it
seemed to her a more alarming symptom than the
other, for the ladies-in-waiting had done nothing to
annoy him. Something had driven him meaninglessly
to assert his power over them, some obscure necessity
to see them in fear of him. But there was nothing she
could do except to move the weapons out of reach. In
point of fact he had no repetition of his waking fit for
some time, till again one morning he woke up with a
peculiar lowering expression. Under the Queen's instructions a tray of fruits had been substituted for the
weapons. The desire to throw coming over him, he
began to fling mangoes, limes, melons and guavas.
During this comparatively harmless fusillade his women
scattered, not much the worse, though one young girl,
who was pregnant, was struck in the stomach by a
melon, which caused a miscarriage.

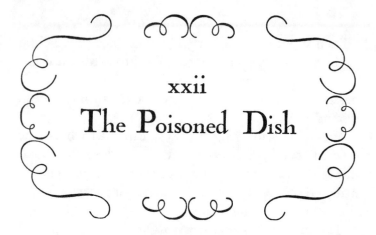

xxii
The Poisoned Dish

Before he became Chief Minister, Chang Hsien Ch'ung had given Narathihāpaté detailed descriptions of the palace at Hangchao, descriptions which fired the King with a desire to improve his own palace. His fancy had been particularly taken by an account of the bathing pool which the Emperor of the Sung had built. A covered way connected his private apartments with the pool, at which magnificent bathing picnics were held. Chang received orders to copy the covered way and the pool as far as he could with the materials available at Pagān.

The work was carried out in a lavish manner. Indeed, the expenses involved were very large, and it was to finance it that Narathihāpaté was guilty of some of those illegal exactions against individuals and the Church to which reference has been made. The pool was situated in the Irrawaddy, a part of which had been

screened off from public view. Beside it stood a fine
pavilion with a seven-tiered gilded roof, which contained a dining hall, as well as smaller rooms. The
covered way, connecting it with the main palace, was
paved with brick and had a balustrade of dragonish
monsters in painted stucco. On each side of the way
were small pavilions of carved wood, standing in
gardens of fruit and flowers, in which Narathihāpaté
accommodated some of the concubines who had been
added to the personnel of late, again in emulation of the
Chinese Emperor's great household.

The work was finished in the tenth year of the reign.
Chang Hsien Ch'ung had been able to avail himself of
the services of a number of first-class artists, builders
and carpenters, for during the preceding two centuries
so much interest had been taken by rich people in
religious building that a standard of taste and technical
ability prevailed which had not existed before and was
never to be seen again.

Narathihāpaté decided to celebrate the completion
by a picnic on the full moon night of April, the middle
of the hot weather. To make the picnic resemble an
occasion of the kind at Hangchao he departed from the
usual practice of the court of Pagān and arranged that
only women were to be present.

When the fierce heat of the middle hours of the day
had declined and the sun's rays were slanting low
across the river, he left the main palace in procession
and entered the covered way. All the attendants were
female, even the bearers of his palanquin, burly women
from the hills with powerful and rather bandy legs, and
his guard, a force of fifty amazons.

Behind him was carried Queen Saw, whose early taste for such festivities had largely evaporated and whose wit and high spirits no longer bubbled over as in the past. She sat up, aloof and faintly smiling, like Kwan-Yin, the Chinese goddess of mercy, as Chang Hsien Ch'ung had once chanted in an ode.

Next came Queen Sawlon, well-bred, supercilious, who never conceded an inch of dignity, never laughed and rarely spoke but to depreciate. She had not slept well the previous night and had awoken in a bad humour. It was the heat, perhaps, or a touch of liver, but she ascribed it to a fantastic dream, in which a dog as large as an elephant had sneezed in her face.

A few paces to the rear of her litter was borne Queen Shinshwé. This woman, though her day was somewhat over, had retained all her cheerfulness. She thoroughly enjoyed life's panorama, and never ceased to congratulate herself on the happy chance that had once set her upon the trunk of the King's elephant. Had she not made that climb she might now be approaching the battered and early middle age of the touring actress. Back again in Cambodia, she would be travelling the villages, the butt, certainly, of the country lout, viewing only from afar the moated walls of Angkor. It was beyond articulation fortunate to be inside a capital, to have a legal position at a king's side. So she went by, unspoilt and humble, on her lap a pet dog with a ribbon round its neck.

There followed the two other queens, maternal figures, shadowy personalities, with the concourse of ladies-in-waiting and the concubines in their grades. Most of these women were walking, though Uhsauppan, at their head, was carried in a litter. She was as beautiful as she had ever been. The passage of time had done nothing to that splendid face but to seal its perfection. Hard as a diamond, she passed on down the causeway. Narathihāpaté had ceased to occupy himself with her; many other beauties had come and gone. But her position was assured, for it was she who trained future favourites. Her knowledge of the art of love was founded upon the theory of the Hindu masters and upon her own extended practice. Likely recruits to the concubinate were placed under her instruction. From her classes they emerged infinitely skilled. By hard work and attention to detail she had raised over a course of years their standard of execution, until Chang Hsien Ch'ung himself declared one night after dinner that some of her girls might have applied with success for admission to the Jade Pavilions of the Son of Heaven.

In addition to these leading figures and the many striking women who accompanied them, were dancers and musicians. As the procession passed the gardens which opened on the causeway, it was swelled by further ladies who emerged from the pavilions. Some of these paced solemnly in their gorgeous silks, others sang and posed in a set measure. It was a spectacle of beauty and, like all beauty, very strange with that latency which forever haunts and eludes the onlooker.

When they reached the platform of the bathing pool the sun sank behind the western mountains and simultaneously in the east appeared the moon, blood-red as it climbed from the dusty horizon. A faint air was moving from the river, refreshingly moist and with a

tang of the night. The King took his seat on the edge
of the pool and as the light of day waned, giving place
to a moonlight which modulated every colour, threw
surfaces out of focus, some of the concubines laid aside
their clothes and plunged into the water. They were
distinguished as much for their agility as swimmers as
for the perfection of their form. While the moonbeams
silvered the pool and turned the drops of water on arm
or breast into falling pearls, a spirited music was played
and singers placed on the far side began their songs.
Wine was served to the King and to the queens, who
sat near him. He felt his spirits rise and called to Uhsauppan to tell some of the girls to wrestle or struggle
together where the water was shallow. This caused
amusement, and as a girl was thrown and fell in the
water, the drums gave a roll and the graded gongs a
flourish.

When more drink had been consumed, the fun in the
pool became more fanciful, the girls romping in gym-
nastics and exhibiting their limbs in every attitude.
Queen Sawlon, with unusual condescension, was
showing particular interest, having moved to the edge
of the pool, the better to see. Narathihāpaté noticed
this and beckoned to Uhsauppan. The beauty, who was
clad only in a rope of pearls, was standing in water up
to her knees. She looked enquiringly at the King.
'Splash Queen Sawlon,' he said. Everyone heard.
Uhsauppan, having the King's direct warrant, bent
and with both hands sent a cascade of water over her.
The Queen's elaborately piled hair was disordered, the
powder was washed in streaks from her face and her
dress was ruined. Narathihāpaté laughed loudly.

Shinshwé's dog barked. There was merriment among
the crowd on the platform, and in the water women,
mounted on the shoulders of others, threw out chal-
lenges as if they were amazons. For a moment Sawlon
stood there in the moonlight, a bedraggled figure, and
then ran crying into one of the rooms of the great
pavilion behind.

The entertainment at the pool, however, continued
as if nothing had happened. The great moon rose
higher, dimming the lights which spangled the pavilions. Facing the royal party on the other side of the
bath was now a living frieze of Cambodian dancers,
who posed and pounced and fell to strings and drums,
now muted, now sending their notes among the bamboos. Queen Saw, though aware of the beauty that en-
compassed her, was not wrought upon by it, could not
enter into it. She felt pent away when she thought of
the love which she had to give and which she could not
let free. If she could loose it, the splendour of a night
like this would take meaning. She would accomplish
the universal dream and prevent the escape of beauty.
'Nirvana only abideth, the calming of the law of rise
and fall,' she quoted to herself. As a woman it was
possible for her to enter the Whole by means of love.
But she was held apart, like an earth-bound spirit
which cannot rise up nor yet turn back to participation
in this world.

Someone came to announce that supper was ready.
Shaking off her regrets, nebulous fancies alien to her
normal mind, she informed the King. They all ad-
journed to the dining hall of the pavilion.

Narathihāpaté's table was apart from the rest. On it

were three hundred small dishes, the number always provided. These were arrayed antithetically. Thus, salted curries were set against spiced, sweet against sour, bitter against hot, and luscious against parching. In this manner the judicious diner at the conclusion of a meal had in his stomach a balance of food, and was thereby able to digest better than had he eaten at random. The service consisted of small glazed bowls with some vessels of gold or lacquer. The practice was for the queens to wait on the King until he was finished, when the dishes were removed and distributed among the rest.

Narathihāpaté took his seat. The green Chinese platter which had been brought from Martaban years previously was in front of him. He had grown to like it and the orders were for it always to be laid. Sawlon appeared to have got over her wetting. She had made a fresh toilette and was standing at the table when they came in. As soon as the King was ready, she and Shinshwé began offering him the dishes in the usual way. In accordance with his choice, they placed the food on the green plate. Shinshwé's pet dog was under the table.

The meal had been proceeding in this way for a short time when Sawlon, taking up a bowl of prawns, gave it into Shinshwé's hands, saying: 'The King has asked for this. Will you serve him? I am not feeling very well —it may be the wetting—and am going to lie down.' At which she left the hall.

Shinshwé accordingly helped the prawns without asking further. They lay, a little pink heap, in the centre of the green plate. Narathihāpaté was just about to lean forward and eat them, when the dog sneezed violently under the table. He started. His objection to sneezing was to some extent real. He had an undefined terror of it. Hence, he started when he heard the dog and looked at his plate, but not with any conscious intention of observing it. As he looked, however, he became aware that it had now turned a bluish tinge. With more concentration he looked again, and though less sure whether the plate was blue or green, he could not get over the feeling that at first glance it had looked blue. Instinctively he took some of the prawns in his fingers and offered them to the dog. The animal swallowed them at once and sat up with its ears cocked, expecting more. In a few seconds, however, it seemed to sway, a foam gathered at its mouth and, yelping loudly, it ran a few paces and fell. When they took it up it was dead.

The King had turned very pale. 'There was something in the prawns! You gave me the prawns, Shinshwé!'

Shinshwé's eyes were straining out of her head. 'Sawlon handed them to me!' she cried. 'I had no notion there was anything wrong. She said you'd asked for them.' Some of the others were witnesses of what had happened, and they said: 'Sawlon gave her the prawns.' Shinshwé was popular. Everyone knew she would not hurt a fly. She now added: 'My poor dog saved you.'

'Where is Sawlon?' asked the King, who was shaking.

'She left the room the moment after she had given Shinshwé the poison,' they said.

Narathihāpaté ordered her to be found. She was brought in a few minutes later by some of the amazons.

'What is this!' he exclaimed. 'You put poison before me! Had not something warned me, I should now be a dead man.'

Sawlon retained her wits. She appeared calm, surprised. 'What poison?' she asked, and as the King pointed to the prawns, she said 'I never helped you to those.'

'You gave them to Shinshwé.'

'Really, I cannot remember among so many dishes. I took up a bowl at random and asked Shinshwé to offer it. If there was poison, you should examine the cook.'

'Why did you give it to Shinshwé? Why did you leave the room?'

'I was drenched this evening at Your Majesty's instance and felt feverish and light-headed.'

The King hesitated, but when he recalled the look of rage and then of humiliation on her face as she stood regarding her dripping clothes, and afterwards her presence in the dining hall before he came in, he was certain of her guilt.

'You did it!' he exclaimed. 'I know you did it. You told Shinshwé I had asked for the prawns, but I had not. And I know why you did it. You thought you were insulted, you with your grand airs and your biting tongue! How dare you be insulted! Whatever I might do, how can I, Narathihāpaté, insult you?'

'I will tell you how you can insult me!' cried Sawlon, who, seeing that the truth was out, let her tongue go. 'I am descended from princes and I was the wife of a legitimate king. You took me to bolster your state, to give an air to your commonness, you, a casual bastard, your mother a slut out of a village, daughter of a tinker, a woman you were so ashamed of that, when you usurped the throne, you refused to recognise her and drove her to suicide. And you want to know how you can insult me? Your very existence has been one long insult!'

These words had an appalling effect upon Narathihāpaté. Not only did they cut deep into the quick, sneering at his origin, his usurpation, and his meanness to his mother, emphasising the sense of inferiority against which he had always sought to assert himself, but the force with which they were delivered seemed to rend his disordered nervous system. The perspiration poured from his skin. A frenzy seized him and, taking up one of the bowls from the table, he flung it into Sawlon's face. The ware broke and cut her; the contents were scattered over her features and neck. But she stood fast and, wiping away the food, said in a level voice:

'If I have failed to poison you, you miserable cur, I am happy to see that my words have unhinged your mind.'

It almost looked as if she had spoken the immediate truth, for with both hands he began to hurtle bowls about the room. Some of them hit members of the court, some smashed against pillar or wall or sailed out of the windows. There was utter consternation, many of the women lying prostrate, while others drifted from the room like flower-petals in a storm. The more experienced, however, waited for the frenzy to pass, and the amazon guard secured Sawlon, binding her hand and foot. Queen Saw, on a little dais behind, watched the scene without allowing any expression to pass over her face. When there remained no more vessels except the green dish, which the King clasped to himself like a breastplate, he fell into a stupor, head drooping forward, mouth open, blank eyes fixed on the dead dog. Quietly, then, Queen Saw gave orders that he was to be carried back to the palace. They helped him into his litter and, at a trot, the bandy-legged women bore him away.

xxiii
The Burning of Sawlon

The next day Narathihāpaté was sufficiently recovered from the double shock of Sawlon's attempt on his life and his reason to order her execution. It was to be no easy despatch: she was to be burnt.
In his horror of the danger he had escaped, in his necessity of asserting himself, he ordered his smiths to forge
an iron cage, under which the fire would be lighted
and wherein the Queen was to meet her death. He
directed that the burning should take place in the presence of the court. His calculation was that when she
felt the floor of the cage scorching her feet, she would
run about in a distracted manner, losing her dignity
and so restoring to him what her words had taken away.

When his intentions were known, an effort was
made by many people to induce him to commute the
sentence to decapitation. Sawlon, no doubt, deserved
to die; even the King's detractors could not deny that

he had the law on his side. But the sentence was shocking to an easy-going court. Those who petitioned for
mercy, however, had no success, for Narathihāpaté's
fright and humiliation combined to give him strength
to resist all appeals. As a last hope they tried to enlist
Queen Saw's help. But unexpectedly she hesitated to
intervene. She was afraid her suit would be in vain. If
she failed her influence in matters of graver import to
the state might be shaken. The individual must give
way. She herself had had to sacrifice her own feelings
for the public service.

The smiths were bribed to induce them to take seven
days over the construction of the cage. When Sawlon
perceived that hope of reprieve was gone, she decided
to devote the time that remained to religion and to
seek in the Buddhist doctrines a solace for her predicament. Accordingly she sent the Royal Chaplain an
urgent message.

That mystic had now reached an advanced age. It
was difficult to know, indeed, what age he was. But
though emaciated and pale, some inner vigour seemed
to animate him. His body, too, appeared to be func-
tioning rhythmically. On receiving the Queen's summons, he left his monastery on foot and, attended only
by a novice to hold up his parasol, walked the distance
into the royal city. Lightly entering the chamber where
Sawlon was confined, he took his seat on a mat. The
Queen threw herself before him and, touching the bare
floor with her forehead, said: 'Master, misfortune has
overtaken me.'

'Relate to me the nature of your misfortune.' He
understood the healing value of confession.

She began to tell him the whole story of the fatal evening. When she had described her drenching, she said: 'The King jeered at me. I could not stand it. I rushed into the dining pavilion where they were laying supper and, not realising what I was doing, mixed arsenic with the food. And now I must burn! How can such a frightful thing happen to me?'

The old sage said gently: 'My disciple, misfortune is one of the three aspects of life in this world. The other two are impermanence and illusion.'

'Instruct me,' begged the Queen. 'In this frivolous court there has been no time for religion. I have forgotten what I was taught as a little girl. I long to know now.'

The Chaplain continued: 'I was speaking of the three aspects of life. *Anissa, Dokha, Anatta*—to give them their classical names—dominate us here. Of these *Anissa*—impermanence—is the first. It is the nature of all things, except truth and the knowledge of truth, to pass away. When this passage has the form of a transit from wealth to poverty, from health to sickness, from high place to the shadow of death, it is called unhappiness or pain, the state in which you now lament. But as your present state is founded in the transitory nature of things, it is as ineluctable as the rhythm of the world.'

'That my predicament partakes of all impermanence is cold comfort, Master.'

'Listen. I spoke of a third aspect, illusion, that is, the unsubstantiality of rise and fall themselves. The world with its rhythm is no more than an appearance. There is no movement from joy to sadness nor from evil to good fortune within the core of truth. If you could

understand the truth, you would see that impermanence and misfortune relate only to outer consciousness;
they disappear when one attains the inner knowledge.
If you can glimpse that knowledge, then the misery you
feel now, the horror with which you view your death,
will be blotted out.'

'Can a poor distracted woman reach that state?'

'It is possible to approach it. I can speak by experience. Once I did not know that poise, where there is
truce from the illusion of rise and fall. But I sought it
and am marvellously embattled now against what may
come.'

Sawlon listened to his words, striving to understand,
as a man might listen to and try to memorise a formula
for the elixir of life. But she could not make her own
what he said, penetrate into the woof of words. His
comforting remained words flapping beyond her.
'Master,' she said plaintively, 'you have spent years at
this study. How can I damp down illusion when it
takes the form of the pangs of fire?'

'There is but one way,' he replied gravely, 'the way
of meditation. Horror and pain can be overcome by the
mind which has passed out of active consciousness.
Contemplate sufficiently truth in meditation and no
man has any power to touch you.' With these words he
seemed himself to fall into a state which was far from
the place in which he sat. The Queen and her guards
waited with respect. The novice was at the window,
watching the butterflies. After some little time the old
man turned compassionate eyes upon her, called the
novice and left the room.

When the Queen was alone, she thought deeply over

what had been said. The sense was clear enough, but she felt no aptitude for applying it to her case. At this distracting moment she could never concentrate sufficiently for the entry into meditation. It was too late now to train her mind. She must fall back on what power of soul she already possessed. Coming to this conclusion, she saw what she could do. She had never bowed to the King, she never would bow to him. She remembered with satisfaction the effect on him of her anger. Though he had on his side all the temporal power, she had broken in with deadly effect. If he calculated to cure himself of his deep wound by seeing her plead, give way to horror and panic in the cage, he was mistaken. He would get no nursing from her; she would wound him again. She felt that she had the power to do this. She could not lift herself from pain by meditation, she was too deeply immersed for that in illusion's sea, but, holding to something unconquerable in her soul, she would give that despicable Narathihāpaté a psychic stab, the haemorrhage of which he would never be able to staunch.

Greatly comforted by this resolution, she awaited death, filling in the time by dwelling on the Three Gems, saying again and again, as she told the beads of her rosary, 'I take refuge in the Buddha, I take refuge in his Law, I take refuge in his Church.' The words soothed her, gave her a feeling of ultimate safety, brought her unwittingly to the threshold of that meditation which at first she had thought she could not approach. But she went no further than the threshold, for, her mind more quiet, she pondered long how in the moment of trial she would beat down the King.

⋆ *The Burning of Sawlon* ⋆

On the seventh morning the cage was erected in one of the quadrangles. There, in accordance with orders, the courtiers assembled in the afternoon. The King's seat was near the cage. When all was in readiness, the executioners went to call Sawlon. She had been confined very closely to prevent sympathisers giving her opium and thereby baulking the King's design. They found her kneeling in white clothes before a little shrine, wherein stood a figure of the Buddha, with his hand raised, holding the *mudra* that takes away fear. They paused a moment in respect for her prayers. At length the senior executioner urged her get up. 'Your Majesty,' he said respectfully, 'the King is in his seat. We dare not delay longer. He is a sudden man.'

After a last prostration before the smiling countenance of the Blessed One, she rose to her feet, saying: 'I am ready to face the King, but will he, I wonder, be able to face me?'

They led her into the courtyard at a gentle pace. The sky overhead was clear, but there was a black cloud to the southward. It looked like the coming of the monsoon, which breaks with a violent storm. When she saw the cage, the iron frame heated by the embers below, she hesitated for a second, for there is a cruel difference between the mind's picture and what the eyes perceive. 'Can I bear this?' she thought, but noticing that the King looked in her direction, she overcame terror and marched on again. To reach the cage it was necessary to pass close by him and the nearer she approached, the more haughty was her step. He was seated uneasily, his face twisted. 'You are going to the fire,' he cried, as if to establish something in his own mind. 'But even now I may have mercy. Will you not beg for it, Sawlon?'

She stood still, but she would not bow, she would not answer. It was evident he was trying to relieve himself of his hurt. If he could get her to beg for life, abjectly, in the face of all, he would refuse the boon and draw from her humiliation the refreshment he needed. That she did not speak or plead alarmed him. 'Take her on,' he said hurriedly. 'Put her in the cage.'

The executioners now seized her and, the door of the cage being pulled open by an iron hook, they pushed her in. The King leaned forward. It was for this moment that he had been waiting. He expected that when her bare feet touched the heated iron of the floor she would dance about shrieking and that he could laugh and recover himself. But this was not so, she stood where she was, and, looking at him through the bars, said in what sounded to him a terrible voice: 'You have my contempt now, but one day you will have the contempt of the whole nation.' The sneer on her lips was so withering that he half rose and cried out. She laughed in his face.

The fire below the cage was glowing charcoal, for the King's intention had been to roast her slowly. But now in his horror of what she might say more, feeling his mind disintegrating under her glance, he called hoarsely, 'Heap up the fire! Heap it up, I tell you! Burn her, quick!' They flung on dry wood. A great flame and smoke rose up instantly, veiling her from sight.

At that moment—it was all over, for Sawlon was not seen again alive—the threatened storm burst on the city. In clouds of dust it came billowing through the courtyard, making the fire roar and covering the spectators with grit. Hard on its tail was a downpour of rain. There was a rush for shelter. Narathihāpaté, who had continued to sit watching the fire, dust and leaves flying round him, was caught and immediately drenched to the skin. When he looked at his dripping garments, his mind was dully conscious of a parallelism, the meaning of which he tried to decipher. In the rencontre just over there had been two actors, Sawlon and himself. They had both been drenched with water; had both of them also been humiliated by the other? And if he had burnt her body, had she scorched his soul? He could not formulate the answers, but darkly feeling that he was involved in a mystery, allowed himself to be hurried back to his apartments.

Queen Saw, who had gravely observed the proceedings throughout, bending her attention more upon Narathihāpaté than upon Sawlon, had entered a closed palanquin before the rain poured over. When she heard that the King had retired, she followed him. He was lying on a couch in a state of collapse. The women had changed his clothes. Two of them were massaging him. Others tried to tempt him with light refreshments. The Queen took up a position at the back of the room. Silently she watched him, as he lay motionless. How would the tension go? She would wait.

As night drew on, he fell into a restless sleep, though the air was fresher after the storm. She remained in the room. Her ladies had made her comfortable under a silk coverlet by a window whence she could view the sky, brilliantly lit with stars. Not far off was the gilded cone of a pagoda, its tiny bells tinkling as puffs from the river agitated their winged tongues. She was beginning to feel drowsy, when suddenly Narathihāpaté sat bolt upright in his bed and screamed: 'Sawlon, come and watch beside me.'

The Queen rose at once and went to his side. He panted: 'What is that?—who is that? Oh, it is you! I've had such a dream!' One of the maids wiped the sweat from his forehead. 'I was falling, I had fallen to some dark hollow, I do not know where. There were bushes, I heard rustling, I could not ward off what was coming. No one could ward it off but Sawlon, and I cried for her help.'

'Lie down again,' said Queen Saw. 'These are imaginings. Sawlon is dead. What can she do for you now, your dead wife?'

They gave him a drink of water and he lay down. They fanned him carefully and he fell asleep. Queen Saw continued by the bed. She saw his face twitch, such a weak face. In a little while he started up once more, saying inarticulately: 'I was in the hollow again. Why is only Sawlon able to protect me? I had to beg her to come. And then I saw her eyes. They were the same eyes that looked at me from the cage; the same disdain was there. What can I do? I dare not sleep again.'

'Try and compose yourself,' said Queen Saw, mixing him a sedative draught. 'You will be better in the morning. We will sit by you here.'

'I cannot sleep, I dare not sleep! What was it that I saw? Can it be that her spirit is about? Can she harm me now? An old man told me once in a forest monastery that, by killing a woman, sometimes one but increases her power. Can that be so?'

The Burning of Sawlon *
* *The Burning of Sawlon* *

'It cannot be so, if you control your mind. But if you let it drift with every influence, then what is most extravagant may seem true.'

'How can I control my mind when I am asleep? It is then that spirits make their assault. I tell you, I felt myself lying there helpless; as plain as day I was lying in a hollow place helpless with her circling about me. I should not have called her. My cry called her from I know not where. You saw her face through the bars to-day. The agony of her burning feet was held back. She loosed something at me, as from a bow.'

Narathihāpaté continued to rave in this manner through the night. Once or twice they induced him to compose himself for sleep, but now he could not sleep. The dawn came at last, another day of dazzling light. In the small hours Queen Saw had sent a messenger to the Royal Chaplain. When the sun was just risen, he arrived at the palace.

The King was now much dejected. Shadows lay under his eyes; he started at every sound. His irritability with the servants was intense. When he saw the Chaplain, he fell on his knees. 'Master,' he said, touching his feet, 'comfort me. I do not know what has happened. As I had the right, I put Sawlon to death. She tried to poison me, she tried to trample on me. Other kings have done the like and so got rid of what troubled them, but I have not been able to void my torment. I feel it darting and throbbing within me. How can I dull it, be easy again, feel assured?'

The Chaplain's old face was calm and happy.

'A king cannot publish innocuously the turmoil of his heart,' he began. 'Sawlon said some hard things, but

224

the people will say harder, if they see that you continue
to mind what she said. How the Sung Emperor would
smile if he heard of your present state! You must control your agitation by reflecting that, if you do not,
there will soon be much more about which to be agitated. Instead of one woman, the whole country will
scant you respect. Remember the Law of Right Effort
preached by the Lord Omniscient. "Strive to avert the
spreading of evil that hath arisen. Strive to avert the
arising of evil that hath not arisen. Strive to aid the
arising of good that hath not arisen. Strive to aid the
spreading of good that hath arisen." Evil has arisen.
Do not spread it by your lack of control.'

These words had an effect. When the Chaplain left,
Narathihāpaté felt stronger for a time. But unfortunately he did not fully understand his own case. He
could not void his torment because in his inmost self
he believed that what Sawlon had said was true. She
had, as she had hoped, dealt him a mortal wound.

xxiv
The Propitious Pagoda

The rainy season which followed the death of Queen Sawlon was a melancholy time, because Narathihāpaté's moods became more incalculable. One day, however, a happy suggestion was made. Would His Majesty build a pagoda?

No royal pagoda had been built since the previous reign. Narathihāpaté fell in with the idea at once. Yes, he would build a pagoda, a magnificent pagoda, a better one than the Ananda, the Incomparable, built by the hero king, Kyansittha, a pagoda which would carry his name down the years, as a great king, a defender of the faith. The Chaplain's words—'Strive to aid the arising of good that hath not arisen'—weighed with him, too, as did the reflection that in the past he had not always been scrupulous in respecting Church property.

It was the fashion—had been for centuries—to build

pagodas as an insurance against the risk inherent in bad actions. The whole area outside the walls for miles and miles was a maze of them. Everyone who could afford it built pagodas and dedicated slaves to keep them in repair. The Duke of Martaban, for instance, had been dedicated. All these years he had acted as head gardener in one of the more fashionable shrines.

This pagoda-building was well suited to a rich and elegant court. It was expensive; it had a pleasant flavour of the arts; and it was profitable, not in a vulgar sense, but metaphysically. The profit was connected with the current theory of salvation by works, a theory which mystics like the Royal Chaplain found shallow, but which was suitable for laymen. According to it all actions were indestructible facts which, accumulated, became the personality of the actor. To build a pagoda was assumed to be a meritorious act and, therefore, to make the builder to that extent a meritorious person. It balanced, and overbalanced, unmeritorious acts. Thus, if a court lady felt that her tongue had been running away with her and thereby she was accumulating a demerit which threatened to hold her back from that ultimate enlightenment which was the aim of the religion, it became very proper for her to build a pagoda. An expensive pagoda would cancel a great deal of malicious scandal. At some time an ingenious lordling had invented a method of increasing the merit that might normally be expected. It was the practice to set up a dedication tablet in stone, whereon the donor expressed a wish to acquire the full merit due. The gentleman in question put forward the idea that the donor should ask in the inscription to be allowed to share the merit with a number of other people, say, his uncles and aunts. The very fact of stating his desire to share merit, rightly his own, was itself an added merit, and it was calculated that the device, without increasing the cost of the structure, doubled the merit that might accrue from it alone. This new practice became the rule until, at a later date, an even more ingenious person suggested, on the same grounds as before, that a maximum merit might be won if the donor, on stone, gave the whole of his merit to others, not even reserving a minor share for himself. In short, the building of pagodas was as elegant a pastime as any invented.

Narathihāpaté announced that he proposed to call his work of merit 'The Propitious Pagoda', intimating that its propitious character was to be shared not only by himself but by the whole realm. It was no easy task to find an unoccupied site, but by clearing away the ruins of certain old pagodas, the attendant slaves of which had died—an arbitrary course, as some dared to say—he acquired an area suitable to his purpose.

The building was going rapidly forward when an unfortunate interruption occurred. One of those sayings the origin of which no one could ever give began to go the round. It passed from mouth to mouth, till at last he heard it. 'The pagoda is up, the kingdom is down.'

He caused enquiries to be made. Some alleged that the saying, engraved on metal, had been found in the rubble of the old pagodas he had demolished, others that a woman had uttered it. Either alarmed him and, to cut a long story short, he stopped the work.

The stoppage irritated the court, the ladies particularly. They declared the saying to be the sort of nonsense which might excite rustics, and that to suppose a work of merit could do other than give merit to the persons concerned was contrary to the established religion. The fact was that they were disappointed. The completion of the pagoda would have meant a fête.

Accordingly one evening, when the King had taken rather more wine than usual to quiet his nerves, they induced an elderly monk to remonstrate with him. This man, who was called Panthagu, enjoyed an immense popularity with the women because he claimed to have invented a permanent cure for superfluous hair. As he insisted that unless he applied the preparation with his own hands it would not work, his acquaintance with the other sex was notoriously intimate. He now came in smiling and was respectfully received.

In the usual way the desired subject was duly brought up by a third party.

'The Supporter of the Religion is running a personal risk in not completing the "Propitious Pagoda",' observed the monk thoughtfully.

'How so?' asked Narathihāpaté, his nervous eyes winking.

'We all have done things we ought not to have done,' explained Panthagu plaintively. 'I know I have myself. The Supporter even, though of course less than others, has had his lapses. Such acts mount up. It is hard in this life to calculate precisely such a debit account. But one discovers it afterwards. A king has a right to expect that his status in his next existence, be it here or elsewhere, will not be inferior to his present rank. When all this can be insured so easily by completing a work of merit, it seems risky to neglect it.'

Narathihāpaté was listening anxiously. If he finished the pagoda, it might damage his future here and now; if he left it unfinished, his further future was uncovered. To Panthagu he said haltingly:

'I stopped the work because I was afraid of endangering the realm.'

'That shows', replied the monk, 'that Your Majesty has not fully considered the Law of Impermanence. The true Buddhist is not concerned with preserving a kingdom, which, in a last analysis, is nothing but impermanence, sorrow and illusion. Where he is concerned is with his own advance towards the bliss of truth. Did not the Lord himself, when he was a prince, desert his kingdom, intent only on becoming the Lord? Hence it is more important to finish the pagoda than to bother about the state. In the one your aim is real, in the other illusory.'

Narathihāpaté, impressed by this specious argument, directed the work on the pagoda to be completed.

In due course the ladies had the gala day they wanted. A covered way was constructed from the palace to the pagoda, a distance of two miles. The flooring of the way was composed of a groundwork of bamboos overlaid with matting, on top of which were spread silk and woollen Chinese carpets. The roof was palm-leaf thatch with a ceiling of long tapestries. At the sides was bamboo lattice-work, with pots full of lilies, living plantain-trees and sugar-cane to form a fence. As an old pundit remarked, quoting a classic: 'It was passing fair and pleasant even as the spirits' highway in Sudassana.'

The day began by a promenade of the court down the covered way. In front on litters were carried gold statuettes of all those persons who in the past had attained to the final illumination, each shown in one of the seven postures, such as that one which takes away fear or bestows the peace. Together with the shapes of those persons, twenty-eight in number, were representations of the chief disciples in characteristic poses. Carried after these were silver statuettes, eighteen inches high, of the fifty-one kings of the Pagān dynasty, each seated upon a throne, and of Narathihāpaté himself and his queens. In addition, there were two figures representing his two sons, the Prome-Min and the Bassein-Min, now boys in their teens.

At a point further down the procession came the White Elephant, housed in a rich caparison overwrought with jewels. The creature was full grown, had a smug expression and seemed in perfect health. It passed at a soft and easy pace. On its back was a cabinet, shaped like a pointed shrine, in which was placed a gold reliquary studded with rubies, emeralds and pearls. This contained relics of the Blessed One, which at one time or another had been procured from Ceylon.

Behind the White Elephant came the court. Everyone walked, as if they were a body of primitive disciples. This made the occasion more animated, for the ladies could show off their clothes to better advantage. Towards the end of the line there was a good deal of talk and laughter. But Veluvati, whom Queen Saw had taken back onto her staff after her escapade with Tharepyissapaté, was in one of her tearful moods.

'I can see the illusion of it all,' she said.

When they reached the pagoda the usual ceremony of enshrining the relics was conducted. In the relic-chamber were also placed the numerous figures and statuettes. But there was to be a sequel not altogether so agreeable. Narathihāpaté took off the jewellery he was wearing and placed it among the objects in the chamber. He then caused word to be passed round that he expected all members of the court to do the same. There was some consternation, for several ladies had been foolish enough to wear their best jewels.

The day ended with a grand entertainment at the palace, which was illuminated, as was the covered way and the pagoda. Countless oil lamps and candles in shades of coloured paper were lighted. Viewed from the tower, it was an enchanting scene. The night was moonless, scented and mild. At every window, on every ledge of the palace the lights showed, picking out the shape of the great building. The tall central roof seemed to float among the stars; the covered way, like a burning finger, pointed out to the new pagoda. Afterwards people remembered that it was the last gala night ever held at Pagān.

XXV

The Sound of Arrows

Events now began to close in. One day the news reached Pagān that Hangchao had surrendered to the Tartars and that the Sung Emperor had fled. Queen Saw sent for Chang Hsien Ch'ung.

'How will this affect Burma, do you imagine?' she asked him.

'It will give the Tartars leisure to think about us,' he replied. 'We are on their borders, and their usual policy towards border states is first to demand tribute as an earnest of good behaviour. But, of course, the demand may not come in our time.'

'It would complicate the internal situation,' said the Queen wearily. 'The country is difficult to hold together as it is. Much discontent prevails against the King's rule. Both the Church and the Mandarinate are disaffected. An external shock, even of the limited kind you suggest, might upset the equilibrium. If a demand is made, what would you advise?'

'That it be met,' said he promptly. 'Burma cannot stand against Kublai Khan.'

They continued to discuss the problem at length. It bristled with difficulties.

When the King was informed of Hangchao's fate, he was not much disturbed, because his grasp of affairs was very weak. But he said:

'We shall be making shortly the usual pilgrimage to consult the Mahagiri. Though all these years they have had little to say, perhaps on this occasion, if, as you pretend, the foreign situation is really threatening, they will give us a warning.'

In this state of mind he set out for Pōpa a month later. Queen Saw was of the party. Her intention was to visit afterwards her father at Kanbyu. Since her mother's death some time back she had made a yearly practice of going there.

As the procession entered the plain, the countryside seemed as calm and lovely as ever. The rice crop had just been reaped. The stubble was fresh and bristly; cattle had not yet eaten it down; it filled the air with a smell of bran. Men were by the threshing floors, women by the wells. Peace and content softened their faces, for the out-turn had been good, the festivals were near. That anything portended there was no sign at all. An immemorial air was over the land. It would never change, no matter what happened in high places. When the rain fell, the earth would bring forth. Centuries would go by and the same pigs, the same cows, would be there; the same grain would be planted, would grow to the same ear; men would bend on the same task, thinking the same thoughts. So it seemed, that countryside, and the royal train, as it passed through, looked in comparison fleeting and unsubstantial.

The village at the foot of Pōpa was reached as on previous occasions, and on the third morning at dawn the ascent was begun. When the sun rose the procession was still winding its way up towards the shoulder where lay the shrine of the Mahagiri. At a point where the trees had thinned out into a region of park-land, the King, whose palanquin was near the front, suddenly called a halt. He was observed to sniff and, turning to those about him, said quickly:

'Did you smell that scent? An intolerably sweet odour seemed to drift over me for an instant.'

No one had smelt anything, though there had been many walking beside him.

'The perfume was very strange,' he continued, 'as if it came from another world of being.'

As he said this, the men near him noticed a change in his face. It grew curiously impassive; the eyes were wider open than usual but more opaque. All stared at him in alarm.

Presently a voice came from his lips, unlike his usual voice, a voice that screeched:

'I hear the sound of arrows, I hear the sound of clouding arrows!' At this he seemed to fall forward in a fit, for when they raised him he was unconscious.

The Queen, whose palanquin was close behind, saw and heard everything. If ever there was a woman, calm and sophisticated, it was she, but the occasion was so strange and sudden that she was deeply shaken. She looked, almost it seemed for help, at Chang Hsien Ch'ung, who was near by.

'What does all this mean, what has happened?' she cried.

'The King before he spoke was in a trance, that I can swear,' answered the minister. 'But what happened then, who knows? This sacred mountain, its spirits did they possess him? You should ask your experts; they have experience of such things. But that he should speak of arrows is curious, of clouding arrows, of hearing the sound of clouding arrows, that is very curious. It made me think at once of the Tartars.'

Queen Saw ordered the procession to turn about. To proceed to the normal séance was out of the question. It was also perhaps unnecessary, she reflected. Maybe they knew already all that they required to know. Moreover, the King was unconscious, must be attended to. So they turned back. On the way down she consulted certain persons.

'What about the perfume?' she asked.

'As to that,' they replied, 'it is our experience that spirits sometimes become manifest so to persons of particular faculty. We did not know that the King was endowed with such faculty.'

But the Queen knew that he was psychic; his detection of poison in the green dish had been clairvoyant.

'You think, then, that the Mahagiri met him on the mountain and communicated their message to him direct?' she enquired.

'There is no doubt,' they replied. 'The Mahagiri came down a distance to meet him. Maybe the message was so urgent.'

When they reached the foot, the King's faint had passed, but he was weeping and hysterical. He did not know what he had said, but he knew something strange had happened. He was frightened and very low. The Queen said no more to him then, but directed his people to carry him back to Pagān. She felt a strong desire to see her father and left at once for Kanbyu village.

xxvi
The Visit

Queen Saw's periodic visits to the place of her birth gave the villagers much pleasure. Her generosity to them had been wide and judicious. The village was now provided at her expense with fine brick wells, roofed over with wooden kiosks, and with cement platforms for bathing. A reservoir supplied the cattle with water in the dry season. The pagoda had been embellished, the wooden monastery recarved in so imaginative a fashion that it seemed to shimmer in the air like a fairy-tale. Moreover, no taxes were levied; the place was a little paradise.

On her arrival at the gateway in the bamboo stockade she was met by all the notabilities who, though they prostrated themselves in the dust of the roadway to the detriment of their clothes, were quite at their ease, smiling and uttering words of greeting.

A Burmese wooden Monastery of the Eighteenth Century
By courtesy of the Royal Asiatic Society

★ *The Visit* ★

'The moment of Your Majesty's gracious condescension to notice Kanbyu' (the headman was making his little speech) 'is always an occasion of unbounded happiness for us, your obliged humble servants.'

The Queen smiled back, recognised one or two elderly men and then directed them to follow her to her father's house. After passing down the village road they entered his garden through the hedge over which, the Queen always remembered, she had noticed the head of Usana's elephant. The bush which had once grown flowers of three colours was still there. Alighting from her palanquin, she desired all, her guard, her attendants, the villagers who had escorted her, to stay below while she mounted the stairs alone to the upper room, where her father was awaiting her.

She came into his presence with a fresh and darling air of affection and respect; with an exquisite grace she knelt before him, joining her two hands together like a lotus bud and bending her forehead. 'Come and sit on the carpet with me,' he said.

She did not immediately introduce what was on her mind, but began:

'How did the crops do this year?'

'There was a wonderful out-turn,' he replied. 'The first, second and third rains were all equally good. The vivid green of August turned naturally to the yellow of October. Such heavy ears—it was a sight of gold.'

'You still plough yourself and sow?'

'Why, yes; I believe it makes a difference. I have always felt a communion with the earth. Turning the furrow seems to me a rite. Some virtue goes out of me

239

as I tread the mud. I could not look for a like result if I left it to others.'

'But your household does the reaping, I suppose?'

'That is less important. Yes, they reap, those of them you have not enticed to the capital with your offers of position.'

'My brothers and sisters and that herd of cousins, they expected me to do something for them.'

'I know, I know; you did well. I am not lonely; I was always a solitary.'

That was very true. Not her most cunning offers had induced him to live at court. She often wondered why. Was it that he would never accept anything from a child of his, could not imagine himself his children's debtor? Was it that he valued freedom beyond wealth and ease? Or did farming seem to him more important than society? Perhaps there was something of all three in his attitude. But more especially he was a man of the imagination. What interfered with his dreams palled with him soon.

'Have you still the field', she asked, 'where the hamadryad came that day when I was a child?'

'Indeed, yes! It is my best field.'

'That was a strange episode. Tell me again, what exactly did the man you consulted afterwards say about it?'

'That you would be great.'

'He gave no details, said nothing about an eventual fall from greatness?'

Her father looked at her thoughtfully and told her no.

'And the bush that once had different coloured flowers—it is still there, I see—what was said in that case?'

'Only that your greatness was at hand, and that it would have three periods.'

Then she burst out: 'I don't know what's going to happen. Things have been getting more and more difficult. I've often told you what the King is like. He is half mad. For years I have struggled for a sane administration. But you can never foresee what he is going to do next. Discontent has been steadily increasing. When his sons are a little older they will head a rebellion. You have no idea what is being hatched underground. Already one of the princes and his mother may be in the hands of plotters. Perhaps I could manage to hold down all that, but there is something outside I cannot hold down.'

She then told him shortly of her recent conversation about the Tartars with Chang Hsien Ch'ung.

'Wondering whether the Mahagiri would give any hint,' she went on, 'I joined the expedition to the mountain. A most unheard-of event there took place this morning. On his way up the King fell into a trance and said something which seemed to refer to a Tartar invasion. I cannot convey to you the extraordinary atmosphere. Telling it to you like this, it sounds all nonsense. But I, who have never been much impressed by the occult, was deeply shaken. It was so sudden, I suppose, and startling the way it happened.'

There was silence between them. At last her father observed:

'Chang Hsien Ch'ung's view, you say, was that if the

Tartars looked in this direction, it would be only guarantees they were after?'

'So he said. That is the Tartar procedure.'

'In that case your power at court should be able to ensure a satisfactory agreement.'

'So it would seem,' she answered with a kind of impatience at the complexity of the problem. 'But think of the King's state of mind. He is as incalculable as a wild beast. How can I be sure sanity will prevail? No, no,' she went on, a vehement note creeping into her words, 'I am much shaken. I will confess to you what I can say to no one else. I feel that a threat to Burma is imminent. You know my life. I was lucky to be queen, you will say, but at least I have given myself entirely to the state. Everything else has been cut out. Is it all to be in vain?'

"If evils are to be', replied her father, his expressive face animated by some inner glow, '—and I myself have had curious intimations as I walked alone on the mountain—you will be none the less for their coming. Character, not success, is the measure of greatness. Should the kingdom you have striven to preserve go down, you will still be a light for those who come after.'

Saying this, he embraced her. She was much comforted.

Conversing a short time longer, she took leave and descended to the garden. The headman and elders were waiting for her, but on this occasion she felt unable to listen to petitions or go into their affairs. To their disappointment, though respect prevented them from showing it, she entered her palanquin and with hardly a word was carried away.

xxvii
The Tartar Embassy

When Queen Saw reached Pagān she found Narathihāpaté more normal, and she thought it best to give him an account of what had happened on Pōpa. In the course of her remarks, she chose to say: 'There is no reason to be alarmed, but we should be prepared, both with a strong army and a sound policy. At the moment we have nothing definite to go on. Your Majesty's experience on the mountain was certainly a strong hint, but it was somewhat vague. The various submissions which have been made by the Chief Minister suggest that we may expect a Tartar embassy demanding guarantees sooner or later, but it may not be in our time. Meanwhile my advice is to increase the elephantry, our best arm, and to make up our minds at the same time that if the Emperor Kublai Khan asks us to recognise his general overlordship we should comply. This last in theory

243

may be derogatory, but in practice it can amount to nothing, for our virtual independence will be unaffected.'

Narathihāpaté listened dully to this masterly analysis. Everything in his nature rose up against the advice. Though he knew himself to be incapable of handling a crisis, if it arose, though in the depths of his soul he was miserably alarmed, his ache to assert himself was greater than ever. All he said was: 'The Chief Secretary is waiting outside with some business.'

As the Queen left, Mahabo was shown in. He had received instructions to invent a new title for the King, a magnificent title, a title more grandiloquent than any other king had ever borne, a title which would express at once both temporal and spiritual lordship.

'You have the draft with you?' enquired Narathihāpaté eagerly. He was longing to see the title.

'I have, Your Majesty,' replied the secretary, spreading out a paper.

The King scanned it with attention. The title was SIRITRIBHAVANATITYAPAVARADHAM-MARAJA.

'I think that will do very well,' he said, repeating it several times with great satisfaction. 'Have it cut in gold and set up over my head here, and insert it in my dedicatory inscription at the Propitious Pagoda.'

When the Chief Secretary had departed to carry out his instructions, the King lay back with a pleased smile. He spent the day teaching the title to anyone who came in.

In futilities of this kind the year passed. Not a word was heard of China; some even began to hope that the long series of hints which had culminated on Pōpa might lead to nothing, when suddenly one November morning a messenger arrived to report that a Tartar embassy had crossed the northern mountains. So it was true after all, a crisis was approaching, a crisis the resolution of which no one could foresee, but which might be disastrous. At the moment there was nothing to be done but to receive the embassy. Accordingly orders were immediately issued to provide it with boats for descending the river.

In December, on the tenth waning day of the moon, the flotilla carrying the Tartars and their horses came into Pagān roadstead. Chang Hsien Ch'ung had instructions to meet and conduct them to their quarters within the palace. An advance report on their identity and numbers was in his hands. It appeared that the Emperor Kublai Khan had seen fit to appoint as head of the embassy so important a mandarin as the Grand Secretary to the Board of Rites. This official was a Chinaman who, like many others, had entered Tartar employ. His name was Lu Chia. Supporting him, as advisers or colleagues, were two other personages, one of them a Tartar cavalry general called Kiluken, the other an adventurer from the extreme west, who had won the Emperor's favour, a man named Marco Polo. Lu Chia was a gentleman, a Taoist and a scholar. Dressed in a blue silk figured gown and a round black hat, he sat fingering an antique jade and murmuring the old poem beginning 'At fifteen I went with the army,' as the flotilla swung round with the current to make the landing stage. Kiluken was a very different type of man. His experience had been exclusively of

war. As a young soldier he had fought in the ranks at
the battle of Liegnitz, had seen the Tartar arrows
pierce the chain mail of the Knights Templar, and used
to claim that it was he who had singled out of the press
and killed, sword to sword, the Grand Master of the
Teutonic Knights, who had perished on that field. He
even used to state, for there was no one now to con-
tradict him, that on his lance after the battle the head of
Henry the Pious of Silesia had been carried into the
city of Liegnitz. Later, as a sergeant of the Imperial
Guard, he had assisted in the sack of Bagdad, when he
entered the Caliph's harem and carried off for his own
use two girls, a Caucasian and a Greek, which booty did
not prevent him during the sack, which lasted ten days,
from raping seven other women whom he had dragged
from private houses. With this wide experience behind
him, he had risen steadily, during the campaign against
the Sung distinguishing himself greatly. He admitted
to only one great disappointment—that Hangchao,
their fairy capital, had not been sacked after its surrender. On his promotion to the rank of general it was
currently agreed that he was the toughest guy in Asia.
He had never washed in his life and could neither read
nor write. From his barge, as she put in, he looked with
a critical eye at the fortifications and with a calculating
eye at the gilded shrines. He was dressed in a long coat,
loose trousers and riding boots. On his head was a cap
with flaps turned back, in which were egret feathers.
A heavy sword swung at his hip.

The second of Lu Chia's colleagues, Marco Polo,
though from the far west wore a costume similar to the
ambassador's. His black beard looked incongruous,

but he had a clever nose. Though he did not yet wash
as often as Lu Chia could have wished, his ablutions
were far more frequent than they had been during his
first years in China. The Emperor had sent him to Burma because he had a reporter's eye and could be de-
pended on for a detailed account of the embassy. Lu
Chia found him quite uncultivated. He had no interest
in literature or in antiquities.

Chang Hsien Ch'ung, as he waited on the wharf with
the numerous courtiers who supported him, did not
know all these facts, but he knew some of them. He had
met Lu Chia twenty years before at a literary dinner-
party at Hangchao, and though he had found him affected, now thought it as well to brush up his classical
quotations. Kiluken he had never come across, nor
Marco Polo, but had heard of the first as a barrack-
room swashbuckler and the second as a merchant-tra-
veller turned administrator. When the ambassador's
barge was alongside, he stepped forward and stood with
the ends of his sleeves meeting, his hands concealed.
The three personages aforesaid came ashore at once,
Kiluken, before he did so, cursing one of the Burman
oarsmen and kicking him into the river. This struck
Chang Hsien Ch'ung merely as bad manners, but some
of the attendant courtiers regarded it as an ominous sign.

After the customary exchange of courtesies, in which
Kiluken took little part, Chang Hsien Ch'ung announced that the King had sent down a number of the
state elephants and expressed the hope that their Ex-
cellencies would mount them and so be carried to the
palace. At this Kiluken said that he never rode elephants and was not going to move off the wharf till his

horses were unshipped. Without caring to see whether the others agreed, he began with a great flow of opprobrious language to superintend their disembarkation. In a remarkably short time a groom led up his horse, a small stallion, into the saddle of which he swung himself in a second. As neither the ambassador nor Polo were in riding kit, they mounted an elephant. When all was ready, a procession was formed, at the head of which were carried the Tartar banners, the pennant with the risen sun and the yak-tail standard. The guard, a force of one hundred men, all mounted archers, followed immediately behind their masters. Kiluken did not leave till he had satisfied himself that the hay and grain would be sent after him at once.

When they reached the apartments which had been reserved for them, Chang Hsien Ch'ung had a private talk with Lu Chia. At the start their conversation was stilted, for the Chief Minister was determined to show that his long residence in Pagān had not turned him into a provincial. He capped every quotation of the other until they both felt able to get to grips with the matter in hand.

'I shall have to arrange an audience for you as soon as possible,' said Chang Hsien Ch'ung. 'What exactly are your instructions?'

'We have a letter addressed to your King and signed with the Vermilion Pencil,' replied Lu Chia. 'The Emperor wants hostages for your good behaviour and the usual tribute presents. An alliance would then follow, which would be in the interests of both China and Burma.' The ambassador did not show him the letter. It was not as tactfully worded as his paraphrase.

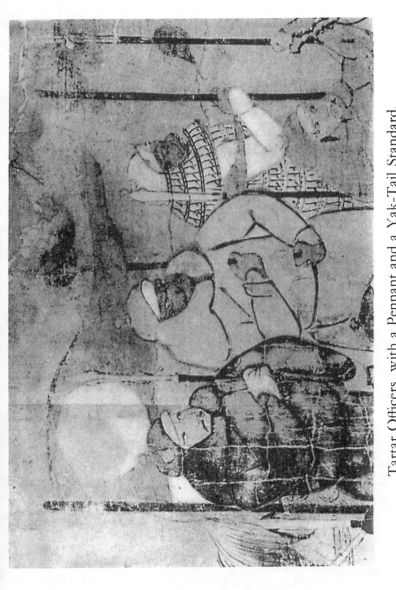

Tartar Officers, with a Pennant and a Yak-Tail Standard,
watching a Battle

From the Japanese contemporary scroll painting of the Mongol invasion of Japan
By courtesy of the British Museum

Chang Hsien Ch'ung waited on Queen Saw immediately after this conversation. 'It is as I supposed,' he said. 'The Emperor simply wants guarantees. These take the form of hostages and a nominal tribute of presents. I see no difficulty.'

'I hope there is none,' said she. 'We must now get the King round.'

They set off for his apartments, where they found him sitting under his new title. The Queen outlined the position. It was clear that he boggled at the idea of tributary presents. Chang Hsien Ch'ung admitted that it was unpleasant, but urged that it was necessary.

'How can it be necessary for Siritribhavanatityapavaradhammaraja to send tribute?' he asked idiotically.

Queen Saw began all over again from the beginning. 'It is easy enough to refuse the Emperor's demand,' she argued. 'What will be difficult comes afterwards—to face his troops. Can you do that?' He did not reply. Then she advanced an argument which turned the scale. 'Agree now,' she said. 'At a later date you can renounce your agreement when opportunity offers.' This appealed to him. It would be clever to cheat Kublai. 'Very well,' he replied at last, 'we had better agree.'

In an effort to impress the ambassador, Narathihāpaté postponed the date of the audience three times. But Lu Chia remained calm and bland. He was a difficult man to ruffle, because he took nothing personally. Marco Polo, with his wide experience of courts and men, was also quite easy. He spent his time exploring the city and making notes. But Kiluken did not take the delay so well. His temper, never good, became atrocious. There were several incidents. For instance, when walking in the circumambulatory of the Ananda, the Incomparable Pagoda, he stopped in front of a statue, that of King Kyanzittha, and after enquiring jocularly who the fellow was, laughed heartily and made an indecent gesture. The matter, of course, was reported. King Kyanzittha was a national hero. When questioned by the ambassador, Kiluken said he was laughing at a joke which had suddenly occurred to him. As to the indecent gesture, nothing was intended, a flea had bitten him. That night his men burnt down a monastery—by mistake.

However, the day arrived for the audience at last. The main hall was the venue and the occasion was to be formal. It was, of course, usual to receive ambassadors in public audience. The fact was, however, that the Tartars were rather envoys carrying a demand than ambassadors seeking mutual agreements. The ceremonial of public audience had been invented to give the impression that those received were suppliants. The King was shown above in his window, the rest prostrate below him on the ground. To apply such a ceremonial on the present occasion was discordant. His staff pointed this out to Narathihāpaté, but in his clouded mind he thought that if he could oblige the Tartars to conform to the etiquette of public audience, their demand would appear, however worded, a petition by force of ceremony. This, he felt, would save his face.

When the form of the reception was explained to Lu Chia, he showed no sign of resentment. If the King wished to hear the Emperor's letter as if it was a petition, no harm was done; that could not alter its manda-

Contemporary Statue of King Kyansittha of Pagān,
Crowned and kneeling before the Figure of the
Buddha in the Ananda Pagoda, Pagān
By courtesy of the Royal Asiatic Society

tory nature. Calling it a petition did not absolve him from obeying it. Moreover, the astute Chinaman knew that in point of psychological fact the letter would sound more startling when delivered in that make-believe fashion than when presented discreetly in private audience. There seems little doubt that this point escaped Queen Saw. Perhaps it amounted to the only major mistake of her life. 'If the ambassador does not mind, let the King have his public audience; it will help him to cover his mortification.' So she is reported to have said. Her eyes, of course, were fixed on the extreme necessity of complying with the Tartars' demands. If this was the only manner the King could be brought to agree, it was best to let him have his way.

The hour for public audience was dawn, and while it was still dark Lu Chia and his two colleagues got out of bed, if that term can describe Kiluken's habit, for he could not sleep except on the ground with a saddle for pillow. They had all agreed to wear Chinese robes for the occasion, the better to conform with Burmese etiquette; that is to say that Kiluken, when Lu Chia put to him the inwardness of the occasion, consented to dress in the same manner as his colleagues. But when at 5 a.m. he saw the silk clothes which his pages held out to him, he felt his stomach turn and refused to put them on. Instead he donned his trousers, top boots, long coat and heavy sword. Giving his face a wipe with a dirty cloth, he joined the other two.

Lu Chia was surprised. 'They won't admit you like that,' he remarked.

'We shall see,' growled Kiluken, drawing his sword absently and rubbing it against his boots.

'I thought we had arranged to wear court dress,' urged the ambassador.

'You're too subtle for me,' sneered the Tartar. 'We're presenting an ultimatum, and this is the dress for it.'

Like many intellectuals, Lu Chia loved to watch the clash of contraries. Accordingly, he said no more and shortly afterwards they left their quarters accompanied by a staff bearing the Emperor's letter in a gold box.

There was the usual press of spectators in front of the palace, and passing through these they mounted the steps. At the entrance to the great hall they were stopped by myrmidons. These indicated to Lu Chia and Marco Polo where to leave their sandals. They noticed Kiluken's boots, but not realising that he was one of the envoys, said nothing. It never occurred to them that he was going to enter. When he strutted in with the others they preferred not to make a scene, supposing he would be stopped by the attendants who showed the embassy to its place.

Inside the hall everyone else was in position. Chang Hsien Ch'ung knelt on a low dais with bannisters just under the veiled window through which the King would be visible. The rest of the Council, the mandarin-ate and the lesser officials lay ranged in ranks face down-wards on the carpets. No ladies were present. As the visitors were rather late, the attendants hustled them to the place reserved near the Chief Minister. Kiluken had three or four secretaries with him. Their robes hid his boots and sword. Not until he sat down in the Tartar fashion, with his legs crossed under him, were his boots noticed. The attendants immediately whispered to him to leave, but he paid no attention, looking about the hall in his hardy manner. The whispering increased, for the attendants were agitated. Chang Hsien Ch'ung turned round and saw Kiluken's boots. In the second occupied by his glance he had the intuition that he was looking at one of those events, apparently insignificant, upon which sometimes turns the fate of a kingdom. He was on the point of telling Kiluken to cover his boots with a scarf when there was a burst of music, the curtain over the window was drawn up and the King appeared seated above them dressed in full regalia. The attendants evaporated and the Chief Minister with everyone else, except Kiluken, bowed to the ground. The Tartar sat upright, a smirk on his powerful and brutal features, his boots clearly visible, and his long sword, the wearing of which in audience was as great a rudeness, sticking out behind him.

Narathihāpaté looked towards the embassy, but much oppressed by the weight of the regalia and the unpleasantness of the occasion, did not at once take in details. After a prescribed series of questions and answers between him and the ministers of a general character and treated antiphonally, the Tartar ambassador was asked to present the Emperor Kublai Khan's letter. This he did, advancing on his knees a yard or so till immediately below the window, when he stood up and, holding the golden box high over his head, placed it in the King's hands. The King opened the box and took out the paper, at the bottom of which the touch of the Vermilion Pencil was clearly visible. It was then passed to the heralds and read out first in Chinese and then in Burmese. The gist of it was in the following sentence:

'If you are resolved to fulfil your duty towards the

All-highest, send one of your brothers or senior ministers to show men that the wide world is linked with Us, and so enter our perpetual alliance. This will increase your reputation and advance your interest. Ponder well, for if it comes to war, who will be victor?'

An advance copy of this letter had not been submitted to Narathihāpaté. He had only heard the paraphrase known to Chang Hsien Ch'ung. Wherefore, the full text, with its lofty tone, its open threat, struck him like a blow. As Lu Chia had foreseen, he was deeply concerned that such a document should have been read out at public audience. There below him was the mandarinate, stretched on the floor indeed, but were they laughing at him? No ceremonial could transform for them such a letter into a petition. He let his eye travel on till it came to the envoys. He saw Kiluken—for the first time he saw his boots and sword. On the Tartar's face was an open sneer. The extreme insolence of his manner seemed to affect the King more than the contents of the letter. His intention had been to say, after the reading, that the Emperor's application would receive favourable attention, but now he felt unable to carry through this subterfuge. At his sign the curtain was lowered and he disappeared from view.

While the audience broke up, Kiluken striding out of the hall, his hand on his sword hilt, daring anyone to touch him, Narathihāpaté returned to the private rooms. The heavy crown, dress and orders were removed. His expression indicated the approach of an emotional crisis. It was a question whether he would commit some violence or break into weeping. The attendants slunk about nervously. A message was sent to Queen Saw, but she did not come. Apparently she had realised that a grave mistake had been made in allowing the King to expose himself to public discomfiture, and she was in agitated conference with Chang Hsien Ch'ung.

Narathihāpaté, however, did not ease himself at once by some outbreak. It might have been better had he done so. He sat for hours in silence on his cushions, his mouth open, occasionally digging his nails into the breast of one of his girls. The shock had stunned him. He refused to see anyone. Later in the day, however, he recovered slightly. He must do something. He was King, he would show them. . . . There was a knock at the door.

They told him that Panthagu was outside and wanted to speak to him, Panthagu, the seraglio priest, the women's favourite. Since the occasion he had induced the King to finish the Propitious Pagoda, he had become rather an intimate; a disreputable influence, he had suggested new amusements. Narathihāpaté was more at ease with him than with his regular advisers. From time to time the priest had given advice. He came in now with his taking smile. Narathihāpaté felt he was the very man to advise him at this juncture.

They sat down together, Panthagu beginning with his flatteries. What a wonderful name that was—and he glanced at the gold style above the King's seat—a finer name than that borne by the famous king of Ceylon, Abhayadutthagamani, or his successor Ghatatanalayaka, a style comparable to that of the forever victorious Alaungsithu's—and he repeated with a rolling fluency, Siritaribhavanadityapavarapunditasudhammarajamaha-dipatinarapatisithu.

'You think my title's as good as Alaungsithu's?' asked the King, anxious to hear the assurance again.

'Better,' replied the cleric promptly. 'Apter and more compact. The great Alaungsithu's sprawls somewhat.'

'That is true. I could, of course, have given myself a longer screed, but I forebore. Kings should be modest; one should not sprawl when one is great.'

'Of course not. Your Majesty's style, as it stands, is very telling. I hear the Tartar embassy was much impressed by it.'

The girls poured out wine. One of them, on whom Panthagu's hair-killer had been very successful, gave him a certain look as she filled his cup.

'You have just alluded to the embassy,' observed the King. 'I am glad you did. I have been feeling rather put out all day. You heard, I suppose, what happened in audience this morning. General Kiluken wore his field boots.' He decided to say nothing about the letter. He would take his stand on the general's rudeness.

Panthagu's face expressed astonishment and annoyance. 'I heard nothing of that,' he replied. In point of fact the episode had been reported to him within the hour.

'Yes, he wore his boots, and his sword. He did not even bow. He just leered.'

'The Tartars are barbarians. Your Majesty, I presume, has ordered some punishment?' Panthagu knew it was a delicate situation and that Queen Saw wanted an agreement. If he could bend the King the other way, it would be proof of his power. He was quite irresponsible. Motioning to the girls to fill the King's cup again, he repeated his question.

'You think I should punish?' the King now asked. There was a harsher, an excited tone in his voice.

'It seems hardly possible to let the incident pass unnoticed. One remembers how years ago Yazathingyan caused Thihathu to be torn by elephants for spitting on him at an audience. General Kiluken's action was worse than spitting on a Chief Minister. He affronted a king, a great king.'

'I like to hear you talk like that, Panthagu. I have had a terrible day. The persons of ambassadors are sacred. I know, of course, all that; I know there is a view that we should settle with the Tartars. But to settle at any price!'—his eyes began to get bloodshot, his voice to rise—'to settle at the price of honour, of self-respect! no, you are right!'

He rose from his seat. Panthagu, alarmed at such a sudden turn, began to go. He did not want to be seen urging the King to violence. But Narathihāpaté shouted: 'Stay where you are!' And turning to a cringing footman at the door bellowed: 'Send Rantapyissi here. I want to see the Captain of the Guard.' When the man had hurried on the errand, Narathihāpaté advanced on Panthagu and caught him by the ear. 'You shall see, you shall see!' he screamed. 'I shall slaughter them all! People can't come here and insult me—I don't care for the Emperor—what do they take me for!' and he twisted Panthagu's ear in a frenzy.

While he was running on in this way, Rantapyissi appeared. Letting go Panthagu, who crawled out of the room holding his ear, Narathihāpaté turned round to the captain.

'Take a thousand men of the guard, at once, this very

257

instant—d'you hear what I say, you fool?—take a thousand men and surround the quarters in which the Tartar embassy is lodged. If they resist, cut them down. Otherwise, bring them here. I have a word to say to them.'

Rantapyissi did not question the order. His intelligence had never been marked. He had no idea of the bearings of such instructions—and departed immediately to carry them out. In the corridors he happened to meet his brother, Anantapyissi, and repeated the orders. They struck that general as so far unusual that he mentioned them to Chang Hsien Ch'ung, whom he met further on. Cursing himself that he had allowed such a situation to arise, that, having seen the shock sustained by the King over the morning's proceedings, he had left him alone all day, the Chief Minister despatched an urgent messenger to Queen Saw, whom he had only just left. He also sent a hint to Lu Chia of what was in the wind, and hastened himself to the King's apartments.

Narathihāpaté received him and, calmer now that he had given his orders, said: 'Were you responsible for letting the Tartar general enter the hall this morning in his boots?'

'General Kiluken', replied the minister, 'seems to have slipped into the hall unnoticed at the last moment. I have ordered the arrest of the attendants responsible. The Tartars' conception of ceremonial differs from ours.'

'Does it include insolence?' enquired Narathihāpaté violently, adding: 'I have taken my measures. I have directed the household troops to bring the ambassadors here.'

'That is a very extreme measure. If they resist there will be bloodshed, and who can foresee the consequences of that? Surely it would be better to summon them in the customary manner and demand an explanation?'

Queen Saw was announced at this point. She had not had time to dress as carefully as usual. The day-long discussion with the Chief Minister and the other officials had tired her. She was not looking her best.

'What is it?' asked the King, irritated by her presence. 'I did not send for you. I am busy with the Chief Minister.'

The Queen perceived that it would take all her tact to cope with the crisis. She blamed herself deeply for not having used her influence against the public audience from the start.

'I came to condole with Your Majesty', she began in her reasonable and modulated way, 'on a tiresome incident of this morning's audience. I think we should call on the Ambassador for a formal apology.'

'Your proposal is both insufficient and too late,' replied the King. 'I have taken my measures.'

She replied: 'I hope those measures are not violent. I have had the honour of pointing out to Your Majesty the extreme delicacy of the present situation. Too vigorous a stroke now may bring consequences with which we are not equipped to deal. The King will show himself a master of statecraft if in this matter, where the embassy is clearly at fault, he makes a dignified protest in the proper quarter, which protest will strengthen his hands considerably in the negotiations which may be expected to follow.'

What she said was unquestionably so true that Nara-thihāpaté, had he listened, might yet have been saved. But he was not listening; he was acting the part of the great king. With ridiculous gravity he replied: 'You will learn that I have ordered out the guard. Events must take their course. There may be something in what you say, but it can be considered later.'

This nonsensical answer came to her as a shock. She looked at Chang Hsien Ch'ung, but he had no suggestion to make. Accordingly they withdrew to a neighbouring room to confer.

It was of the utmost importance to take some action at once, for by now news had come in that Rantapyissi was parading the guard in the courtyard and might start at any moment. But no course suggested itself. As a last resort it occurred to the Queen that Theimmazi might be able to do something. Occasionally he was successful with the King when all else failed. They hastened to his quarters. Unfortunately, it was now six o'clock in the afternoon. By that hour he was never sober. When his agitated servants hastened to tell him that the Chief Queen and the Chief Minister desired speech with him urgently, he belched in their faces. They were obliged to inform the distinguished visitors that their master was indisposed. By that time Rantapyissi had marched his men out of the courtyard.

The house where the embassy lodged was within the palace enclosure, but about half a mile from the royal apartments. When the ambassador received Chang Hsien Ch'ung's warning message, he had been much alarmed. Fortunately both his colleagues were at home, nor had any leave been granted to their men. He hurried to Kiluken and said: 'Thanks to your antics this morning, they've turned on us.'

Now Kiluken had been in sixty-eight battles and three hundred and forty-one skirmishes. He had fought against everybody in the known world who mattered, and he had never been on the losing side except at Tsu Shima, a few years previously, where he had met the Samurai of Japan. Lu Chia was inclined to argue that for all his adventures he had had no experiences of the spirit, but that judgment disclosed a limitation in the Chinaman's own mind, for Kiluken's medium was action, and in action he experienced the ecstasy of the artist in creation, of the lover with his mistress. When, therefore, Lu Chia told him that the Burmese guard was about to attack them, his habitual bad temper, rough manner, left him; he became jovial, animated, and with the utmost confidence took charge of the situation.

Within fifteen minutes the embassy guard of a hundred mounted archers had fallen in. Kiluken made a rapid inspection. Before leaving China he had picked the men himself. They were all veterans, ancient companions in arms, small fellows of herculean build, great marksmen with the arrow, long tried swordsmen, who were armoured in plates of lacquered hide, as resistant but lighter than steel, and carried three full quivers slung from their shoulders.

'Men,' said Kiluken, addressing them in the happiest manner imaginable, 'the Burmese guard is about to attack us. We are roughly three hundred miles from anywhere. But that is nothing like as far as we have been in the past. We are going to get home and report to the Khan.'

He then ordered Lu Chia and Polo to mount. The
guard formed round them and they set out for the
river. The general had taken the precaution to place a
squad of men on the bank with orders to keep a fifty-
oared boat provisioned and floating in readiness for
emergency. It was his intention now to reach that boat,
abandon his horses and row up the river. He considered this more feasible than a mounted retreat
through forest and swamp, a three hundred mile march
in the tropical hot season. The two-mile march to the
boat would be long enough—and hot enough too—he
expected.

As he had got moving with such speed, he met no
opposition in the neighbouring streets and was able to
take his troop through the inner gate into the outer
city, the sentinels having as yet no instructions to stop
him. Hardly had he passed the moat, however, than he
saw signs that the guard was on his heels. Cavalry began to pour through the gate on to the bridge. To check
them he wheeled thirty of his men, ordering them to
send three flights over the moat. They did this like
lightning, while the main body continued the retreat.
The arrows caused havoc, the bridge being choked
with struggling horses. The wooden balustrade was
broken in the press and many fell into the water among
the red and white lotus flowers.

Kiluken took the next stage of his retreat at the gallop. He passed like a ball of iron through the bazaar,
which was crowded with people. Many stalls were over-
turned; the women fled when he had passed. The cohesion of his force gave this impression of a ball. Lu
Chia and Polo were swept along in its centre. The am-

Tartar Archers
*From the contemporary Japanese scroll painting of the
Mongol invasion of Japan
By courtesy of the British Museum*

bassador was not a good rider, but he held on desperately. They approached the outer gate. If this was closed they were done for. But Rantapyissi's routine order to close all the gates had not yet reached the sentinels. The gate was open and they careered through it.

The river bank was now a quarter of a mile away. There were only a few huts about, and the ground was open and flat. Kiluken's intention was to raise a high tempo of manœuvre on this little plain, long enough to enable him to embark his force. The squad at the boat was standing by, for an advance messenger had warned them of the evacuation. By the time the Tartars had reached the bank, their pursuers were already through the gate.

In action Kiluken was conscious of a rhythmical beat. His most successful manœuvres were always effected by identification with that beat. So highly trained were his soldiers, that they appeared to him like an instrument upon which a harmony can be played. When the harmony was truly developed, the result was, as it were, absolute and he became irresistible. At this moment he heard in his being a lively air. In the phenomenal world it took form as follows.

Directing Lu Chia and Polo to enter the boat, which, lying under the high bank, was invisible from the bridge, he placed himself at the head of his men and began galloping south along the bank. When the Burmese cavalry of the guard saw this they pursued him diagonally across the plain. As they approached him at an angle which became more acute the farther he went, they exposed their right flank more and more to his archers. The Burmese could not shoot from horseback at speed, but the Tartars, excelling in this, poured in volley after volley with deadly effect. Before his opponents could close with him he wheeled east from the river across their front and then wheeling north, before they were on him, galloped up their other flank. This utterly confused them, for they had now no front. In this way he rounded their original rear and was back again near the boat, where he detached twenty of his men with orders to embark. They dismounted at speed, their horses continuing to gallop in the centre of the troop, which had begun again to circle the royal troops. Plying his arrows faster and galloping at a greater pace, he rolled up the thousand men of the guard into a force facing four ways and without cohesion. Such arrows as they discharged flew wide. They could not hit such a moving target. Again and again the Tartar arrows struck them in heavy wedges. Kiluken continued to gallop round his opponents, compressing them ever tighter. When from time to time a section of them made a dash to close with him, he retreated hurling his arrows like the sleet of his plateaux. From first to last he maintained his rhythm. These tactics continued until the guard broke and made for the gate, intending there to form again and advance with support. Circling and swooping after them, he kept up his arrow-stroke, now close, now farther away, till, seeing his moment when he was opposite the boat, he dismounted his men and they dipped under the bank. From there the flight of arrows continued while the embarkation was taking place. Straining his eyes through the dust into the setting sun Rantapyissi saw horses without riders and arrows rising from invisible bows. In a minute or so the

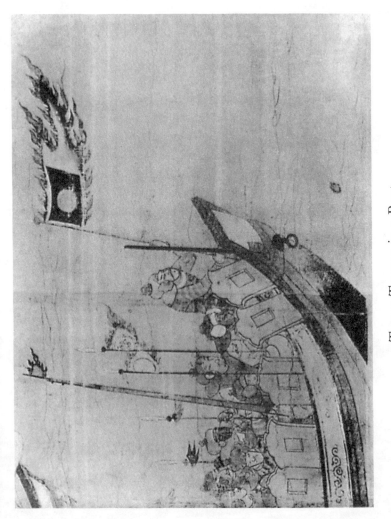

Tartar Troops in a Boat

From the contemporary Japanese scroll painting of the Mongol invasion of Japan
By courtesy of the British Museum

arrows ceased and he beheld a long boat out in the stream, paddled vehemently by the Tartars, the south wind streaming forward their banners. Kiluken was amidships, glaring at the shore. He was pleased enough with his little masterpiece. But there was one annoying detail. Lu Chia was dead. A stray Burmese javelin had struck him in the throat.

The Tartar Invasion

When Rantapyissi returned and reported that, though the main body of the Tartars had escaped, Lu Chia was dead, his master was satisfied. 'I'm sorry it was not Kiluken,' he said, 'but Lu Chia was a scoundrel too. He may have set up the other to insult me. Well, we've taught them a lesson; they had to run for their lives!' He tittered foolishly.

Queen Saw and Chang Hsien Ch'ung, who had no illusions about the gravity of the situation, tried to enlighten him. The Emperor was bound to take his revenge.

'Let him try,' retorted Narathihāpaté. 'He has no elephants. You don't seem to understand our great tactical advantage. I have five thousand elephants of the line. What effect can his cavalry have upon them? Armoured and endorsed with turrets full of bowmen, they are mobile forts. Who ever heard of cavalry taking a fort? As for infantry, it could never reach them.'

'But his archers,' they urged, 'they can outshoot us. A hundred of them held up the whole guard.'

'That was a rough and tumble on the bank,' he laughed. 'The guard had no time to deploy. But leave it to me. I am not afraid. I shall shortly be in consultation with my generals, Anantapyissi and Rantapyissi.'

The Queen and the minister were obliged to give it up. You could do nothing with such a man, a man who held his folly to be a vigorous counter-stroke, in which he had played the part of a strong king standing up for his honour. They now perceived he would remain in this delusion until alarmed by the sequel. He would then probably go to pieces. Unfortunately, the country would go to pieces with him.

They were far from being alone in their view of the situation. The King's two sons, the Bassein-Min and the Prome-Min, did not conceal their opinion that he was leading the country to disaster. They were still very young, but the Prome-Min was precocious. The adventurers who surrounded him had got him to believe that he could save Burma. Queen Saw had secret information that he was in a plot to overthrow his father, seize the throne and by a timely arrangement with the Tartars avert the blow which everybody knew was imminent. She was even sounded indirectly on the project. While admitting that there was something to be said for it in theory, she refused for reasons which will appear to have anything to do with it.

In case the Emperor might attack, Narathihāpaté devoted some time to the army. It was still loyal. Like all armies, it wanted a fight and was confident of success. He now added to it; there were reviews; the generals were in and out of the palace all day. When he saw his elephants march past, his confidence overflowed. His only dread now was that Kublai Khan would be afraid to attack him.

With the close of the rains in October, the army was sent north to the frontier. The men were in high spirits. Narathihāpaté, to see them go, took up his position near the Tharaba gate. The two generals, Anantapyissi and Rantapyissi, rode magnificently by on their war elephants, umbrellas, fans and whisks borne beside them. They were covered in gilded armour, high pointed helmets on their heads. Queen Saw, who also watched, half wished they had not assumed so fierce an air; it accorded more with the stage than the inclement altitudes of pure strategy. The march out took many hours. If Tepathin was in the gate, he made no sign that lovely morning, but curious to relate, certain of the common soldiers, talking the same night in the first bivouac, swore they had seen him at noon striding in the van.

After the departure of the army, Narathihāpaté had less to do and, without the daily spectacle of his elephants, his confidence began to sag. He had a way of sending for Queen Saw at all hours to enquire whether she thought the army would win.

'You have no doubts now, I suppose?' he would say.

As she saw little use in depressing him, knowing indeed that it would be futile to make a criticism, she would reply with any words that occurred to her.

'You are quite sure?' he would press her. 'We are bound to win, are we not?'

She managed some answer, which comforted him for a time. But his agitation would return. He would sit in the tower watching hour after hour for despatches, but sometimes when letters came he was afraid to unseal them.

On the full moon day of December there was a storm. The sun had gone down behind the western mountains and was throwing up on to what strips of cloud were there a scarlet of exceptional tone, when suddenly a bank of inky vapour lit with flashes rose from the eastern horizon on a rushing wind. This wrack, bellying over the blue that lay before the sunset, soon burst in a deluge, which, caught in the reflection from the west, turned pink as it fell, came teeming down a reddish flood.

That night Narathihāpaté could not sleep and sent for Queen Saw. They sat playing chess. Three times he was mated. 'I can play no more,' he said. 'Where are the musicians? Have they no songs to sing? Let me have martial music, old songs of triumph, what an army sings when it comes home victorious.' They began to play an air of the hero Alaungsithu. 'I cannot hear that!' he cried. He did not know what ailed him.

Near midnight those on duty by the door announced that a novice was in the ante-chamber, the young novice who often went with the Royal Chaplain. 'He has an urgent message,' they said. 'He desires Your Majesty's ear, he is straight from the Chaplain.' The boy was let in, a child of twelve in the yellow robe of the order. He remained silent when he saw the King.

'What is it, novice? Tell me!' Narathihāpaté was shivering.

'I have a message from my master. He says that the army has perished.'

'How does he know this thing?' cried Narathihāpaté.

'To-night Tepathin, the guardian spirit of the Tharaba gate, came from the battle. He gave news of it to my master.'

'Speak out, say all you know, how was it?' the King questioned him incoherently.

The young boy then said with fear in his voice: 'When darkness was come after the storm, my master composed himself to sleep. I lay down not far off. In a little while, it seemed, I was roused from my doze, for the building was shaken by a tremor, like a slight earthquake. I looked towards the Chaplain. In the light of the moon, which streamed into the eastern window, I saw the shape of a man bending over his bed. It was shaking him by the foot. The Chaplain started from sleep. 'Who shakes me?' he said. 'It is I, Tepathin, the guardian spirit of the Tharaba gate of Pagān,' replied the shape. 'I come from the battle. The army has perished. Anantapyissi and Rantapyissi are dead. See, I myself am wounded by an arrow.' As we looked closer, we saw that he was pierced by an arrow, that he was shot through and through by a Tartar arrow. He seemed then to grow more indistinct, until I could see him no longer. Thereafter, my master told me to hurry to the palace and inform Your Majesty.'

At this frightful intelligence, shocked further by the manner of its presentation, Narathihāpaté fainted.

When they had attended to him, Queen Saw, deeply perturbed and anxious for more light, desired the novice to pray his master to come at once to the palace.

At dawn the old monk appeared. He seemed weary, more fragile.

'Your novice related an extraordinary tale!' exclaimed the Queen. 'Tepathin was with the army? He was wounded by a mortal bolt? Must we assume for sure that disaster has overtaken us?'

With a melancholy sweet smile the Master replied: 'I once said—whether to you or to someone else, I cannot remember—that as a younger man I had made a study of the phenomenal side of concentration, but that I had discarded it as clogging approach to the higher consciousness. I thought it discarded for ever and took increasing pleasure in long periods of meditation. But these latter events, the Tartar embassy, the threat to this country, which is the repository of the true religion, distracted me from the contemplation of the One Light. While you were organising the army, the shades of those men who in the past were buried under the gates or elsewhere gathered about me. Though I condemn the practice which chained them, I was moved to use my power over them. There were paraded under my hand Tepathin and the Kanshi spirit, the Ngatinkyeshin spirit and Wetthakan, the guardian of Salin. Many others too were there whose names are unknown to you. These marched out of the city in the van of the army. It is a true report which Tepathin has given this night.'

'How came he to have a bolt sticking in him?' she asked.

'The Tartar shamans had loosed their own spirits,' he said gravely. 'Tepathin was struck by an arrow shot by them.'

An official account of what had taken place on the frontier became available within a week of the Chaplain's report. The first batch of fugitives from the battle arrived by boat. Chang Hsien Ch'ung examined them at length and from their often contradictory statements compiled a narrative of events which he placed before the King. This document showed that Anantapyissi and Rantapyissi on reaching the border took up a strong position behind the stockade of a town called Ngahsaung-gyan. Thereafter, hearing that the Tartar army consisted only of twelve thousand mounted archers, they left the shelter of their entrenchments and sought to attack, instead of waiting to be attacked. The Tartars retired until they had enticed the Burmese on to ground favourable to cavalry, namely an open plain fringed with forest. At first the day went well for the Burmese. The elephantry, led by Anantapyissi, advanced in a solid wedge masking the foot, with cavalry supporting them on the two wings. This moving wall of great beasts alarmed the Tartar horses, which had never seen or smelt elephants before. They shied and bolted, making it impossible for their riders to manœuvre with precision. Perceiving that the usual tactic of swoop and encirclement would have to be abandoned, the Tartars dismounted in the forest, to the trees of which they tied their horses. Emerging from the wood on foot, while the elephants were still on the great plain, they disposed themselves in a series of lines, one behind the other, with intervals of fifty yards. As the elephants advanced they came within bowshot of the first line, before the men in their turrets could range on their opponents. In result, the Burmese were spattered with arrows without being able to hit back. They continued, however, to press on, in order to bring the range down to the capacity of their bows, but when their arrows began to reach, the first line of the Tartars ran back behind the second line, which opened on the elephants with the same tactical advantage.

It was a curious spectacle. The elephants, numerous and well disciplined, continued to advance, but as far as the Tartars' safety was concerned they were no more dangerous than targets. The bowmen on their backs never got the range. The superiority of the Tartar bow was absolute. Had the elephants been more heavily armoured they might eventually have brought their riders within striking distance, but the Tartar arrows pierced their mail. Agonisingly covered with them, like porcupines, they broke and stampeded into the forest. There the boughs carried away their turrets.

The Tartars then remounted and swept over the plain, disposing rapidly of the Burmese horse and foot. The battle ended in a fierce hand-to-hand. Though the Burmese fought courageously, they were without cohesion, while the Tartars wheeled and thrust with measured accuracy. A carnage resulted, followed by the advance of the Tartars upon the stockade of Ngahsaung-gyan. This was occupied without difficulty. All the Burmese commanders were dead.

Such was the substance of the report which Chang Hsien Ch'ung laid before the King. The fugitives had added that the enemy were pressing down on the capital.

When the full bearing of this news was publicly known, despair and panic spread through Pagān. The

Tartars were alleged never to spare the population of a city which resisted. Terrible were the stories which circulated of their sack of other capitals. People began leaving in large numbers. When Narathihāpaté learnt this, he spoke of evacuating the capital, falling down the river to Bassein, where was the fief of his eldest son, and there, protected by the network of deltaic rivers from the Tartar cavalry, rallying the south.

During these days of decisions taken, revoked, altered and renewed, he exhibited in an intensified degree all those opposing characteristics of vacillation and precipitancy, optimism and despair, conceit and lack of self-confidence, which had marked his progress from the beginning and precipitated the tragedy. The whole weight of the crisis rested upon Queen Saw. He could not lead, he would not follow; he opposed sense with nonsense; it took hours to get the simplest point settled.

It became clear at last that the court must leave the capital. To stand without an army was impossible. But what should have been an orderly evacuation became a disorderly flight, as the King first delayed his sanction and, when a rumour was brought that the Tartars were within a few days' march, ordered the embarkation to take place on the morrow.

A quantity of craft of all kinds was alongside the wharves or at anchor offshore. The treasury and the regalia were first loaded under a strong guard. The White Elephant followed, being led down and placed on a raft without ceremony, for its reputation had suffered at this moment of misfortune. The harvest, which had all been garnered, was transferred to barges. Then there was the embarkation of the queens with their suites, of the concubines and the maids of honour. After a time it became evident that the boats were insufficient. The mandarins had not scrupled to take as many as they could lay hands on. Tharepyissapaté had departed one night not only with his household and attendants, but with all his furniture and livestock, down to his hens. When it was announced that no more boats were available, the slave-women of the inner palace still remained to be taken off.

The scene on the riverside was one of great confusion. The King himself sat in his barge, Thonlupuzaw, which was moored close in to the river bank. From its carved and gilded stateroom he watched the embarkation, frequently issuing orders to make haste, but impeding haste by the contradictory nature of the orders. Queen Saw's barge, Nawarat, was anchored by him, but she remained on shore in a temporary pavilion, from which she strove to manage what was passing beyond management. When this difficulty about the insufficiency of boats to accommodate the slave-women was reported, there was consternation.

The women in question, who numbered several hundreds, were those who had been captured years before at Martaban, women selected for their rank or beauty to reside in the palace from the bulk of the prisoners devoted as pagoda slaves. They were in a little crowd on the bank, seated as best they could on the dusty grass. Those who had parasols held them up against the blazing sun. It was a sweltering afternoon; they were dazed and thirsty. Each had a little woven bag containing the trifling valuables they had been able to

take with them. Some of them had tiny children on
their laps. They had not been very happy as under-ser-
vants in the palace, but as they thought of it now, it
seemed pleasant enough. Since dawn they had been
sitting there waiting to embark. Some had had a banana
and some a few nuts. The subordinate officials had been
rude and inconsiderate, though certain charitable persons, seeing them so helpless, had brought them water.
Now it was announced that there was no room for
them.

In due course the King noticed that they were not
being embarked.

'No boats for the slave-women?' he said angrily.
'Well, we cannot leave them behind. I have no intention of making any presents to the Tartars. I want them
to find Pagān empty, a shell of a place, without a stick
in it.' He ran on in this way, his officials crouching before him. 'You've got to take them,' he concluded.
'Make a raft.' But there were no bamboos left. Though
the officials murmured compliance, nothing was done.

This threw Narathihāpaté into one of his rages.
When it was clear that no raft could be made, he cried:
'Why didn't you tell me there was no wood? You're
wasting time. Throw them into the river! The Tartars
are not going to have them. Bind them hand and foot
and throw them into the river. They're only slaves anyway; I could have put them to death years ago after
the triumph, but I was too good-natured.'

The officials were relieved at this way out of the difficulty, and the orders were passed on to the subordinate
police. These went up to the women and, seizing some
of them roughly, began to bind their hands and feet.

There was a general outcry and a few rushed towards Queen Saw's pavilion and, making their way in, threw themselves at her feet. When she heard their prayer for mercy, she was deeply moved. That the King's last act in his capital should be to drown his servants seemed despicable.

The Royal Chaplain happened to be in the crowd on the bank. It was not his intention to leave Pagān. To flee from Tartars to save his comfort or his body was for him a simple irrelevancy. He had but come to the shore to take leave of the King and Queen. He was with the latter when the slave-women made their petition.

'Master,' said she, 'can you take up this matter? Go aboard Thonlupuzaw and reason with the King.'

Wrapping his yellow robe about him, he was paddled to the barge.

Fright and the nervous exhaustion caused by directing all day in the heat the loading of his possessions had reduced the King to a state of irritation bordering upon frenzy. He was looking out eagerly to see the women drown. But when the Chaplain, gaunt and quiet, entered his cabin, he felt the support of his anger leaving him.

'I have come to say farewell', said the Chaplain, 'and to have a last word with you. You know the text: "It is hard indeed for any creature traversing the illusion of this world to become a man: should he become a man it is still very hard for him to be born in the dispensation of the Buddha." If the present is a rout, a moment of despair, at least you are fortunate to have been born a man and a Buddhist. But now you contemplate an act which is so cruel, so unnecessary, that, if you do it, you will prevent yourself from being born a man again, and rightly so, for you would have become unfit to be a man. Why heap despair on despair? Why go down the river not only disgraced in this life but doomed for ages to a lower existence? By drowning the slave women you commit a suicide worse than killing your body, a suicide that perhaps for ever will prevent you from having a man's body again.'

'Master,' replied Narathihāpaté, who had fallen on his knees, 'what then should I do with the slave-women?'

'They can be distributed among the pagodas.'

That was the Chaplain's last public act in Pagān. At dusk the flotilla weighed anchor. He watched it round Lokananda point, the great barges, Thonlupuzaw and Nawarat, in front. No expression of any kind passed over his aged face as he saw it go. Only a rash man would have dared to guess his thoughts, but he gave some clue to them, for as he turned away one of the novices heard him utter a quotation from the classical books: 'Not even the universal monarch, King Mandhata, sovereign ruler of the four great Islands and two thousand lesser isles surrounding them, and of the two limbos of the world of spirits, was free from rise and fall, separations and the breach of death.'

Striding from the bank, he began the walk home to his monastery. To reach it he chose to pass through the city. The gateway was no longer guarded, and within the walls he saw the result of the court's flight. A great part of the population had deserted their homes to seek safety in distant villages. Bands of marauders were parading the streets, searching the houses for buried valuables. If the owners were still there, they tortured them to disclose their wealth; if they had gone they probed the garden with pointed stakes in the hope of striking a box of treasure. Flames mounted up in various directions. The public thoroughfare was clearly very dangerous. Desperate men could be seen everywhere, many drunk and all of them brandishing weapons.

But the Royal Chaplain passed along, his eyes on the ground. Some last glow from the western heavens illumined his yellow robe. His pace was even, he appeared unaware of danger. The two novices with him became alarmed. It would be better, they urged, to return to the gate and, making circuit of the walls, come round to the monastery. But the Chaplain paid no attention to their prattle and continued to advance through the heart of the town. When he reached the main bazaar he saw evidence of much looting. The shopkeepers had not been able to remove their goods in time. At one point brocades were strewn in the gutter. Turning a corner he came upon one of the bands of desperadoes, an ugly crowd, dancing and shouting, waving sticks and spears, some dressed in court silks, others draining pots of wine. They had just killed a woman; her body was in the roadway.

The Chaplain, however, did not alter his pace. It was now late dusk, made darker by overspreading trees, but the yellow of his robe was visible enough. The men knew well that a monk was walking towards them, but they were past respect for the robe and the Church.

As the Chaplain approached them, the novices huddled against him. They were in the place of death;

they felt death fingering at them. But suddenly a change
came over the roughs. Their eyes, hitherto fixed on the
monk, were fixed on something that went behind him.
As he came up, they flung themselves on the ground.
They seemed to be terrified; some of them writhed with
terror or screamed. The Chaplain passed through them
and on down the street. What they saw behind him
threw them into this panic. As the light of the fire-fly
flickers in and out, now clear, now gone, so flickering
at his back there appeared to be strange figures, the one
that stepped closest upon him being pierced through
and through with an arrow. Further shapes there were,
some loosing arrows that streamed away, others
marching, riding, some flying, some gnashing teeth or
pointing north. It seemed to the ruffians and to others
who saw him pass that night that the Royal Chaplain
led on through the city, as marshal of the world of
spirits, followed by Tepathin, guardian of the Tharaba
gate, by the Kanshi spirit, the Ngatinkyeshin spirit and
by a multitude of others, dedicated over centuries to
the defence of the capital, and that these defenders were
now, like the court, departing, that they were abandon-
ing great Pagān for ever. In what sense the Royal Chaplain would have admitted the truth of this it is difficult
to say, as it is to say whether he would have admitted
that the apparitions saved his life, for his values were
not phenomenal and what value he would have attached to the ordinary conception of an escape from
death is unknown.

XXIX
Queen Saw's Harangue

The court made first for Prome, to which the Prome-Min, the King's second son, had gone ahead. That town lay just north of the delta of the Irrawaddy. As it was within reach of the Tartars, no halt was made, the flotilla entering the maze of waterways of which the delta was composed and dropping down to Bassein, the headquarters of the elder prince's fief. Here a temporary palace was under construction and the court moved in when it was ready. As far as attack by the Tartars was concerned, they were as safe, moated by dozens of creeks running in every direction through marsh and jungle, as if they had reached another country. The Tartar cavalry could not get within two hundred miles of them.

News gradually filtered in from the north. The Tartar army advanced on Pagān, which was looted and burnt. A pursuit down the river was organised, but called off when the country became unsuitable for horses. As nothing more could be done, the Tartars withdrew, but left a garrison in Pagán. It was clear that they intended to wait until the situation settled down, when they would recognise any man, prince or otherwise, who had the support of the country and who would hold it as a king tributary to Kublai Khan, in the sense of the letter which had so much upset Narathi-hāpaté.

The Prome-Min had already made it clear that he considered himself that man. He had even, as has been said, sounded Queen Saw through third parties, for she was the most influential person in the country, and if she joined him the whole court and all the leading men would follow. But she had refused even to consider the project. One practical reason was that she had no opinion of the prince, and she had many other reasons. For instance, if the prince succeeded, his mother, a stupid tiresome woman who was now fourth queen, would move into a dominating position. Queen Saw felt that, even if left with the title of Chief Queen, she would never be able to work satisfactorily with two people like that. But she had a further reason, a less practical and more intimate reason. She was not going to stoop to betray Narathihāpaté when he was down. She did not love him, like him, respect him, she could hardly bear him, but she could not visualise herself going over to his son, deserting the man she had propped up all these years, handing him over, perhaps to death, certainly to degradation.

What then did she propose to do? No one could believe that Narathihāpaté had any chance of recovering his position. The country had been against him before his flight; his flight had turned dislike into contempt. He would never now be able to form a new army and return to Pagān. In the face of these facts what was going to be her policy? As she sat in the temporary palace at Bassein she made up her mind. She would stand by Narathihāpaté to the end, an end which she knew could not be very far off. When that happened, she would be released from the duty which had lain heavily upon her since Yazathingyan's death; she would be a free woman, and she would know how to employ that freedom.

One morning in August Chang Hsien Ch'ung came in to see her. All these years he had respected with the utmost loyalty her decision that they could be no more than friends and close colleagues, but he had not ceased to admire her as the most remarkable woman he had ever met, a woman whose breadth of intellect was evenly balanced by the depth of her heart. He was utterly happy to be her Chief Minister, and if during these latter days, when events had drawn in, he had begun to perceive that an end of some kind was approaching, he was more excited than depressed, for he dared to hope that in some way it might bring him closer to the woman he loved. He had come to speak to her now on an urgent matter.

'Despatches have just been received from the Prome-Min,' he said.

The prince had been backwards and forwards to Bassein and had outwardly professed the warmest devotion to his father, pretending that the army he was raising at Prome would eventually be placed at Narathihāpaté's disposal.

'What is he writing about now?' the Queen asked.

'He proposes that His Majesty should move up to Prome at once, as he argues that an advance on Pagān can be made in a month or so, when the rains are over.'

'And what did the King say to that nonsense?'

'That he intended to go.'

'Is he completely mad?' she exclaimed. 'No, I suppose, he is no worse, he is just as he always was. I have told him a hundred times he cannot trust the Prome-Min. Yet he calmly tells you he is going to put himself into his power. Has the Bassein-Min been informed?'

'The Bassein-Min was present when the despatches were opened. He begged his father not to go.'

'How did the King take that?'

'He was rather disagreeable. He told the Bassein-Min that he couldn't stay here all his life, that the prince had failed to raise an army in the delta, and that he was going to some one who had an army.'

'This is too much,' said the Queen angrily. 'Come with me. I must speak to the King at once.'

They crossed the courtyard to Narathihāpaté's rooms, and found him still looking over his son's despatch. He seemed glad to see the Queen and said:

'I have good news here. The Prome-Min thinks we can safely advance in October. We might go up to Prome now and help him to complete his preparations. When I arrive there, everyone will rally to me. What do you say?'

The Queen sat down. She was impatient with his folly, but covered her feelings in a weighty manner.

'Let me take the general question first—whether you should now attempt to re-establish your dominion,' she began. 'It is easy enough to say we shall advance, but how are we to do it? Consider the state of the kingdom. Many of the inhabitants of the upper part have been killed by the Tartars or have fled into distant villages. None of them have come down to join you here. And in the lower part, what do we see? At Bassein, which you have made your seat, hardly a man has rallied to you. The headmen have kept aloof, and Martaban, which Yazathingyan took for you, has revolted again.'

'Certainly the delta is surprisingly backward,' admitted Narathihāpaté.

'There is nothing surprising about it,' cried the Queen. 'You were a hard master. Your old subjects do not want to bear your yoke again. How often did I warn you in the past that this might happen! But you would not alter your ways, and now no one will help you. Can you forget how I quoted to you that famous passage? "Bore not thy country's belly. Abase not thy country's forehead. Fell not thy country's banner. Pluck not out thy country's eyes. Break not thy country's tusk. Sully not thy country's face. Cut not thy country's feet and hands." But you have done all those things. How then can you be surprised that no one has rallied to you?'

'I have never heard your quotation before,' said the King sullenly. 'What's it all about?'

'You have heard it before, but I shall explain it to you again. "Bore not thy country's belly"—to seize the goods of the rich, to the exclusion of their heirs, and squander them till all is gone, that is to bore your country's belly, and you have done it; you did it to obtain funds for your buildings, your bathing pools, your fêtes.'

'I deny that,' said the King. 'Any money I took was by process of law.'

'Listen to me; you have asked me to explain and I shall do so. I have been too sparing in the past, but you shall hear all now. "Abase not thy country's forehead" —that is, do not turn away contemptuously from those who have sought to advise you. Have you ever done anything but spurn advice?'

'I don't know what you are talking about,' said he. 'Have you come in to abuse me?'

'No,' she retorted, 'I've come to tell you a few truths in the hope that you will realise your position. Let me go on. "Fell not thy country's banner"—your country's banner is the Church, the Church that brought true religion to this country, the monks of which by their lives demonstrate for us all the high state of holy living. Your predecessors protected the Church, but what have you done?'

'I built the Propitious Pagoda,' he interrupted.

'Yes, you built the Propitious Pagoda, and you cut down the estimate, with the result that the very next year cracks appeared in the walls. I pass over that. You did worse to the Church than cheat. But I must finish. "Break not thy country's tusk"—the members of your family, they are your country's tusk—what did you do to Sawlon, your Queen? You tortured her to death.'

'I cannot listen to any more of this,' he said. 'You are just abusing me. I shall go to Prome and from thence to the capital.'

'You will go to Prome at the risk of your life. That

son of yours is as crooked as a maze. His despatch is a feint to get you into his hands.'

'I have said that I cannot listen to any more of this. I am going to Prome. Chang Hsien Ch'ung, make the arrangements.'

As she left, Queen Saw wondered why she had bothered to argue with him. He was impenetrable. The end could not be far off.

XXX

The End of Narathihāpaté

Before the week was out, the court again embarked on the flotilla. The monsoon was at its height and the weather in consequence very bad, with downpours which lasted for days, followed by fine periods, when the heat was intense. A more uncomfortable time for travelling could not have been chosen. The distance by water between Bassein and Prome was nearly two hundred miles, and as the creeks were tidal a great part of the way, progress was mostly made in bouts of six hours. When the tide turned, as a rule they anchored, unless a strong wind was blowing aft. There they would swing on the ebb in some dismal creek, fringed with mangrove and infested with mosquitoes, as the sun beat down on the murky water and the mud banks slowly were exposed to view. These glistened like an unwholesome skin; horrible creatures crawled over them, half fish, half mammal, wallowing in the ooze.

Sometimes a crocodile floated by or a flight of horn-bills laboured over. So the ebb would slowly run out, the rank stench of the flats gradually increasing, till at last the anchor-ropes began to ease and the flood came pushing up from the sea. Then the oars would come out again and the boats be forced another thirty miles.

When they were a day out from Bassein, the discipline deteriorated. The guard boats, which had orders to keep level with the royal barge, fell behind. At the occasional straggling villages they passed, the soldiers went ashore and got drunk on palm-wine. Largely unescorted, the King and his entourage reached Prome on the third day shortly before the time of the evening meal.

As they entered the roadstead and came to anchor, the Prome-Min put out from the shore accompanied by numerous boats filled with armed men. On reaching the royal barge, he disposed his boats around it, himself stepping on board accompanied by a small staff. With him also were a number of menials carrying dishes of great variety. Entering the stateroom, where his father was seated with Queen Saw and some of the mandarins, he made the usual prostration, though a little carelessly, and said: 'Your Majesty is welcome to Prome. I fear the journey was long and tiresome. Those delta creeks are like a nightmare the way they wind through the mangroves with never a vista. But you will be happy here. Though damper, it is not unlike the capital. What a fine view it is looking westward to the mountains, and on shore eastwards how fine are the hills crowned with pagodas.'

Queen Saw was not listening to this flow of light

talk, for her attention was occupied by the armed boats. But Narathihāpaté was delighted to see his son and said: 'Yes, it is good to be free from the constriction of the creeks. This open prospect is very delightful.'

'I have ventured', went on the Prome-Min, 'to bring you ready cooked some of your favourite dishes, for I suppose fresh provisions on the journey were not easy to obtain. It is just supper time and, perhaps, Your Majesty will flatter me by sampling a few.'

The bowls were laid out, their covers taken off and an appetising smell filled the cabin. The Prome-Min intimated that he proposed to do himself the honour of serving his father. Selecting a dish from one of the trays, he offered it, saying: 'I am sure you will like this.'

'Very well, let me try it,' said the King. 'Threaded liver, yes, I like that very much.'

He settled himself to eat, when suddenly, just as he was about to take the first mouthful, he felt a violent spasm in the stomach. Half rising to his feet, he exclaimed: 'What's happened to me? I have a dreadful pain!' The spasm passing, he sat down again bewildered.

The Prome-Min, after a momentary start, looked at him steadily, but Queen Saw, who had a deep understanding of his mind, of the strange faculty he sometimes exhibited, whispered quickly: 'Don't touch the food; I believe it's poisoned!'

The Prome-Min overheard the whisper. 'You are right,' he said in level tones. 'I had wished to spare him the shock, but now you have said it. Yes, the food is poisoned, but he will have to eat it.'

At these startling words there was dead silence. The King's staff with terrified faces looked at the Prome-Min. Had the words come from that thin youth with damp hands, hardly eighteen? He looked back at them all with bravado. 'Eat it up, father,' he said. 'You'll have to take it.'

'What's this!' cried Narathihāpaté, very pale. 'He says there's poison—he wants to poison me. Hey, there! Where's my guard? Arrest the prince! Are we all mad?

'You are too late,' sneered his son. 'Your guard-boats have been stopped further down. And look about you. Those men in canoes there, they are my soldiers. You are surrounded.' As he spoke, he gave a sign. His men stood up in the boats and waved their swords. They gave a sullen shout, which echoed on the river. At that moment the sun dipped under the mountains and the golden pagodas on the eastern shore seemed more distant.

Narathihāpaté, who had grown haggard and was panting, said: 'You do not mean this. It is a joke!'

'Well, treat it as a joke, and eat the liver!'

'You cannot force me to eat,' said the King now; 'no man can be forced to swallow against his will.'

'Quite,' agreed the prince, 'but that will not save you. If you do not eat what is in this bowl,' and he pushed it towards him, 'my soldiers will come aboard and kill you.'

At these words Narathihāpaté broke down and weeping, turned to Queen Saw. 'What shall I do?' he moaned. 'Can you not save me? Why did you let me come to this place? You warned me, I know, but why did you not stop me?'

The Queen then addressed the Prome-Min in that manner which had won so many diplomatic victories, urging him to moderation as she enlarged on the dreadful crime of parricide. 'Let him go into a monastery,' she begged. 'He can never be a danger to you, because he has no followers.'

But the prince replied: 'I cannot take the risk. My elder brother would go to his assistance. He must die, and does he not deserve death? He has ruined the country, and until he is dead nothing can be done.'

Narathihāpaté was clinging to Queen Saw's arm. There was a dreadful broken look on his face. 'What shall I do, Saw?' he was gasping. 'I cannot put the food in my mouth. If I must die, is it not better to let them cut me down?'

The Queen could not bear to see him so abject before his son. 'Listen,' she whispered, as he held on to her with both hands, 'your weakness, your intransigent ways have brought you to this. I tried my best to save you; now I am powerless. All I can do is to advise you how to die. If you die with some dignity, it will wipe out much.'

'I cannot, I cannot,' he sobbed. 'I have no strength left.'

'Face your son,' she urged. 'Do not let him see he has cowed you. Even now you are still King.'

While the Queen was speaking, the Prome-Min had withdrawn a few paces, for he held her in profound respect. Now he approached again and, pointing to the bowl, said: 'I can wait no longer.'

But Narathihāpaté with the Queen's help had gained some little hold. He trembled pitifully, he was ashen pale, but he faced his son. 'Wait on the deck outside,' he said with a semblance of dignity. 'When I am ready, I shall take the poison. Leave me, I say; you can enter when I have gone. I do not wish to see your face in my pain.'

The prince stepped back as he had been desired, not out of consideration for his father, but for the Queen.

When he was gone and Narathihāpaté was left alone with Queen Saw, the momentary strength he had shown seemed to leave him and he wept again. Recovering somewhat, but profoundly miserable, he said: 'That it should be my own son! When he was an infant at the breast, I remember he would smile at me. I'd hold him and his tiny hands would grasp my jacket. Had I dropped him then, it would have saved me this.' He lapsed into the silence of utter disillusion. Queen Saw was silent too; she felt creeping over her a horror of public life.

Presently Narathihāpaté took the ring from his finger, a great emerald cut as an octagon, and while he let fall drops of water upon it uttered this solemn wish: 'In all the lives wherein I wander through the worlds of illusion until I reach Nirvana's ultimate truth, may a son never again be born to me.' He gave the ring to the Queen, saying: 'If that wish is granted, this ordeal at least cannot be mine a second time.'

His mind had been distracted a moment by these other thoughts. Now he had to face back to death, the immediate bleakness of violent death. He was dismally afraid.

'Help me, now, Saw,' he groaned. 'Give me all your strength. Where is the bowl?' He panted wretchedly.

'I must take it. Let me smell it. The food smells as usual. One would never think there was death there. And I was hungry a few moments ago—how curious that seems now!'

He laid down the bowl. 'What poison has he put in? Some of them strike through you, like a flame; others are more slow. It is strange, one cannot imagine what poison is like to take. Do you think it will hurt me much? I was foolish not to have ready by me an instant poison. Some of the kings in India always carry a poisoned pin. One prick of it, I have heard, renders them insensible. Had I such a pin now, it would be easy. But to eat this food—I cannot move my jaw and swallow, my throat is too dry.'

He became silent, staring at the bowl. Then suddenly in some access of desperation he seized it and, with a golden spoon filling his mouth, swallowed quickly. Terrified by his own act, he fell back on to Queen Saw's breast.

It was not long before he felt the clash within him. A searing pain shot through his stomach. He started violently and rolled from her arms. Looking down at him with compassion, uttering words to give him fortitude, she raised his head. As spasm followed spasm, shaking him as if he had been struck by a hammer, he moaned piteously, a foam gathering on his violet lips. She lifted him again, murmuring the verse: 'All suffering creatures who wander in the Three Worlds must needs endure the Eight World-Predicaments.' But his suffering was over; the eighth predicament had been endured.

The Prome-Min, informed that his father was dead,

walked in, remarking: 'He took his time. Well, I am king now.'

The Queen's humour was not accommodating. 'How so?' she asked. 'Your brother is lawful heir.'

'If my brother has a word to say, he shares my father's fate.'

'What about the country? A king without a country is more amusing than important.'

'There I have a proposition. Will you not second me? The interests of the country demand our collaboration. You and I, we can re-establish the dynasty.'

'But I consider you only a mountebank,' said the Queen with cool insolence. 'This murder of your father, somehow it does not impress me. It is a dirty deed, that's all, and you are a dirty scoundrel, mountebanking as a hero, the saviour of your country.'

'I can force you, you know,' he replied, though much dashed. 'I have captured the whole court.'

'I thought you were a fool,' said she. 'Press me, and the country will never rally to you. You have little support now, you would have none then.'

He knew this was true and, in a very flat manner, asked what she proposed to do.

'That is my business,' said she. 'Now, get out of my sight!'

He left without a word.

xxxi
The Third Period

When the reverberations of the last scene had died away, Queen Saw asked Chang Hsien Ch'ung to meet her on her barge, Nawarat. The Chinaman had found the last few years pitched very high. He was not so wholly a man of the imagination as the Queen's father, but he loved the quiet of books and papers, polished conversation and the intellectual approach. In affairs of state he moved as a gentleman. The crash of a dynasty hardly suited him. Rather weary, he obeyed the Queen's summons. He did not know her intentions with precision, but for some time she had hinted, when he pressed her to say what she would do if Narathihāpaté did not survive, at a course of action which would recompense her—she did not say him— for the long years of duty done at the expense of her heart.

Ushered now into her stateroom on the barge, he found her smiling and animated; indeed, he had rarely seen her with such a playful air. What a bewitching girl she must have been, he thought, when she was plain Ma Saw. To know her as that, what an intoxication it would be!

'Since I ordered the Prome-Min out of my sight I have been thinking hard,' she began with a little pout.

'Your Majesty has been thinking—that is about your own future?'

'Of course! To think about public affairs any more is silly. That particular game is up. No, I have been thinking of indulging myself.'

'And in what does Your Majesty intend to indulge?'

'I intend to indulge in a holiday, a long holiday, and at home.'

'Will Your Majesty explain?'

'I want to settle in Kanbyu,' she said, 'build myself a house there, develop my land, read, think, dream, be a free woman.'

'Your Majesty will not feel dull after court life?'

'That is a point and I have considered it. I want to bring with me at least one of my courtiers.'

'And who is that person?' he enquired, though a soft tone which had crept into her voice had enlightened him.

'I intend to invite my Chief Minister.'

'As Chief Minister?'

'Well, no; there would be a little work, of course. But if he would like to come as . . . in a private capacity . . . in short as . . .'

'He would like to come in that capacity!'

This point settled, the Queen turned her attention to details with her usual force. The Prome-Min had given up any thought of trying to prevent her retirement. He also found himself unable to prevent her taking her household, private property and guard. And no one informed him she had just appointed a new Comptroller, and that the Comptroller was Chang Hsien Ch'ung.

The day came for her departure. Her farewell to the court was an affecting scene. The queens, concubines, maids and officials felt extremely uncertain about their future. Like her, they had no confidence in the Prome-Min. The most tearful parting was with Shinshwé.

'I thought I had a safe contract for life,' she cried. 'But it just shows—you never can tell! I might have been safer on the stage after all.'

The Queen's property was all on her barge, Nawarat, and its tenders, smaller country boats. It consisted of gold, silver, gems, a quantity of table vessels, silks, carpets, furniture, books, together with elephants, horses and palanquins. She had a private guard of two hundred soldiers armed in the most advanced fashion of the day. Her staff amounted to ten ladies-in-waiting and forty maids, and she had ample servants and slaves to man her barge and boats, undertake the household duties and manage the animals. There was a long journey before them, a hundred miles upstream to the little port of Mi-gyaung-ye; from there thirty miles overland to Taungdwingyi, where the governor, now independent, was an old adherent of the Queen's; and thence seventy miles north to Pōpa. In that way they avoided Pagān and its Tartar garrison and, by travelling through the territory of a lord friendly to them, minimised the risk of attack by the bandits who now prowled on the country roads.

At last they were off. The Queen did not creep away. Far from it, she let the Prome-Min watch her state, pennants flying, umbrellas spread, as she swept up the reach on the following wind. Disembarking at Mi-gyaung-ye, she proceeded by palanquin over the sandy downs with their clumps of toddy palms to the rice valley of Taungdwingyi. Received there with every respect by the ruler of the town, who was awaiting her at the gate kneeling on a mat, she turned north and a few mornings later reached Shwebandaw, the village of the Royal and Golden Flower. From there she could see Pōpa in the far distance. Its cone was dipped in the monsoon cloud, which a high wind from the south-west drove over the sky. The prospect was wide and invigorating. The rice was coming into ear. She was nearly home.

Messengers had been sent ahead to warn the head-man of Kanbyu. That village had not been touched by the Tartars. It was off their track. But like every other village, with the breakdown of the central government it had been exposed to bandit attack. The headman, however, was very competent and by strengthening his stockade and increasing his guards, had discouraged malefactors with complete success. In spite of this, his position remained precarious enough, and when he re-ceived news that the great Queen Saw was coming to take up her residence within the village, accompanied by a strong force of trained soldiers, he was much re-lieved.

In due course the royal procession arrived at the

stockade. When the Queen's palanquin was set down at the gateway, the headman and the village council were there to meet it. They knelt by the roadside, as they had always done. Behind them were many villagers at full length on the ground. From their lips went up a murmur of welcome and gladness. It was more than they had ever hoped to see. Some of the older men and women who had known the Queen as a child were weeping with joy. That their daughter, their mother, their benefactor, their goddess should have come at last to live amongst them seemed like the return of the golden age. What a living loving darling she was! She had not changed from the old days; she had just as beautiful, just as sweet a smile. And as, wiping their eyes, they dared to raise their heads and gaze with adoration, they felt sure that they saw rising from her a dazzling light.

After a suitable interval the Queen went on to her father's house. There, descending from the palanquin, she asked whether he was upstairs. They told her, no, that he had gone out to see his crops.

'I shall go to the field and meet him there,' she told Chang Hsien Ch'ung.

Entering the house for a moment, she caused her maids to take off her grand clothes; her headdress was undone; she removed her jewels. Then in a simple gown, her hair in a knot and without her slippers, she stepped from the porch.

'I am going alone,' she announced, 'just as I once was. No one should follow me.'

They understood her very well and watched her leave the garden.

She walked down the village street towards the gate. Word had been passed on and everyone knew where she was going. Nobody obtruded, somehow no one was in the street. She went through the gate and so out of sight.

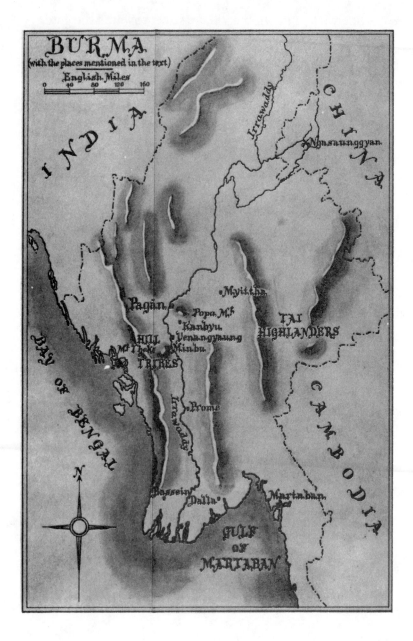

BURMA
(with the places mentioned in the text.)

English Miles
0   40   80   120   160

INDIA

CHINA

Irrawaddy

Ngasaunggyan

Pagán

Popa, M.ᵗ

Myittha

Kanbyu

TAI
HIGHLANDERS

Yenangyaung

M.ᵗ Theka

Minbu

HILL

TRIBES

BAY

OF

BENGAL

Irrawaddy

Prome

CAMBODIA

N

Bassein

Dalla

Martaban

GULF
OF
MARTABAN